A NOTE ON THE AUTHOR

SUSANNA CLARKE lives in Cambridge with her partner, the novelist and reviewer Colin Greenland. *Jonathan Strange & Mr Norrell* was published in 2004 in more than thirty countries and shortlisted for the Whitbread First Novel Award and the Guardian First Book Award. It won the British Book Awards Newcomer of the Year, the Hugo Award and the World Fantasy Award in 2005.

BY THE SAME AUTHOR

Jonathan Strange & Mr Norrell

SUSANNA CLARKE
THE LADIES
of
GRACE ADIEU

and other stories

ILLUSTRATED BY CHARLES VESS

BLOOMSBURY
LONDON · OXFORD · NEW YORK · NEW DELHI · SYDNEY

Bloomsbury Paperbacks
An imprint of Bloomsbury Publishing Plc

50 Bedford Square
London
WC1 3DP
UK

1385 Broadway
New York
NY 10018
USA

www.bloomsbury.com

BLOOMSBURY and the Diana logo are trademarks of Bloomsbury Publishing Plc

First published in Great Britain 2006
This paperback edition published in 2007

© Susanna Clarke, 2006

Illustrations © Charles Vess

Susanna Clarke has asserted her right under the Copyright, Designs and Patents Act, 1988, to be identified as Author of this work.

"The Ladies of Grace Adieu" was first published in *Starlight 1* edited by Patrick Nielsen Hayden, pub. Tor, New York, 1996. "On Lickerish Hill" was first published in *Black Swan, White Raven* edited by Ellen Datlow and Terri Windling pub. Avon, New York, 1997. "Mrs Mabb" was first published in *Starlight 2* edited by Patrick Nielsen Hayden, pub. Tor, New York, 1998. "The Duke of Wellington Misplaces His Horse" was first published in *A Fall of Stardust*, pub. Green Man Press, Virginia, 1999. "Mr Simonelli or the Fairy Widower" was first published in *Black Heart, Ivory Bones* edited by Ellen Datlow and Terri Windling, pub. Avon, New York, 2000. "Tom Brightwind or How the Fairy Bridge Was Built at Thoresby" was first published in *Starlight 3* edited by Patrick Nielsen Hayden, pub. Tor, New York, 2001. "Antickes and Frets" was first published in *The New York Times*, 31st October 2004

British Library Cataloguing-in-Publication Data
A catalogue record for this book is available from the British Library.

ISBN: PB: 978-0-7475-9240-2
       ePub: 978-1-4088-0933-4

13

Typeset by Hewer Text UK Ltd, Edinburgh
Printed and bound in Great Britain by CPI Group (UK) Ltd, Croydon CR0 4YY

To find out more about our authors and books visit www.bloomsbury.com. Here you will find extracts, author interviews, details of forthcoming events and the option to sign up for our newsletters.

Acknowledgements

These stories would never have come into being had it not been for the following people: Colin Greenland and Geoff Ryman (who made me write my first short story when I really didn't want to), Neil Gaiman, Patrick and Teresa Nielsen Hayden, Terri Windling, Ellen Datlow and Charles Vess. My love and thanks to them all.

For my parents, Janet and Stuart Clarke

For my parents, Jane and Stan Clark

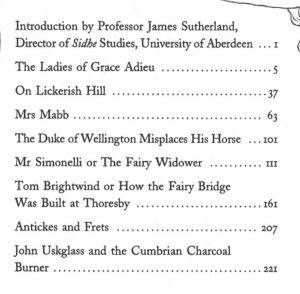

CONTENTS

Introduction

by Professor James Sutherland, Director of
Sidhe *Studies, University of Aberdeen*

I HAVE APPROACHED THIS collection with two very modest aims in mind. The first is to throw some sort of light on the development of magic in the British Isles at different periods; the second is to introduce the reader to some of the ways in which Faerie can impinge upon our own quotidian world, in other words to create a sort of primer to Faerie and fairies.

The title story, "The Ladies of Grace Adieu", falls into the first category, with a poignant depiction of the difficulties faced by female magicians during the early nineteenth century – a time when their work was simply dismissed by their male counterparts (here amply represented by Gilbert Norrell and Jonathan Strange). The events of the story were referred to in a somewhat obscure novel published a few years ago. Should any readers happen to be acquainted with *Jonathan Strange and Mr Norrell* Bloomsbury, London, 2004), then I direct their attention to a footnote in chapter 43 which describes how Jonathan Strange went to some trouble to extract his clergyman brother-in-law from a living in Gloucestershire and get him a different living in Northamptonshire. "The Ladies of Grace Adieu" provides a fuller explanation of Strange's rather enigmatic actions.

"On Lickerish Hill" and "Antickes and Frets" both describe the somewhat easier, less fraught relationship with fairies and magic which our English and Scottish ancestors once enjoyed.

"Mr Simonelli or the Fairy Widower" is an extract from the diaries of Alessandro Simonelli. Simonelli is, of course, a monstrously irritating writer; at every turn he displays the conceit and arrogance of his race. (And I am talking here of the *English* and not of anyone else). An editor is advised to approach his diaries with caution. Simonelli published them first in the mid-1820s. Twenty years later he revised them and published them again. He did the same thing in the late 1860s. Indeed throughout the nineteenth century and early twentieth century his diaries and memoirs were being continually rewritten and brought out in new editions; and at each stage Simonelli reworked his past in order to promote his latest obsession – whether that be ancient Sumerian history, the education of women, the improvement of *Sidhe* (fairy) morals, the provision of bibles for the heathen or the efficacy of a new sort of soap. In an attempt to circumvent this problem I have chosen an extract from the first edition which describes the beginning of Simonelli's extraordinary career. We can but hope that it bears some sort of relation to what actually happened.

In the years that followed Waterloo dealings between the *Sidhe* (fairies) and the British increased. British politicians debated the "Fairy Question" this way and that, but all agreed it was vital to the national interest. Yet if these stories demonstrate nothing else it is the appalling unpreparedness of the average nineteenth-century gentleman when he accidentally stumbled into Faerie. The Duke of Wellington is a case in point.

Women do seem to have fared somewhat better in these perplexing circumstances; the heroine of "Mrs Mabb", Venetia Moore, consistently demonstrates an ability to intuit the rules of Faerie, which the older and more experienced Duke is quite without.

"Tom Brightwind or How the Fairy Bridge Was Built at Thoresby" remains a tale replete with interest for the student of Faerie. However I see no reason to revise my earlier assessment of the story given in 1999 (and deserving, I think, to be more widely known). The reader will find it prefacing the tale itself.

I have chosen to finish with a story from that wonderful writer, John Waterbury, Lord Portishead. Apart from the period 1808–1816 when he was under the thumb of Gilbert Norrell, Waterbury's writings and in particular his retelling of old tales of the Raven King are a continual delight. "John Uskglass and the Cumbrian Charcoal Burner" is an example of that genre of stories (much loved by the medievals) in which the rich and powerful are confounded by their social inferiors. (I am thinking here of the tales of Robin Hood or the ballad, "King John and the Abbot of Canterbury"). In medieval Northern England no one was richer or more powerful than John Uskglass and consequently Northern English folklore abounds with tales in which Uskglass tumbles down holes in the ground, falls in love with unsuitable ladies or for various complicated and unlikely reasons finds himself obliged to cook porridge for harassed innkeepers' wives.

The sad truth is that nowadays – as at all periods of our history – misinformation about Faerie assails us from every side. It is through stories such as these that the serious student of *Sidhe* culture may make a window for herself into Faerie and snatch a glimpse of its complexity, its contradictions and its perilous fascinations.

James Sutherland
Aberdeen, April 2006

THE LADIES

OF GRACE

ADIEU

A BOVE ALL REMEMBER this: that magic belongs as much to the heart as to the head and everything which is done, should be done from love or joy or righteous anger.

And if we honour this principle we shall discover that our magic is much greater than all the sum of all the spells that were ever taught. Then magic is to us as flight is to the birds, because then our magic comes from the dark and dreaming heart, just as the flight of a bird comes from the heart. And we will feel the same joy in performing that magic that the bird feels as it casts itself into the void and we will know that magic is part of what a man is, just as flight is part of what a bird is.

This understanding is a gift to us from the Raven King, the dear king of all magicians, who stands between England and the Other Lands, between all wild creatures and the world of men.

From *The Book of the Lady Catherine of Winchester* (1209–67), translated from the Latin by Jane Tobias (1775–1819)

When Mrs Field died, her grieving widower looked around him and discovered that the world seemed quite as full of pretty, young women as it had been in his youth. It further occurred to him that he was just as rich as ever and that, though his home already contained one pretty, young woman (his niece and ward, Cassandra Parbringer), he did not believe that another would go amiss. He did not think that he was at all changed from what he had been and Cassandra was entirely of his opinion, for (she thought to herself) I am sure, sir, that you were every bit as tedious at twenty-one as you are at forty-nine. So Mr Field married again. The lady was pretty and clever and only a year older than Cassandra, but, in her defence, we may say that she had no money and must either marry Mr Field or go and be a teacher in a school. The second Mrs Field and Cassandra were very pleased with each other and soon became very fond of each other. Indeed the sad truth was that they were a great deal fonder of each other than either was of Mr Field. There was another lady who was their friend (her name was Miss Tobias) and the three were often seen walking together near the village where they lived – Grace Adieu in Gloucestershire.

Cassandra Parbringer at twenty was considered an ideal of a certain type of beauty to which some gentlemen are particularly partial. A white skin was agreeably tinged with pink. Light blue eyes harmonized very prettily with silvery-gold curls and the whole was a picture in which womanliness and childishness were sweetly combined. Mr Field, a gentleman not remarkable for his powers of observation, confidently supposed her to have a character childishly naive and full of pleasant, feminine submission in keeping with her face.

Her prospects seemed at this time rather better than Mrs Field's had been. The people of Grace Adieu had long since settled it amongst themselves that Cassandra should marry the Rector, Mr Henry Woodhope and Mr Woodhope himself did not seem at all averse to the idea.

"Mr Woodhope likes you, Cassandra, I think," said Mrs Field.

"Does he?"

Miss Tobias (who was also in the room) said, "Miss Parbringer is wise and keeps her opinion of Mr Woodhope to herself."

"Oh," cried Cassandra, "you may know it if you wish. Mr Woodhope is Mr Field stretched out a little to become more thin and tall. He is younger and therefore more disposed to be agreeable and his wits are rather sharper. But when all is said and done he is only Mr Field come again."

"Why then do you give him encouragement?" asked Mrs Field.

"Because I suppose that I must marry someone and Mr Woodhope has this to recommend him – that he lives in Grace Adieu and that in marrying him I need never be parted from my dear Mrs Field."

"It is a very poor ambition to wish to marry a Mr Field of any sort," sighed Mrs Field. "Have you nothing better to wish for?"

Cassandra considered. "I have always had a great desire to visit Yorkshire," she said. "I imagine it to be just like the novels of Mrs Radcliffe."

"It is exactly like everywhere else," said Miss Tobias.

"Oh, Miss Tobias," said Cassandra, "how can you say so? If magic does not linger in Yorkshire, where may we find it still? 'Upon the moors, beneath the stars, With the King's wild Company.' *That* is my idea of Yorkshire."

"But," said Miss Tobias, "a great deal of time has passed since the King's wild Company was last there and in the meantime Yorkshiremen have acquired tollgates and newspapers and stagecoaches and circulating libraries and everything most modern and commonplace."

Cassandra sniffed. "You disappoint me," she said.

Miss Tobias was governess to two little girls at a great house in the village, called Winter's Realm. The parents of these children were dead and the people of Grace Adieu were fond of telling each other that it was no house for children, being too vast and gloomy and full of odd-shaped rooms and strange carvings. The younger child was indeed often fearful and often plagued with nightmares. She seemed, poor little thing, to believe herself haunted by owls. There was nothing in the world she feared so much as owls. No one else had ever seen the owls, but the house was old and full of cracks and holes to let them in and full of fat mice to tempt them so perhaps it were true. The governess was not much liked in the village: she was too tall, too fond of books, too grave, and – a curious thing – never smiled unless there was some thing to smile at. Yet Miss Ursula and Miss Flora were very prettily behaved children and seemed greatly attached to Miss Tobias.

Despite their future greatness as heiresses, in the article of relations the children were as poor as churchmice. Their only guardian was a cousin of their dead mother. In all the long years of their orphanhood this gentleman had only visited them twice and once had written them a very short letter at Christmas. But, because Captain Winbright wore a redcoat and was an officer in the _____ shires, all his absences and silences were forgiven and Miss Ursula and Miss Flora (though only eight and four years old) had begun to shew all the weakness of their sex by preferring him to all the rest of their acquaintance.

It was said that the great-grandfather of these children had studied magic and had left behind him a library. Miss Tobias was often in the library and what she did there no one knew. Of late her two friends, Mrs Field and Miss Parbringer, had also been at the house a great deal. But it was generally supposed that they were visiting the children. For ladies (as every one knows) do not study magic. Magicians themselves are another matter – ladies (as every one knows) are wild to see magicians. (How else to explain the great popularity of Mr Norrell in all the fashionable drawing rooms of London? Mr Norrell is almost as famous for his insignificant face and long silences as he is for his incomparable magicianship and Mr Norrell's pupil, Mr Strange, with his almost handsome face and lively conversation is welcome where ever he goes.) This then, we will suppose, must explain a question which Cassandra Parbringer put to Miss Tobias on a day in September, a very fine day on the cusp of summer and autumn.

"And have you read Mr Strange's piece in *The Review*? What is your opinion of it?"

"I thought Mr Strange expressed himself with his customary clarity. Any one, whether or not they understand any thing of the theory and practice of magic, might understand him. He was witty and sly, as he generally is. It was altogether an admirable piece of writing. He is a clever man, I think."

"You speak exactly like a governess."

"Is that so surprizing?"

"But I did not wish to hear your opinion as a governess, I wished to hear your opinion as a . . . never mind. What did you think of the ideas?"

"I did not agree with any of them."

"Ah, *that* was what I wished to hear."

"Modern magicians," said Mrs Field, "seem to devote more of their energies to belittling magic than to doing any. We are constantly hearing how certain sorts of magic are too perilous for men to attempt (although they appear in all the old stories). Or they cannot be attempted any more because the prescription is lost. Or it never existed. And, as for the Otherlanders, Mr Norrell and Mr Strange do not seem to know if there are such persons in the world. Nor do they appear to care very much, for, even if they do exist, then it seems we have no business talking to them. And the Raven King, we learn, was only a dream of fevered medieval brains, addled with too much magic."

"Mr Strange and Mr Norrell mean to make magic as commonplace as their own dull persons," said Cassandra. "They deny the King for fear that comparison with his great magic would reveal the poverty of their own."

Mrs Field laughed. "Cassandra," she said, "does not know how to leave off abusing Mr Strange."

Then, from the particular sins of the great Mr Strange and the even greater Mr Norrell, they were led to talk of the viciousness of men in general and from there, by a natural progression, to a discussion of whether Cassandra should marry Mr Woodhope.

While the ladies of Grace Adieu were talking, Mr Jonathan Strange (the magician and second phenomenon of the Age) was seated in the library of Mr Gilbert Norrell (the magician and first phenomenon of the Age). Mr Strange was informing Mr Norrell that he intended to be absent from London for some weeks. "I hope, sir, that it will cause you no inconvenience. The next article for the *Edinburgh Magazine* is done – unless, sir, you wish to make changes (which I think you may very well do without my assistance)."

Mr Norrell inquired with a frown where Mr Strange was going, for, as was well known in London, the elder magician – a quiet, dry little man – did not like to be without the younger for even so much as a day, or half a day. He did not even like to spare Mr Strange to speak to other people.

"I am going to Gloucestershire, sir. I have promised Mrs Strange that I will take her to visit her brother, who is Rector of a village there. You have heard me speak of Mr Henry Wood-hope, I think?"

The next day was rainy in Grace Adieu and Miss Tobias was unable to leave Winter's Realm. She passed the day with the children, teaching them Latin ("which I see no occasion to omit simply on account of your sex. One day you may have a use for it,") and in telling them stories of Thomas of Dundale's captivity in the Other Lands and how he became the first human servant of the Raven King.

When the second day was fine and dry, Miss Tobias took the opportunity to slip away for half an hour to visit Mrs Field, leaving the children in the care of the nursery maid. It so happened that Mr Field had gone to Cheltenham (a rare occurrence, for, as Mrs Field remarked, there never was a man so addicted to home. "I fear we make it far too comfortable for him," she said) and so Miss Tobias took advantage of his absence to make a visit of a rather longer duration than usual. (At the time there seemed no harm in it.)

On her way back to Winter's Realm she passed the top of Grace and Angels Lane, where the church stood and, next to it, the Rectory. A very smart barouche was just turning from the high road into the lane. This in itself was interesting enough for Miss Tobias did not recognize the carriage or its occupants, but what made it more extraordinary still was that it was driven with great confidence and spirit by a lady. At her side, upon the barouche box, a gentleman sat, hands in pockets, legs crossed, greatly at his ease. His air was rather striking. "He is not exactly handsome," thought Miss Tobias, "his nose is too long. Yet he has that arrogant air that handsome men have."

It seemed to be a day for visitors. In the yard of Winter's Realm was a gig and two high-spirited horses. Davey, the coachman and a stable boy were attending to them, watched by a thin, dark man – a very slovenly fellow (somebody's servant) – who was leaning against the wall of the kitchen garden to catch the sun and smoking a pipe. His shirt was undone at the front and as Miss Tobias passed, he slowly scratched his bare chest with a long, dark finger and smiled at her.

As long as Miss Tobias had known the house, the great hall had always been the same: full of nothing but silence and shadows and dustmotes turning in great slanting beams of daylight, but today there were echoes of loud voices and music and high, excited laughter. She opened the door to the dining parlour. The table was laid with the best glasses, the best silver and the best dinner service. A meal had been prepared and put upon the table, but then, apparently, forgotten. Travelling trunks and boxes had been brought in and clothes pulled out and then abandoned; men's and women's clothing were tumbled together quite promiscuously over the floor. A man in an officer's redcoat was seated on a chair with Miss Ursula on his knee. He was holding a glass of wine, which he put to her lips and then, as she tried to drink, he took the glass away. He was laughing and the child was laughing. Indeed, from her flushed face and excited air Miss Tobias could not be entirely sure that she had not already drunk of the contents. In the middle of the room another man (a very handsome man), also in uniform, was standing among all the clothes and trinkets and laughing with them. The younger child, Miss Flora, stood on one side, watching them all with great, wondering eyes. Miss Tobias went immediately to her and took her hand. In the gloom at the back of the dining parlour a young woman was seated at the pianoforte, playing an Italian song very badly. Perhaps she knew that it was bad, for she seemed very reluctant to play at all. The song was full of long pauses; she sighed often and she did not look happy. Then, quite suddenly, she stopt.

The handsome man in the middle of the room turned to her instantly. "Go on, go on," he cried. "We are all attending, I promise you. It is," and here he turned back to the other man and winked at him, "delightful. We are going to teach country dances to my little cousins. Fred is the best dancing master in the world. So you must play, you know."

Wearily the young lady began again.

The seated man, whose name it seemed was Fred, happened

at this moment to notice Miss Tobias. He smiled pleasantly at her and begged her pardon.

"Oh," cried the handsome man, "Miss Tobias will forgive us, Fred. Miss Tobias and I are old friends."

"Good afternoon, Captain Winbright," said Miss Tobias.

By now Mr and Mrs Strange were comfortably seated in Mr Woodhope's pleasant drawing room. Mrs Strange had been shewn all over Mr Woodhope's Rectory and had spoken to the housekeeper and the cook and the dairymaid and the other maid and the stableman and the gardener and the gardener's boy. Mr Woodhope had seemed most anxious to have a woman's opinion on everything and would scarcely allow Mrs Strange leave to sit down or take food or drink until she had approved the house, the servants and all the housekeeping arrangements. So, like a good, kind sister, she had looked at it all and smiled upon all the servants and racked her brains for easy questions to ask them and then declared herself delighted.

"And I promise you, Henry," she said with a smile, "that Miss Parbringer will be equally pleased."

"He is blushing," said Jonathan Strange, raising his eyes from his newspaper. "We have come, Henry, with the sole purpose of seeing Miss Parbringer (of whom you write so much) and when we have seen her, we will go away again."

"Indeed? Well, I hope to invite Mrs Field and her niece to meet you at the earliest opportunity."

"Oh, there is no need to trouble yourself," said Strange, "for we have brought telescopes. We will stand at bedroom windows and spy her out, as she goes about the village."

Strange did indeed get up and go to the window as he spoke. "Henry," he said, "I like your church exceedingly. I like that little wall that goes around the building and the trees, and holds them all in tight. It makes the place look like a ship. If you ever get a good strong wind then church and trees will all sail off together to another place entirely."

"Strange," said Henry Woodhope, "you are quite as ridiculous as ever."

"Do not mind him, Henry," said Arabella Strange. "He has the mind of a magician. They are all a little mad."

"Except Norrell," said Strange.

"Strange, I would ask you, as a friend, to do no magic while you are here. We are a very quiet village."

"My dear Henry," said Strange, "I am not a street conjuror with a booth and a yellow curtain. I do not intend to set up in a corner of the churchyard to catch trade. These days Admirals and Rear Admirals and Vice Admirals and all His Majesty's Ministers send me respectful letters requesting my services and (what is much more) pay me well for them. I very much doubt if there is any one in Grace Adieu who could afford me."

"What room is this?" asked Captain Winbright.

"This was old Mr Enderwhild's bedroom, sir," said Miss Tobias.

"The magician?"

"The magician."

"And where did he keep all his hoard, Miss Tobias? You have been here long enough to winkle it out. There are sovereigns, I dare say, hidden away in all sorts of odd holes and corners."

"I never heard so, sir."

"Come, Miss Tobias, what do old men learn magic for, except to find each other's piles of gold? What else is magic good for?" A thought seemed to trouble him. "They shew no sign of inheriting the family genius, do they? The children, I mean. No, of course. Who ever heard of women doing magic?"

"There have been two female magicians, sir. Both highly regarded. The Lady Catherine of Winchester, who taught

Martin Pale, and Gregory Absalom's daughter, Maria, who was mistress of the Shadow House for more than a century."

He did not seem greatly interested. "Shew me some other rooms," he said. They walked down another echoing corridor, which, like much of the great, dark house, had fallen into the possession of mice and spiders.

"Are my cousins healthy children?"

"Yes, sir."

He was silent and then he said, "Well, of course, it may not last. There are so many childish illnesses, Miss Tobias. I myself, when only six or seven, almost died of the red spot. Have these children had the red spot?"

"No, sir."

"Indeed? Our grandparents understood these things better, I think. They would not permit themselves to get overfond of children until they had got past all childhood's trials and maladies. It is a good rule. Do not get overfond of children."

He caught her eye and reddened. Then laughed. "Why, it is only a joke. How solemn you look. Ah, Miss Tobias, I see how it is. You have borne all the responsibility for this house and for my cousins, my rich little cousins, for far too long. Women should not have to bear such burdens alone. Their pretty white shoulders were not made for it. But, see, I am come to help you now. And Fred. Fred has a great mind to be a cousin too. Fred is very fond of children."

"And the lady, Captain Winbright? Will she stay and be another cousin with you and the other gentleman?"

He smiled confidingly at her. His eyes seemed such a bright, laughing blue and his smile so open and unaffected, that it took a woman of Miss Tobias's great composure not to smile with him.

"Between ourselves she has been a little ill-used by a brother officer in the _____ shires. But I am such a soft-hearted fellow

– the sight of a woman's tears can move me to almost any thing."

So said Captain Winbright in the corridor, but when they entered the dining parlour again, the sight of a woman's tears (for the young lady was crying at that moment) moved him only to be rude to her. Upon her saying his name, gently and somewhat apprehensively, he turned upon her and cried, "Oh, why do you not go back to Brighton? You could you know, very easily. That would be the best thing for you."

"Reigate," she said gently.

He looked at her much irritated. "Aye, Reigate," he said.

She had a sweet, timorous face, great dark eyes and a little rosebud mouth, for ever trembling on the brink of tears. But it was the kind of beauty that soon evaporates when any thing at all in the nature of suffering comes near it and she had, poor thing, been very unhappy of late. She reminded Miss Tobias of a child's rag doll, pretty enough at the beginning, but very sad and pitiful once its rag stuffing were gone. She looked up at Miss Tobias. "I never thought . . ." she said and lapsed into tears.

Miss Tobias was silent a moment. "Well," she said at last, "perhaps you were not brought up to it."

That evening Mr Field fell asleep in the parlour again. This had happened to him rather often recently.

It happened like this. The servant came into the room with a note for Mrs Field and she began to read it. Then, as his wife read, Mr Field began to feel (as he expressed it to himself) "all cobwebby" with sleep. After a moment or two it seemed to him that he woke up and the evening continued in its normal course, with Cassandra and Mrs Field sitting one on either side of the fire. Indeed Mr Field spent a very pleasant evening – the kind of evening he loved to spend, attended to by the two ladies. That it was only the dream of such an evening (for the poor, silly man was indeed asleep) did not in any way detract from his enjoyment of it.

While he slept, Mrs Field and Cassandra were hurrying along the lane to Winter's Realm.

In the Rectory Henry Woodhope and Mrs Strange had said their goodnights but Mr Strange proposed to continue reading a while. His book was a Life of Martin Pale by Thaddeus Hickman. He had reached Chapter 26 where Hickman discussed some theories, which he attributed to Martin Pale, that sometimes magicians, in times of great need, might find themselves capable of much greater acts of magic than they had ever learnt or even heard of before.

"Oh," said Strange with much irritation, "this is the most complete stuff and nonsense.'

"Goodnight, Jonathan," said Arabella and kissed him, just above his frown.

"Yes, yes," he muttered, not raising his eyes from the book.

"And the young woman," whispered Mrs Field, "who is she?"

Miss Tobias raised an eye-brow and said, "She says that she is Mrs Winbright. But Captain Winbright says that she is not. I had not supposed it to be a point capable of so wide an interpretation."

"And if any thing were to happen . . . to the children, I mean," whispered Mrs Field, "then Captain Winbright might benefit in some way?"

"Oh, he would certainly be a very rich man and whatever he has come here to escape – whether it be debts or scandal – would presumably hold no more fears for him."

The three ladies were in the children's bedroom. Miss Tobias sat somewhere in the dark, wrapped in a shawl. Two candles bloomed in the vast dark room, one near to the children's bed and the other upon a little ricketty table by the door, so that any one entering the room would instantly be seen. Somewhere in the house, at the end of a great many long, dark corridors, could be heard the sound of a man singing and another laughing.

From the bed Miss Flora anxiously inquired if there were any owls in the room.

Miss Tobias assured her there were none.

"Yet I think they may still come," said Miss Flora in a fright, "if you do not stay."

Miss Tobias said that they would stay for a while. 'Be quiet now," she said, "and Miss Parbringer will tell you a story, if you ask her."

"What story shall I tell you?" asked Cassandra.

"A story of the Raven King," said Miss Ursula.

"Very well," said Cassandra.

This then is the story which Cassandra told the children.

"Before the Raven King was a king at all, but only a Raven Child, he lived in a very wonderful house with his uncle and his aunt. (These were not really his relations at all, but only a kind gentleman and lady who had taken him to live with them.) One day his uncle, who was reading books of magic in his great library, sent for the Raven Child and inquired politely how he did. The Raven Child replied that he did very well.

"'Hmmph, well,' said Uncle Auberon, 'as I am your guardian and protector, little human child, I had better make sure of it. Shew me the dreams you had last night.' So the Raven Child took out his dreams and Uncle Auberon made a space for them on the library table. There were a hundred odd things on that table; books on unnatural history; a map shewing the relative positions of Masculine Duplicity and Feminine Integrity (and how to get from one to the other) and a set of beautiful brass instruments in a mahogany box, all very cunningly contrived to measure Ambition and Jealousy, Love and Self-sacrifice,

Loyalty to the State and Dreams of Regicide and many other Vices and Virtues which it might be useful to know about. All these things Uncle Auberon put on the floor, for he was not a very tidy person and people were for ever scolding him about it. Then Uncle Auberon spread the Raven Child's dreams out on the table and peered at them through little wire spectacles.

"'Why,' cried Uncle Auberon, 'here is a dream of a tall black tower in a dark wood in the snow. The tower is all in ruins, like broken teeth. Black, ragged birds fly round and round and you are inside that tower and cannot get out. Little human child, when you had this terrible dream, was you not afraid?'

"'No, Uncle,' said the Raven Child, 'last night I dreamt of the tower where I was born and of the ravens who brought me water to drink when I was too young even to crawl. Why should I be afraid?'

"So Uncle Auberon looked at the next dream and when he saw it he cried out loud. 'But here is a dream of cruel eyes a-glittering and wicked jaws a-slavering. Little human child, when you had this terrible dream, was you not afraid?'

"'No, Uncle,' said the Raven Child, 'last night I dreamt of the wolves who suckled me and who lay down beside me and kept me warm when I was too young even to crawl. Why should I be afraid?'

"So Uncle Auberon looked at the next dream and when he saw it he shivered and said, 'But this is a dream of a dark lake in a sad and rainy twilight. The woods are monstrous silent and a ghostly boat sails upon the water. The boatman is as thin and twisted as a hedge root and his face is all in shadow. Little human child, when you had this terrible dream, was you not afraid?'

"Then the Raven Child banged his fist upon the table in his exasperation and stamped his foot upon the floor. 'Uncle Auberon!' he exclaimed, 'that is the fairy boat and the fairy boatman which you and Aunt Titania yourselves sent to fetch me and bring me to your house. Why should I be afraid?'

" 'Well!' said a third person, who had not spoken before, 'how the child boasts of his courage!' The person who spoke was Uncle Auberon's servant, who had been sitting high upon a shelf, disguised (until this moment) as a bust of Mr William Shakespeare. Uncle Auberon was quite startled by his sudden appearance, but the Raven Child had always known he was there.

"Uncle Auberon's servant peered down from his high shelf at the Raven Child and the Raven Child looked up at him. 'There are all sorts of things in Heaven and Earth,' said Uncle Auberon's servant, 'that yearn to do you harm. There is fire that wants to burn you. There are swords that long to pierce you through and through and ropes that mean to bind you hard. There are a thousand, thousand things that you have never yet dreamt of: creatures that can steal your sleep from you, year after year, until you scarcely know yourself, and men yet unborn who will curse you and scheme against you. Little human child, the time has come to be afraid.'

"But the Raven Child said, 'Robin Goodfellow, I knew all along that it was you that sent me those dreams. But I am a human child and therefore cleverer than you and when those wicked creatures come to do me harm I shall be cleverer than them. I am a human child and all the vast stony, rainy English earth belongs to me. I am an English child and all the wide grey English air, full of black wings beating and grey ghosts of rain sighing, belongs to me. This being so, Robin Goodfellow, tell me, why should I be afraid?' Then the Raven Child shook his head of raven hair and disappeared.

"Mr Goodfellow glanced a little nervously at Uncle Auberon to see if he were at all displeased that Mr Goodfellow had spoken out so boldly to the human foster child, but Uncle

Auberon (who was quite an old gentleman) had stopt listening to them both a while ago and had wandered off to resume his search for a book. It contained a spell for turning Members of Parliament into useful members of society and now, just when Uncle Auberon thought he had a use for it, he could not find it (though he had had it in his hand not a hundred years before). So Mr Goodfellow said nothing but quietly turned himself back into William Shakespeare."

In the Rectory Mr Strange was still reading. He had reached Chapter 42 where Hickman relates how Maria Absalom defeated her enemies by shewing them the true reflections of their souls in the mirrors of the Shadow House and how the ugly sights which they saw there (and knew in their hearts to be true) so dismayed them that they could oppose her no more.

There was, upon the back of Mr Strange's neck, a particularly tender spot and all his friends had heard him tell how, when ever there was any magic going on, it would begin to prickle and to itch. Without knowing that he did so, he now began to rub the place.

So many dark corridors, thought Cassandra, how lucky it is that I know my way about them, for many people I think would soon be lost. Poor souls, they would soon take fright because the way is so long, but I *know* that I am now very near to the great staircase and will soon be able to slip out of the house and into the garden.

It had been decided that Mrs Field should stay and watch the children for the remainder of the night and so Cassandra was making her way back to Mr Field's house quite alone.

Except (she thought) I do not believe that that tall, moonshiny window should be *there*. It would suit me much better if it were behind me. Or perhaps on my left. For I am sure it was not there when I came in. Oh, I am lost! How very . . . And now the voices of those two wretches of men come echoing down this dark passageway and they are most manifestly drunk and do not know me. And I am here where I have no right to be.

(Cassandra pulled her shawl closer round her.) "And yet," she murmured, "why should I be afraid?"

"Damn this house!" cried Winbright. "It is nothing but horrid black corridors. What do you see, Fred?"

"Only an owl. A pretty white owl. What the devil is it doing inside the house?"

"Fred," cried Winbright, slumping against the wall and sliding down a little, "fetch me my pistol, like a good fellow."

"At once, Captain!" cried Fred. He saluted Captain Winbright and then promptly forgot all about it.

Captain Winbright smiled. "And here," he said, "is Miss Tobias, running to meet us."

"Sir," said Miss Tobias appearing suddenly out of the darkness, "what are you doing?"

"There is a damned owl in the house. We are going to shoot it."

Miss Tobias looked round at the owl, shifting in the shadows, and then said hurriedly, "Well, you are very free from superstition, I must say. You might both set up as the publishers of an atheist encyclopedia tomorrow. I applaud your boldness, but I do not share it."

The two gentlemen looked at her.

"Did you never hear that owls are the possessions of the Raven King?" she asked.

"Do not frighten me, Miss Tobias," said Captain Winbright, "you will make me think I see tall crowns of raven feathers in the dark. This is certainly the house for it. Damn her, Fred. She behaves as if she were my governess as well."

"Is she at all like your governess?" asked Fred.

"I do not know. I had so many. They all left me. You would not have left me, would you, Miss Tobias?"

"I cannot tell, sir."

"Fred," said Captain Winbright, "now there are two owls. Two pretty little owls. You are like Minerva, Miss Tobias, so tall and wise, and disapproving of a fellow. Minerva with two owls. Your name is Jane, is it not?"

"My name, sir, is Miss Tobias."

Winbright stared into the darkness and shivered. "What is the game they play in Yorkshire, Fred? When they send children alone into the dark to summon the Raven King. What are those words they say?"

Fred sighed and shook his head. "It has to do with hearts being eaten," he said. "That is all I recall."

"How they stare at us, Fred," said Winbright. "They are very impertinent owls. I had always thought they were such shy little creatures."

"They do not like us," said Fred sadly.

"They like you better, Jane. Why, one is upon your shoulder now. Are you not afraid?"

"No, sir."

"Those feathers," said Fred, "those soft feathers between the wing and the body dance like flames when they swoop. If I were a mouse I would think the flames of Hell had come to swallow me up."

"Indeed," murmured Winbright, and both men watched the owls glide in and out of the gloom. Then suddenly one of the owls cried out – a hideous screech to freeze the blood.

Miss Tobias looked down and crossed her hands – the very picture of a modest governess. "They do that, you know," she said, "to petrify their prey with fear; to turn it, as it were, to stone. That is the cruel, wild magic of owls."

But no one answered her, for there was no one in the corridor but herself and the owls (each with something in its beak). "How hungry you are, dearest," said Miss Tobias approvingly, "One, two, three swallows and the dish goes down."

About midnight Mr Strange's book appeared to him so dull and the night so sweet that he left the house and went out into the apple orchard. There was no wall to this orchard but only a grassy bank. Mr Strange lay down beneath a pear tree and, though he had intended to think about magic, he very soon fell asleep.

A little later he heard (or dreamt that he heard) the sound of laughter and of feminine voices. Looking up, he saw three ladies in pale gowns walking (almost dancing) upon the bank above him. The stars surrounded them; the night-wind took their gowns and blew them about. They held out their arms to the wind (they seemed indeed to be dancing). Mr Strange stretched himself and sighed with pleasure. He assumed (not unreasonably) that he was still dreaming.

But the ladies stopt and stared down into the grass.

"What is it?" asked Miss Tobias.

Cassandra peered into the darkness. "It is a man," she said with great authority.

"Gracious Heaven," said Mrs Field. "What kind of man?"

"The usual kind, I should say," said Cassandra.

"I meant, Cassandra," said the other, "what degree, what station of man?"

Jonathan Strange got to his feet, perplexed, brushing straw from his clothes. "Ladies," he said, "forgive me. I thought that I had woken in the Raven King's Other Lands. I thought that you were Titania's ladies come to meet me."

The ladies were silent. And then: "Well!" said Mrs Field. "What a speech!"

"I beg your pardon, madam. I meant only that it is a beautiful night (as I am sure you will agree) and I have been thinking for some time that it is (in the most critical and technical sense) a magical night and I thought perhaps that you were the magic what was meant to happen."

"Oh," cried Cassandra, "they are all full of nonsense. Do not listen to him, my dear Mrs Field. Miss Tobias, let us walk on." But she looked at him curiously and said, "You? What do *you* know of magic?"

"A little, madam."

"Well, sir," she said, "I will give you a piece of good advice. You will never grow proficient in the art as long as you continue with your outmoded notions of Raven Kings and Otherlanders. Have you not heard? They have all been done away with by Mr Strange and Mr Norrell."

Mr Strange thanked her for the advice.

"There is much more that we could teach you . . ." she said.

"So it would seem," said Strange, crossing his arms.

". . . only that we have neither the time nor the inclination."

"That is a pity," said Strange. "Are you sure, madam, that you will not reconsider? My last master found me to be a most apt pupil, very quick to grasp the principles of any subject."

"What was the name of your last master?" asked Miss Tobias.

"Norrell," said Strange softly.

Another short silence ensued.

"You are the London magician," said Cassandra.

"No, indeed," cried Strange, stung. "I am the Shropshire magician and Mr Norrell is the Yorkshire magician. We neither of us own London as our home. We are countrymen both. We have that, at least, in common."

"You seem, sir, to be of a somewhat inconsistent, somewhat contradictory character," said Miss Tobias.

"Indeed, madam, other people have remarked upon it. And

now, ladies, since we are sure to meet again – and that quite soon – I will wish you all a goodnight. Miss Parbringer, I will give you a piece of advice in return for yours (for I am certain that it was given in good faith). Magic, madam, is like wine and, if you are not used to it, it will make you drunk. A successful spell is as potent a loosener of tongues as a bottle of good claret and you will find the morning after that you have said things you now regret."

With that he bowed and walked back through the orchard into the house.

"A magician in Grace Adieu," said Miss Tobias thoughtfully, "and at such a time. Well, let us not be disconcerted. We will see what tomorrow brings."

What tomorrow brought was a courteous note from Mr Wood-hope, expressing his hopes that the ladies of Grace Adieu would do his sister the honour of meeting her at the Rectory that afternoon. On this occasion the invitation included Miss Tobias, although, in general, she did not visit in the village (and was no great favourite with Mr Woodhope).

Despite the misgivings which all the ladies felt (and which Mrs Field had several times spoken out loud), Mr Strange met them with great good manners and a bow for each and he gave no hint to any one that this was not the first time he had seen them.

The talk was at first of the commonest sort and, to the ladies of Grace Adieu who did not know him, Mr Strange seemed of an easy and sociable character, so it was a trifle unsettling to hear Arabella Strange ask him why he was so silent today. Mr Strange replied that he was a little tired.

"Oh," said Mrs Strange to Mrs Field, "he has been up all night reading books of magical history. It is a bad habit that all magicians get into and it is that, as much as any thing, which weakens their wits in the end." She smiled at her husband as if expecting him to say some clever or impertinent thing in return. But he only continued to look at the three ladies of Grace Adieu.

Halfway through their visit Mr Woodhope rose and, speaking his great regret and looking at Miss Parbringer, begged that they would excuse him – he had parish business to attend. He was very anxious that Mr Strange should go with him, so much so that Strange had no alternative but to oblige him. This left the ladies alone.

The conversation turned to the articles Mr Strange had published in the quarterly reviews and, in particular, those passages where he proved that there could never have been such a person as the Raven King.

"Mrs Strange," said Cassandra, "you must agree with me – those are most extraordinary opinions for a magician, when even our common historians write the King's dates in their history books – four or five times the span of a common life."

Arabella frowned. "Mr Strange cannot always write exactly what he pleases. Much of it, you know, comes from Mr Norrell. Mr Norrell has studied magic for many years more than any other gentleman in England, and certainly with much greater profit. His opinion must carry great weight with any one who cares about English magic."

"I see," said Cassandra, "you mean that Mr Strange writes things which he does not entirely believe, because Mr Norrell tells him to. If I were a man (and, what is much more, a magician) I should not do any thing, write any thing, if I did not like it."

"Miss Parbringer," murmured Miss Tobias, reprovingly.

"Oh, Mrs Strange knows I mean no offence," cried Cassandra, "but I must say what I think and upon this topic of all things."

Arabella Strange smiled. "The situation," she said, "is not exactly as you suppose. Mr Strange has studied for a number of years with Mr Norrell in London and Mr Norrell swore at the beginning that he would not take a pupil and so it was considered a great honour when he consented to take Jonathan. And then, you know, there are only two true magicians in England and England is at war. If those two magicians quarrel, what follows? What greater comfort could we offer the French than this?"

The ladies took their tea together and the only slight incident to disturb the remainder of the visit was a fit of coughing which seized first Cassandra, and then Mrs Field. For several moments Mrs Strange was quite concerned about them.

When Henry Woodhope and Strange returned the ladies were gone. The maid and Mrs Strange were standing in the passage-way. Each was holding a little white linen cloth. The maid was exclaiming loudly about some thing or other and it was a moment before Jonathan Strange could make himself heard.

"What is it?" he asked.

"We have found some bones," said his wife, with a puzzled air. "Small, white bones, it would seem, of some delicate little creatures, and two little grey skins like empty pods. Come, sir, you are the magician, explain it to us."

"They are mouse bones. And mouse skins too. It is owls that do that. See," said Strange, "the skins are turned quite inside out. Curious, is it not?"

Mrs Strange was not greatly impressed with this as an explanation. "So I dare say," she said, "but what seems to me far more miraculous is that we found these bones in the cloaths which Miss Parbringer and Mrs Field had to wipe their fingers and their mouths. Jonathan, I hope you are not suggesting that these ladies have been eating mice?"

* * *

The weather continued very fine. Mr Woodhope drove his sister, Mr and Mrs Field and their niece to _____ Hill to see the views and to drink and eat by a pretty, hanging wood. Mr Strange rode behind. Once again he watched all the party carefully and once again Mrs Strange told him that he was in a grave, odd mood and not at all like himself.

On other days Mr Strange rode out by himself and talked to farmers and innkeepers on the highways all around. Mr Woodhope explained this behaviour by saying that Strange had always been very eccentric and that now he had become so great and full of London importance, Mr Woodhope supposed he had grown even more so.

One day (it was the last day of Mr and Mrs Strange's visit to their brother) Mrs Field, Miss Tobias and Cassandra were out walking on the high, empty hills above Grace Adieu. A sunlit wind bent all the long grasses. Light and shade followed each other so swiftly that it was as if great doors were opening and closing in the sky. Cassandra was swinging her bonnet (which had long since left her head) by its blue ribbons, when she saw a gentleman on a black mare, come riding to meet them.

When he arrived, Mr Strange smiled and spoke of the view and of the weather and, in the space of five minutes, was altogether more communicative than he had been in the entire past fortnight. None of the ladies had much to say to him, but Mr Strange was not the sort of gentleman who, once he has decided to talk, is to be put off by a lack of encouragement on the part of his listeners.

He spoke of a remarkable dream he had had.

"I was told once by some country people that a magician should never tell his dreams because the telling will make them come true. But I say that that is great nonsense. Miss Tobias, you have studied the subject, what is your opinion?"

But Miss Tobias was silent.

Strange went on. "I had this dream, Mrs Field, under rather curious circumstances. Last night I took some little bones to bed with me – I happened upon them quite recently. I put them under my pillow and there they stayed all night while I slept. Mrs Strange would have had a great deal to say to me upon the subject, had she known of it. But then, wives and husbands do not always tell each other every thing, do they, Mrs Field?"

But Mrs Field said nothing.

"My dream was this," said Strange. "I was talking to a gentleman (a very handsome man). His features were very distinct in my dream, yet I am quite certain that I never saw him before in all my life. When we came to shake hands, he was very reluctant – which I did not understand. He seemed embarrassed and not a little ashamed. But when, at last, he put out his hand, it was not a hand at all, but a little grey-furred claw. Miss Parbringer, I hear that you tell wonderful stories to all the village children. Perhaps you will tell me a story to explain my dream?"

But Miss Parbringer was silent.

"On the day that I and my wife arrived here, some other people came to Grace Adieu. Where are they now? Where is the thin dark figure – whether boy or young woman I do not know, for no one saw very clearly – who sat in the gig?"

Miss Tobias spoke. "Miss Pye was taken back to Reigate in our carriage. Davey, our coachman, conveyed her to the house of her mother and her aunt – good people who truly love her and who had wondered for a long, long time if they would ever see her again."

"And Jack Hogg, the Captain's servant?"

Miss Tobias smiled. 'Oh, he took himself off with remarkable speed, once it was made plain to him that staying would do no good at all."

"And where is Arthur Winbright? And where Frederick Littleworth?"

They were silent.

"Oh, ladies, what have you done?"

After a while Miss Tobias spoke again. "That night," she said, "after Captain Winbright and Mr Littleworth had . . . left us, I saw someone. At the other end of the passageway I saw, very dimly, someone tall and slender, with the wings of birds beating all around their shoulders. Mr Strange, *I* am tall and the wings of birds were, at that moment, beating around my shoulders . . ."

"And so, it was your reflection."

"Reflection? By what means?" asked Miss Tobias. "There is no glass in that part of the house."

"So, what did you do?" asked Strange a little uncertainly.

"I said aloud the words of the Yorkshire Game. Even you, Mr Strange, must know the words of the Yorkshire Game." Miss Tobias smiled a little sarcastically. "Mr Norrell is, after all, the Yorkshire magician, is he not?"

"I greet thee, Lord, and bid thee welcome to my heart," said Strange.

Miss Tobias inclined her head.

Now it was Cassandra's turn. "Poor man, you cannot even reconcile what you believe in your heart to be true and what you are obliged to write in the quarterly reviews. Can you go back to London and tell this odd tale? For I think you will find that it is full of all kinds of nonsense that Mr Norrell will not like – Raven Kings and the magic of wild creatures and the magic of women. You are no match for us, for we three are quite united, while you, sir, for all your cleverness, are at war, even with yourself. If ever a time comes, when your heart and your head declare a truce, then I suggest you come back to Grace Adieu and then you may tell us what magic we may or may not do."

It was Strange's turn to be silent. The three ladies of Grace Adieu wished him a good morning and walked on. Mrs Field alone favoured him with a smile (of a rather pitying sort).

*   *   *

A month after Mr and Mrs Strange's return to London, Mr Woodhope was surprized to receive a letter from Sir Walter Pole, the politician. Mr Woodhope had never met the gentleman, but now Sir Walter suddenly wrote to offer Mr Woodhope the rich living of Great Hitherden, in Northamptonshire. Mr Woodhope could only imagine that it was Strange's doing – Strange and Sir Walter were known to be friends. Mr Woodhope was sorry to leave Grace Adieu and sorry to leave Miss Parbringer, but he comforted himself with the thought that there were bound to be ladies, almost as pretty, in Northamptonshire and if there were not, well, he would be a richer clergyman there than he was in Grace Adieu and so better able to bear the loneliness.

Miss Cassandra Parbringer only smiled when she heard he was going and that same afternoon, went out walking on the high hills, in a fine autumn wind, with Mrs Field and Miss Tobias – as free, said Miss Parbringer, as any women in the kingdom.

ON

LICKERISH

HILL

WHEN I WAZ a child I lived at Dr Quince's on the other side of Lickerish Hill. Sometimes in a winters-twilight I have look't out of Dr Quince's windowe and seen Lickerish Hill (where the Pharisees live) like a long brown shippe upon a grey sea and I have seen far-awaie lights like silver starres among the dark trees.

My mother was mayde and cook to Dr Quince, an ancient and learned gentleman (face, very uglie like the picture of a horse not well done; dry, scantie beard; moist, pale eyes). This good old man quickly perceived what waz hid from my mother: that my naturall Genius inclin'd not to sweeping dairies or baking cakes or spinning or anie of the hundred thinges she wish'd me to know, but to Latin, Greeke and the study of Antiquities, and these he taught me. He alwaies meant that I should learne Hebrew, Geometrie, the Mathematiques, and he would have taught me this yeare but Time putt a trick on him and he died last summer.

The day after the pore old doctor died my mother baked five pies. Now malicious persons will open their mouths and lies will flie out and buzz about the World, but the truth is that those pies (which my mother baked) were curiously small and, for certaine pressing and private reasons of my owne – to witt a Great and Sudden Hunger – I ate them all, which was the cause of a quarrel betweene my mother and me. Angrilie shee foretold that terrible Catastrophes would befall me (povertie, marriage to beggars and gypsies, etc., etc.). But, as Mr Aubrey sayz, such Beautie as mine could not long remain undiscover'd, and so it waz that I married Sir John Sowreston and came to Pipers Hall.

Pipers Hall is the loveliest old house – alwaies very smiling in the sunshine. It was built long ago (I thinke in the time of King Solomon). About the house are many lawns where stand ancient trees that overtop the roofs like Gracious and Gigantique Ladies and Gentlemen from more Heroique Times, all robed in dresses of golden sunlight. Its shadie alleys are carpeted with water-mint and thyme and other sweet-smelling Plantes so that in a sum-mers-twilight when Dafney and I walke there and crush them with our feet 'tis as if an Angell caress't you with his Breath.

Sir John Sowreston is two-and-thirty yeares of age; size, middling; eyes, black; legges, handsome. He smiles but rarely and watches other men to see when they laugh and then does the same. Since a boy he haz been afflicted with a Great Sadnesse and Fitts of Black Anger which cause his neighbours, friends and servants to feare him. It is as if some Divinitie, jealous of the Gifts Heav'n haz bestowed on him (Youth, Beautie, Riches, etc., etc.) haz putt an eville Spell on him. There waz a little dogge borne upon our Wedding-daye. At 3 or 4 weeks old it would always goe a little sideways when it walked and would climb upon Sir John's shoulder when he sat after dinner and sleep there, as if it loved him extreamlie. But, being frighted by a horse looking in at the windowe, it fouled a coat belonging to Sir John with its excrements and Sir John putte it in a sack and drowned it in the horse-pond. We called it Puzzle because (Dafney sayd) whatsoever happen'd puzzled it sorely. (I thinke it was puzzled why it died.) Now Sir John haz gott 3 great blacke dogges and his greatest pleasure in all the Worlde is to goe hunting on Lickerish Hill.

Two months after Sir John and I were married we travelled to Cambridge to seek a cure for Sir John's melancholie from Dr Richard Blackswann, a very famose Physician. We took with us a little cristall flask that had some of Sir John's water in it. Dr Blackswann went into a little closet behind a curtain of blacke velvet and prayed upon his knees. The Angell Raphael then appearing in the closet (as commonly happens when ever this doctor prays) peer'd into Sir John's urine. Dr Blackswann told us that the Angell Raphael knew straightway from the colour of it (reddish as if there waz bloude in it) that the cause of Sir John's extreame Want of Spirits was a lack of Learned Conversation. The Angell Raphael said that Sir John muste gather Scholars to his howse to exercise their Braines with Philosophie, Geometrie, Rhetorique, Mechanicks etc., etc., and that hearing of their schemes would divert Sir John and make his thoughts to runne in pleasanter courses.

Sir John waz very much pleased with this Scheme and all the way home we sang Ballads together and were so merry that Sir John's three great black dogges raised their voices with us in praise of learned Dr Blackswann and the Angell Raphael.

On the evening that we came home I waz walking in the garden by myselfe among the Heroique Trees when I met Mrs Sloper (my mother).

Mrs Abigail Sloper, widow; person thin and stringy; face the shape of a spoon and the colour of green cheese; cook and nurse to the late Dr Hieronymous Quince; made nervous by Dr Quince's talking Hebrew on purpose to discompose her (she mistook it for incantations) – a cruel Satire on her Ignorance, but I could not gett him to leave off; talkes to herselfe when in a fright; haz two old English Catts (that are white with some blewnesse upon them) – Solomon Grundy (4 yeares old) and Blewskin (10 yeares old) and a Cowe called Polly Diddle (one yeare old); in 1675 she buried a little blew pot of shillings at the

41

bottom of Dr Quince's garden, under some redd-currant bushes, but he dying shortly after and the house being sold very suddenly, she was cast into a Great Perplexitie how to recover her monies which she haz not yet resolved.

"Good Evening, mother, my deare," sayz I. "Come into the howse and have some vittles and drinke."

But she would not answer me and cast her Glances all over the garden, a-twisting and a-twisting of her apron. "Oh!" sayz she (with her eyes fix't upon a Beech-tree, so that she seemes to address it), "my daughter'll be so vex't."

"No, I won't," sayz I, "Why are you in such a pickle? Take time, my deare, and tell me what you're afeard of."

But instead of a Replie she rambled about the Garden, complain'd to a Briar-rose that I am Ungrateful to her, told two little Oringe-trees that I doe not love her.

"Oh, mother!" sayz I, "I doe not wish to be angrie, but you will make me so if you doe not tell me what the matter is."

At this she hid her head in her apron; wept very piteously; then suddenly reviv'd.

"Well!" sayz she (apparently to a monument of Kinge Jupiter that look't downe on her with much contempt), "You remember the day after the pore owd doctor died I baked five pies and my daughter ate 'em all, first and last!"

"Oh! Mother!" sayz I, "Why doe you perpetuate these old quarrels between us? Those old pies waz such tiddly little thinges!"

"No, they warn't," sayz she to Jupiter (as if he contradicted her). "Howsomediver," sayz she, "I were so vex't an' I muddled about an' I told little owd Solomon Grundy and owd Blewskin . . ." (she meanes her Catts) ". . . I sayz to 'em, My daughter haz ate five pies today! Five pies! And I lookes up and I sees Sir John Sowreston a-sitting on his hobby-horse – as bewtiful as butter. And he sayz to me, What are you a-saying of, Mrs Sloper? Well!

I knowed Sir John Sowreston waz extreamlie in Love with my daughter an' I knowed he'd come to looke at har through the owd Elder-hedge an' I didn't like to say as how my daughter had ate five pies. So I sayz, right sly like, I sayz My daughter haz spun five skeins o' flax today . . ."

"Mother!" sayz I, "You never! You never told Sir John such a lie!"

"Well then," sayz she, "I did. An' there ain't nothing but good come to my daughter a'cos of it. Sir John Sowreston lookes at me with his bewtiful Eyes like two dishes o' Chocolate a-poppin' out of his Head and he sayz to me Stars o' mine! I never heerd o' anyone as could do that! Mrs Sloper, I'll marry your daughter on Sunday. – Fair enough, sayz I, an' shall she have all the vittles she likes to eat and all the gowns she likes to get and all the company she likes to have? Oh yes! sayz he, all o' that. But come the last month o' the first year she must spinne five skeins o' flax every day. Or else . . ."

"Or else what, mother?" sayz I in a Fright.

"Oww!" she cries, "I sayd as how she'd be vex't! I knew she would! I have made her a Grand Ladye with such a bewtiful Husband and all the vittles she likes to eat and all the gowns she likes to get and all the company she likes to have – and her never a bitt grateful. But," she sayz a-tapping herselfe upon the nose and lookinge sly, "No harm will come to my daughter. Sir John Sowreston is still extreamlie in Love an' he haz forgott those owd skeins of flax completely . . ."

Then, having vindicated her-selfe in the Opinions of all the rose-bushes and Beech-trees and monuments in the garden, my mother went away againe.

Now Sir John Sowreston does not forget anie thinge and as sure as there are Pharisees on Lickerish Hill, come the first daie of the last month of the first yeare of our marriage, he would aske me for those skeins. At first I waz very much tempted to weep oceans of bitter tears but then I thought of the noble and virtuous Roman matrons of whom Dr Quince told me and how they would not weep no matter how great their sufferings; and I thought how I had a very ingeniose head and alwaies a thousand notions flitting about inside it and waz besides as beautiful as an Angell. I dare say, sayz I, there is some verie cunning way to overcome this Fate. And I determined to discouver what it waz very suddenlie.

Sir John went to London to seek out Ingeniose Gentlemen to cure his Melancholie. In this he waz shortly successful for nothing is so agreeable to a Scholar than to goe and stay in a rich man's howse and live at his expense. Mr Aubrey and Sir John Sowreston gott acquainted, and Sir John waz very pressing with Mr Aubrey to come to Pipers Hall and Mr Aubrey who waz pressed another way (Great Debts he could not Pay and Danger of Arrests!), was glad to come immediately.

Mr Aubrey is writing downe all that he can remember of the customes of former times. He smells of brandy and chalke and is finely spotted all over with Inke. He haz pieces of paper in all his pockets on which he is writing his Histories. He is a Member of the Royal Society. He is my deare Friend. He is putting down all the lives of Great and Ingeniose men so that their Genius may not be forgot. Mr Aubrey sayz that he is like a man plucking out spars and relicks from the Shipwreck of Time and tossing them upon the sand. But, sayz Mr Aubrey, the Waters of Oblivion have the best of it.

For severall years Mr Aubrey haz wish'd to come into this Countie which is stuff't with Ancient Persons who, as Mr Aubrey sayz, may suddenly die and cheat Posterity of their Remembrances, if some Publick-spirited and Ingeniose man does not come and sett them downe; and Mr Aubrey wish'd very much to carry out this Design but was prevented, having no money and no friends residing in this part of the Countrey whom he could suddenly delight by arriving for a good long visit. Mr Aubrey was once a very rich man with lands; estates; pleasant farmes; cowes; sheepe, etc., etc., and (I thinke) great boxes of silver and gold. But he haz lost it all through Law-suites, Misfortunes and the Unkindnesse of his Relations. Mr Aubrey sayz that nothing so distracts a Scholar or drawes so many teares from a Scholar's head as Law-suites. But, sayz Mr Aubrey, I am now very merry, Miranda, my Troubles are at an end. And he asked me to lend him three pounds.

The other noble Scholars arrived shortly afterwards. They are all very memorablie famose. Mr Meldreth, a sweet, shy gentleman the colour of dust, is for Insects and haz 237 dead ones in a box. Mr Shepreth haz discovered the date upon which the Citie of London waz first built. This, being like to its *Birthe-daye*, haz enabled him to caste its horoscope: he knowes all its Future. Dr Foxton haz shewne by Irrefutable Arguments that Cornishmen are a kind of Fishe. His beard curles naturallie – a certaine sign of witt.

All winter the Learned Conversation of the Scholars delighted Sir John extreamlie. But it is part of Sir John's Affliction that whatever pleases him best at first, he most detests at last. In spring he began privately to calle them Raskall-Jacks, Rumble-Guts, Drunke, Ungrateful; complain'd that they ate too much, despis'd their Learning and frowned very blacke upon them at dinner until the poore Scholars had scarcelie anie Appetite to eate so much as a bit of Breade and all satt with a kinde of Lownesse on their Spirits. Summer came againe and it waz almost a yeare since Sir John and I were married. I tried very hard to conjure a cunning Scheme out of my Head but could think of nothing until the verie last daie.

Upon that daie the Scholars and I were sitting together beneathe the great Beeche-tree which stands before the dore of Pipers Hall.

Mr Meldreth sighed. "Gentlemen," he sayz, "We are very poor physick. Poor Sir John is as unhappy as ever he waz."

"True," sayz Mr Shepreth, "but we have made Lady Sowreston . . ." (he meant me) ". . . very merry. She loves to heare our Learned Conversation."

"There is no merit in that," sayz Mr Aubrey, "Miranda is alwaies merry."

"Mr Aubrey," sayz I.

"Yes, Miranda?" sayz he.

" 'Tis a very curious thinge, Mr Aubrey," sayz I. "I have lived all my life neare Lickerish Hill, but I never once sawe a Pharisee."

"A Pharisee?" sayz Mr Aubrey, "What doe you meane, child?"

"They live on Lickerish Hill," sayz I, "Or under it. I doe not know which. They pinche dairymaides blacke and blewe. Other times they sweepe the floor, drinke the creame and leave silver pennies in shoes. They putte on white cappes, crie Horse and Hattock, flie through the aire on Bitts of Strawe – generally to the Kinge of France's wine-cellar where they drinke the wine out of silver cups and then off to see a wicked man hanged – which person they may save if they have a minde to it."

"Oh!" sayz Dr Foxton, " 'Tis *Fairies* she meanes."

"Yes," sayz I. "That is what I sayd. Pharisees. I have never seen one. Dr Quince haz told me that they are not so common as once they were. Dr Quince haz told me that the Pharisees are leaving and will never more be seen in England. For my-selfe I never sawe one. But many Ancient Persons worthy of Belief have seen them on Lickerish Hill, trooping out of the World on Ragged Ponies, their heads bowed downe with Sadnesse, descending into dark hollows and blewe shadowes betwixt the trees. My Opinion is," sayz I, "that there can be no better taske for an Antiquarie than to discouver all he can of the Pharisees and I thinke there can be no better place in all the

World to look for Pharisees than Pipers Hall under Lickerish Hill, for that is where they live. Mr Aubrey," sayz I, "Doe you know anie Spells to conjure Pharisees?"

"Oh, severall!" sayz Mr Aubrey, "Mr Ashmole (who is a noble Antiquary and haz made the Collection at Oxford) haz putt them downe in his Papers."

"Mr Aubrey," sayz I.

"Yes, Miranda?" sayz he.

"Will you shew me the Spells, Mr Aubrey?"

But before he could answer me Mr Meldreth ask'd with a Frowne if they worked?

"I doe not knowe," sayz Mr Aubrey.

"Who shall we conjure first?" askes Dr Foxton.

"Titania," sayz Mr Shepreth.

"A common Pharisee," sayz I.

"Why, Miranda?" askes Mr Shepreth.

"Oh!," sayz I, "they can doe a hundred clever thinges. Bake cakes, gather in flockes of sheepe, churne butter, spinne flax . . ."

All the Scholars laugh't very much at this.

"So can your mayde, Miranda," sayz Mr Shepreth. "No, 'tis fairie politics we chiefly wish to learn. And for this purpose the Queen is best. Besides," sayz Mr Shepreth, "she may give us presents."

"Tut," sayz Mr Meldreth, " 'Tis onlie young men with handsome faces that she woos with presents."

"We are handsome enough," sayz Mr Shepreth.

Dr Foxton sayd that it waz one of the many inconveniences of discoursing with Fairies, that they may at anie moment disappear and so the gentlemen agreed to draw up a list of questions – so that when they discouvered a Fairie willing to speak to them all pertinent questions should be convenient to hand.

Quaere: if the Faeries have anie Religion among them?

Oh! sayd Dr Foxton, there waz a Fairie-woman in Cornwall who heard a Reverend gentleman saying his prayers. She asked him if there were salvation and eternal life for such as shee? No sayd the Reverend gentleman. With a cry of despair she instantly threw herself over a cliff and into the foaming sea. This, sayd Dr Foxton, he gott from a very Pious person who all his life abhorred Lying. Dr Foxton sayd he would not believe it else and Mr Meldreth, who is of a sweet and gentle nature, wept a little to think on't.

Quaere: if they have anie marrying among them?

Mr Shepreth sayd he believed they did *not* live together like Christians and turtle-doves, but had all their ladyes in common. Tut! sayz Mr Meldreth. Ha! cried Mr Aubrey and wrote it down very fast.

Quaere: if it is true (as some people say) that they are a much-decayed people and not so strong as they used to be?

Quaere: their system of Gouvernment: if a Monarchie or a Commonwealthe?

Quaere: if a Monarchie then whether it is true (as we have heard tell) that the Queen and King of the Pharisees have quarrelled?

Quaere: if it is true that the Queen cannot in one thinge gouverne herselfe?

This went on until the Scholars all fell a-quarrelling, having now gott fortie-two questions to ask the poor Pharisee when they found it and Mr Foxton sayd a Christian could not bear to be so putt upon let alone a Fairie. Mr Aubrey sighed and sayd he would trie to reduce the number.

"Here is Sir John Sowreston!" whispers Dr Foxton.

"Mr Aubrey!" sayz I.

"Yes, Miranda?" sayz he.

But I had no time to aske him what I wished because Sir John hurried me into the howse.

"Oh, my deare," sayz I to Sir John, "What is the matter? Do not let the noble Scholars see you looke so Melancholie! They still hope to chear you."

"Where are we going, Sir John?" sayz I. "I never sawe this little staircase before. Is it some secret place that you discouvered when you played here as a boye? Is that what you wishe to shew me?"

"I never saw this room before," sayz I, "And here are your three goode dogges, fighting with each other for some bones. Sir John, doe such great big dogges like to be shutt up in such a little room? And what is this little spinning wheele for?"

"Miranda," sayz Sir John, "You are very younge and for that reason I have often gouverned my-selfe when I should be angrie. Your lookes are often insolent. Your speech is full of Conceit and not womanly."

"Oh no, my deare!" sayz I, "You mistake. Those are lovinge lookes I give you."

"Perhaps," sayz he. "I doe not know. Sometimes, Miranda, I half-believe . . . But then againe, all men lye – and all women too. They drinke in Lyes with their mother's milke. As little children they delight to bear false witness one against the other. The Lyes and deceits that are practised on me every day by the common sort of people . . ." (He meant our Servants, Neighbours, Lawyers, Relations, etc., etc.) ". . . pricke my flesh like the stinges of bees and mosquitos. I scarcelie regard them. But a

Lye from you, Miranda, will be a long, sharp sworde that slippes between my bones and cuttes my Heart. You swore when you married me that you could spinne five skeins of flax every daye for a month . . ."

"Spinne five skeins of flax in a daye . . . Oh, Sir John! I never heard of anie one that could doe that!"

"I hope, Miranda, that you have not lyed. A wife, Miranda, haz her husband's conscience in her keeping and muste so order her actions that they tempt not her husband to sinne. It is a wicked thinge to tempt others to sinne. To kille someone in anger is a sinne."

He wept a little to thinke on't, but it waz not for me he wept but for his owne Unhappy Spirit, thinking that when he murdered me 'twould be all his owne Misfortune and none of mine.

"Oh!" sayz I chearfully, "Doe not be afraid, my deare. I shall spinne you thread so soft and fine. And Dafney and I shall make you shirts of the thread I spinne and at every touch of those shirts you will thinke I kisse you."

But he shutt the doore upon me and lock't it and went awaie.

From the windowe I sawe the Scholars sitting beneath the Beech-tree. They were all very merry now that Sir John waz gone. As the twilight deepen'd they dranke each others healthes and sang a ballad of their youth about a shepherdesse that some gentlemen liked. Then all joined armes and sang againe and off to bed together.

The kitchen door opened and let out a little firelight upon the lavender bushes. Dafney look't out. (Dafney Babraham: mayde to Lady Miranda Sowreston that is my-selfe; yellow haire; smelles of rosemary and other good thinges; haz two gownes, a blew and a redd.) She called faintly, "Madam, Madam." She came along the path; cast her lookes this way and that; seemed quite distracted from not knowing where to finde me. She feared Sir John had alreadie drowned me in the horse-pond.

"Oh!" she cries, spying me, "What are you a-doing up there? Where did that little windowe come from? I'll come to you directly, my deare!"

"No," sayz I, "Go to bed. I shall sleepe in this little room tonight. 'Tis my fancy."

"I heare terrible fierce noyses," she sayz.

" 'Tis onlie some dogges that keepe me safe," sayz I, "Goodnight my deare. God blesse you. I am not a bitt afraid."

But all through the night the three dogges growled and twitched as if in their sleepe they hunted me on Lickerish Hill.

In the morning Sir John brought me flax and vittles. Then he went awaie againe. Outside my windowe a silvery mist like a Cloude cover'd Pipers Hall. Everything in the world (*scilicet* Trees, Hedges, Fountains, Monuments, Dwellings of Men, Cattle, Hens, Bees, Horses etc., etc.) waz grey and faint in the silver Aire. There waz a golden glory all around Lickerish Hill but the Sunne did not yet peepe above the brow of the hill. All the birds sang and all the grey roses hung downe their heads with heavie dew.

Four grey figures in long robes approached the Beech-tree that stood before the doore. One grey figure sneezed and complained of the freshnesse and sharpnesse of the Aire that, he sayd, was not wholesome for Men. Another grey figure regretted eating too much cheese and pickled herring the night before. And a third waz fearful that the Pharisees might steale him awaie.

Dr Foxton had gott a magickal hatt that (he thinkes) once belonged to the old, wicked magician, Simon Forman. He putt it on. The Sunne peep'd over Lickerish Hill. Mr Aubrey beganne to read the Spelle in a clear voice. It waz stuff't as full of magic words as a puddinge is of plumms.

"I, John Aubrey, call thee, Queen Titania, in the name of . . ."

And I listened very carefully and repeated the words after him – but where he sayd "Queen Titania" I sayd "Pharisee Vulgaris."

". . . conjure and straightly charge and command thee by Tetragrammaton, Alpha and Omega and by all other high and reverent . . ."

The miste that cover'd Pipers Hall turned to rose and blew and silver. I heard a noyse in the orchard. But it waz onlie three birds that rose into the Aire.

". . . meekely and mildely to my true and perfect sight and truly without fraud, Dissymulation or deceite, resolve and satisfye me in and of all manner of such questions and commands and demandes as I shall either aske, require . . ."

The miste that cover'd Pipers Hall turned to golde. I heard a noyse by the hen-houses. But it waz onlie a foxe that ranne home to the woods.

". . . quickly, quickly, quickly, quickly, come, come, come. Fiat, Fiat, Fiat. Amen, Amen, Amen . . ." Mr Aubrey paused. "Etcetera," he sayz with a Flourishe.

The miste that cover'd Pipers Hall turned to little droppes of water. I heard a noyse beneathe the windowe but I could not tell what it waz.

There waz a long silence.

Then Dr Foxton sighed. " 'Tis well known that the Queen of the Fairies is not to be trusted. Shee is capricious," he sayz.

"Perhaps," sayz Mr Shepreth (meaning to be Satirical), "Shee did not like your hatt."

Suddenly the 3 dogges beganne to howle and runne and leape in a manner very strange to see as if they had fallen into a kinde of Extascie. It waz so violent and continued for so long that I hid my-selfe in a corner.

"Woman," sayz a Voice, "What are you a-crying for?"

"Oh!" sayz I. "Are you the Pharisee?"

A small black thinge. Hairie. Legges like jug-handles. Face – not a bitt handsome. It had a long, blacke taile – at which I waz much surprized. Irishmen have tailes neare a quarter of a yard longe (as I thinke is commonly known) but I never hearde before that Pharisees have them.

"Are you a good Pharisee or a bad?" sayz I.

The Pharisee, a-twirling and a-twirling of his long, black taile, seemed to consider my inquiry. "Never you minde," it sayz at last. It cock't its head in the direction of the windowe. "There be four peevish old men a-standin' in your meadow, wi' queer old hatts on their heads, all jammerin' together."

"Oh!" sayz I, "They are disappointed in their Spelle which haz had No Success. Whereas mine haz summoned you promptlie to the proper place."

"I don't take no notice o' frimmickin' old Spelles an' such like," sayz the little black thinge, picking his teeth with a bit of old rabbit-bone, "But I waz extreamlie kewrious to know what you waz a-crying for."

So I told him my historie, beginning with the pies (which were so curiouslie small) and ending with the five skeines of flax. "For the truth is, Pharisee," sayz I, "that that my naturall Genius inclines not at all to brewing or baking cakes or spinning or anie of those thinges, but to Latin, Greeke and the study of Antiquities and I can no more spinne than flie."

The Pharisee consider'd my Dilemma. "This is what I'll doe," it sayz at last. "I'll come to your windowe ev'ry morning an' take the flax an' bring it back spun at night."

"Oh, a hundred thousand thankes!" sayz I. "'Tis a very generous turne you doe me. But then, you know, I have alwaies heard that Pharisees doe wonderful kind thinges and never ask for pay of anie sorte or anie thinge in returne."

"You heerd that, did you?" sayz the little black thinge,

a-scritch-scritch-scratching of his armpit. "Well, woman, you heerd wrong."

"Oh!" sayz I.

The Pharisee look't at me out of the corners of its little blacke eyes and sayz, "I'll give you three guesses ev'ry night to guess my name an' if you ain't guessed it afore the month's up, Woman, you shall be mine!"

"Well then", sayz I, "I thinke I shall discover it in a month."

"You thinke so, doe you?" sayz the Pharisee and laugh't and twirl'd its taile. "What be the names o' they old dogges?"

"Oh!" sayz I, "That I doe know. Those dogges are called Plato, Socrates and Euclid. Sir John told me."

"Noo, they ain't," sayz the Pharisee, "One on 'em's called Wicked. The other un's Worse an' the third's Worst-of-all. They told me theerselves."

"Oh!" sayz I.

"Happen," sayz the Pharisee with great satisfaction, "you don't know yer own name."

"'Tis Miranda Sloper," sayz I. ". . . I meane Sowreston."

"Woman," sayz the Pharisee laughing, "You shall be mine."

And he took the flax and flew awaie.

All daye long there waz a kind of twilight in the little room made by the shadowes of leaves that fell over its white walls.

When the twilight in the room waz match't by a twilight in the World outside the Pharisee return'd.

"Good evening, Pharisee," sayz I, "How doe you fare?"

The little blacke thing sighed. "Kind o' middlin' like. My old ears is queer an' I have a doddy little ache in my foot."

"Tut," sayz I.

"I have brung the skeins," it sayz. "Now, woman, what's my name?"

"Is it Richard?" sayz I.

"Noo, it ain't," sayz the little blacke thinge and it twirl'd its taile.

"Well, is it George?" sayz I.

"Noo, it ain't," sayz the little blacke thinge and it twirl'd its taile.

"Is it Nicodemus?" sayz I.

"Noo, it ain't," sayz the little blacke thinge and flew awaie.

Strange to say I did not heare Sir John enter. I did not know he waz there until I spied his long shadowe among the shifting shadowes on the wall. He waz entirelie astonished to see the five skeins of thread.

Every morning he brought me flax and vittles, and whenever he appear'd the blacke dogges seemed full of joy to see him there, but that waz nothing to their Frenzie when the Pharisee came. Then they leap't in great delight and smelled him extremlie as if he were the sweetest rose. I satt thinking of all the names I ever heard, but never did I chuse the right one. Every night the Pharisee brought the spun flax and every night it came closer and closer and twirl'd its taile faster in its Delight. "Woman," it sayz, "You shall be mine." And every night Sir John came and fetched the thread and every night he waz greatly puzzled, for he knew that the three fierce dogges that guarded me obeyed no man but him-selfe.

One daye, towards the end of the month I look't out of my windowe and waz entirelie astonished to see a great many people with sorrowful faces trudging out of Pipers Hall and Dafney's yellow head among them, bent in Teares. Beneathe the great Beech-tree the four Scholars were equally amazed.

"Sir John, Sir John!" cries Mr Aubrey, "Where are all the servants going? Who will take care of Lady Sowreston?" (Sir John had told them I waz sicke.)

Sir John bent low and sayz something to them which I did not heare, and which seem'd to them a great Surprize.

"No, indeed!" sayz Mr Shepreth.

Mr Aubrey shook his head.

Dr Foxton sayz gravely, "We are Scholars and Gentlemen, Sir John, we doe not Spinne."

"Truly," sayz Mr Meldreth, "I cannot spinne, but I can make a pie. I read it in a booke. I believe I could doe it. You take flour, cleane Water, some raisins, whatsoever meate you like best and, I thinke, some Egges and then . . ."

Dr Foxton (who waz once a teacher in a grammar-schoole) hit Mr Meldreth on the head to make him quiet.

After Sir John had gone the Scholars told each other that Pipers Hall had gott very dismal and queer. Perhaps, sayz Mr Shepreth, it is time to goe and take their chances in the wider World againe. But all agreed to wait until Lady Sowreston waz well and all spoke very sweetly of my kindnesse to them. Then Mr Meldreth look't up. "Why!" he sayz, "There is Lady Sowreston at that little window among the leaves!"

"Miranda!" crie the Scholars.

Dr Foxton waved his hatt. Mr Shepreth kiss't his hand to me twenty times, Mr Meldreth putte his hands upon his Heart to shew his devotion and Mr Aubrey smiled chearfully to see my face.

"Good morning, deare Scholars!" I crie, "Have you discouvered the Queen of the Pharisees yet?"

"No," sayz Dr Foxton, "But we have got eightie-four more questions to aske her when she does appeare."

"Are you better, Miranda?" askes Mr Aubrey.

"My Opinion is," sayz I, "that I shall be cured by the end of the month. Meanwhile, deare Scholars, I have had a strange dream which I muste tell you. I dreamt that if a Scholar onlie knew a Pharisee's true name then he could conjure it quite easily."

"Well, Miranda," sayz Mr Aubrey, "many Fairies have secret names."

"Yes but doe you know anie of them?" sayz I.

The Scholars putte their Heads together for Grave Debate. Then they all nodded together.

"No," sayz Mr Aubrey, "We doe not."

Today waz the last daie. Earlie in the morning I look't out of the windowe and sawe a shower of cool rain upon Lickerish Hill that stirr'd all the leaves of the trees. When Sir John brought me flax and vittles I told him what I have seen.

"There are Deer upon Lickerish Hill," sayz Sir John thoughtfully.

"Yes," sayz I, "and many other thinges besides. I remember how when you and I were first married, you used to say that you had no greater pleasure in the world than to goe hunt some wild creature on Lickerish Hill and kille it and then come home and kisse your owne Miranda. And my Opinion is that you should take these goode dogges and let them know againe how grasse smelles. Take your learned guests, Sir John, and goe hunting on Lickerish Hill."

Then Sir John frown'd, thinking that the dogges should still remaine in this little room, for the month waz not yet over. But the breeze that came in through the windowe carried with it the sweet scent of the woods on Lickerish Hill.

In the shelter of the Beech-tree I heard Mr Shepreth tell Mr Aubrey that he waz glad Sir John had so far mended his quarrel with the Scholars that he invited them to goe hunting with him. Dr Foxton haz gott a special Hatt for hunting. He putte it on. Then Sir John and the Scholars and all the grooms gott on their horses and rode out of Pipers Hall with Wicked, Worse and Worst-of-all running on before smelling every thinge.

The rain fell all daie. All daie the new servants that Sir John haz hired muddled their work from not having anie good ancient servant set in authoritie over them to instruct them what to doe. The bread did not rise. The butter did not come in the churne. Knives and sickles were blunted from wrong use. Gates were opened that should be shutt. Cowes and horses gott into the wrong fields; broke fences; trampl'd crops. Some wicked boyes I never sawe before climb'd over the orchard wall and ate the apples, then went home with white sicke faces. All through the house I heard the new servants quarrelling with each other.

It is time for the Pharisee to come and bringe me the spun thread. But he does not come.

Grey rabbits bob and looke about them in the summers-twilight, then creepe into the kitchen-garden to eate our sallade-herbes. Owls hoot in the darkening woods and foxes bark. The last of the light is upon Lickerish Hill. It is time for Sir John to come and kille me. But he does not come.

"Miranda!"

"Good evening, deare Scholares. What have you killed?"

"Why, nothing, Miranda," sayz Mr Meldreth in great excitement. "We have had a strange adventure as we must tell you. From the moment that we reached Lickerish Hill, Plato, Socrates and Euclid . . ." (He meanes the dogges that the Pharisee calles Wicked, Worse and Worst-of-all) ". . . ranne as if their dearest Friend waited on Lickerish Hill to embrace them and our horses raced after and we could not halt them. They tooke us to a part of Lickerish Hill which none of us had ever seen before. A great Stagge with droppes of rain upon his speckled flanks stepp't out before us and look't at us as if he waz the Lord of All Creation and not us Men at all. Foxes cross't our path and watch't us pass. Little grey hares look't up from their cradles of stones with fearless faces. But we had no time to be astonished for Plato, Socrates and Euclid ranne on ahead and our horses followed . . ."

"Yes, indeed!" sayz Mr Shepreth, "And one dark sulkie fellow among us cried out that we must have fallen by mistake into some Fairie-kingdome under the ground where Beastes revenge

them-selves upon Men for the harms done to them on Earth; and Dr Foxton began to speak of wild rides that go on for all Eternity and enchanted riders who cannot jumpe downe for feare of crumbling to duste when they touch the earth. But Mr Aubrey bid us all trust in God and have no feare . . ."

"We stopp't suddenlie in a little green meadow in the dark woods. The meadow waz full of flowers and the sulkie man sayd that such flowers had never before been seen anie-where. But Sir John sayd he waz a fool and Sir John sayd he knew the names of the flowers as well as his own – they were Shepherds' Sun-dialls, Milkmaydes' Buttons and Dodmans' Combs. In the middle of the meadow waz a little chalke pit. This old pit waz mostly hidden by tall grasses and the flowers that Sir John had named. And out of the pit came a noyse of humming. The men held back the dogges – to their very Great Distresse – and we went very quiet to the pit and look't down. And what doe you thinke we sawe there?"

"I doe not know, Dr Foxton."

"A Fairye, Miranda! And what doe you thinke it waz doing?"

"I cannot guess, Dr Foxton."

"Well!" sayz Mr Aubrey, "It had a little spinning wheele and it waz spinning wonderfully fast and twirling its long, blacke taile. Quick! cries Mr Shepreth, Say your Spelle, Mr Aubrey! and he leapt into the pit and we all leapt after him."

"I am entirelie astonished," sayz I. "But what did you learne? What did the Pharisee tell you?"

"Nothing," sayz Dr Foxton crossly. "We asked it our hundred and fortie-seaven questions – which is the reason of our staying so long on Lickerish Hill and coming home so late to dinner – but 'twas the most ignorant Pharisee."

We are all silent a moment.

"But it listened to all your questions," sayz I, "That is strange. It would not so much as come when you summoned it before."

"Quite, Miranda," sayz Mr Aubrey, "And the reason is that we had not gott its name before. The wordes of the Spell and its owne true name held it fast. It waz obliged to hear us out – though it yearn'd to goe on with its worke – it had gott a fearful great pile of flax to spinne. We gott the name by chance. For, as we peep't over the edge of the pit, it waz singing its name over and over againe. We were not at all enchanted by its song. An Ingeniose Spinner, Miranda, but no Poet. Fairies love to sing, but their Inventions are weak. They can get no further than a line or two until some kind Friend teaches them a new one."

We are all silent againe.

"And what did it sing?" sayz I.

"It sang: 'Nimmy, Nimmy Not; My name's Tom Tit Tot.'" sayz Mr Aubrey.

"Well!" sayz I, "I am very glad, deare Scholars, to heare that you have seen a Pharisee, but I am happier still that you have gott safe home againe. Goe to your dinner but I feare it will be a poore one."

Now comes the Pharisee creeping through the evening mist with the skeins of spun flax upon his arme. First I shall guess Solomon then I shall guess Zebedee. But then I must tell him his name and poore Tom Tit Tot must goe howling awaie to his cold and lonelie hole.

Now comes Sir John, all Frowne and Shadowe, on a horse as blacke as a tempest, with Wicked, Worse and Worst-of-all beside him. And when he haz seen the spun flax then he and I shall goe downe together to eate and drinke with the happy Scholars who even now are composing a chearfull song about four gentlemen who once sawe a Pharisee. And all our good Servants shall come home and each shall have sixpence to drinke Sir John's healthe.

"I am writing my historie," sayz I, "Where doe I begin?"

"Oh!" sayz Mr Aubrey, "begin where you chuse, Miranda, but

putte it downe very quick while it is fresh and sprightly in your Braine. For remembrances are like butterflies and just as you thinke you have them flie out of the window. If all the thinges I have forgott, Miranda, were putte into His Majesties Navy, 'twould sink the fleet."

Among the many sources she drew upon for this story the author would particularly like to acknowledge folklorist Edward Clodd's wonderful 1898 rendition of Tom Tit Tot in Suffolk dialect.

I N T H E L A T E spring of 18 ___ a lady in the village of Kissingland in D _____ shire suffered a bitter disappointment.

Mrs Fanny Hawkins to Mrs Clara Johnson:
". . . and I know, my dear Clara, that you will share my vexation when I tell you what has happened. Some months ago my sister, Miss Moore, had the good fortune to captivate an officer in the Regulars. Captain Fox shewed a decided preference for Venetia from the start and I was in great hopes of seeing her respectably settled when, by a stroke of ill fortune, she received a letter from an acquaintance, a lady in Manchester who had fallen sick and was in need of someone to nurse her. You may imagine how little I liked that she should leave Kissingland at such a time, but I found that, in spite of all I could say, she was determined to undertake the expense and inconvenience of the journey and go. But now I fear she is too well punished for her obstinacy, for in her absence the wretched Captain Fox has forgot her entirely and has begun to pay his respects to another lady, a neighbour of ours, Mrs Mabb. You may well believe that when she comes back I will always be quarrelling with her about it . . ."

*　　*　　*

Fanny Hawkins' amiable intention of quarrelling with her sister proceeded, not merely from a general wish to correct faulty behaviour, but also from the realization that if Venetia did *not* marry Captain Fox then she must look to Fanny for a home. Fanny's husband was the curate of Kissingland, a person of no particular importance in the society of the place, who baptised, married, and buried all its inhabitants, who visited them in their sick-beds, comforted them in their griefs, and read their letters to them if they could not do it for themselves – for all of which he received the magnificent sum of £40 a year. Consequently any moments which Fanny could spare from domestic cares were spent in pondering the difficult question of how an income which had never been sufficient for *two* might now be made to support *three*.

Fanny waited for her sister's return and, with great steadiness of purpose, told Mr Hawkins several times a day how she intended to quarrel with her for letting Captain Fox slip his bonds. "To go off like that with the business entirely unsettled between them. What an odd creature she is! I cannot understand her."

But Fanny had a few oddities of her own, one of which was to delight in fancying herself disagreeable and cold-hearted, when in truth she was only ill-used and anxious. When at last Miss Moore returned to Kissingland and when Fanny saw how white and stricken the poor girl was to hear of her lover's defection, all of Fanny's much-vaunted quarrelsomeness dwindled into a shake of her head and, "Now you see, Venetia, what comes of being so obstinate and liking your own way above what other people advise"; and even this she immediately followed with, "There, my dear, I hope you will not distress yourself. Any man who can play you such a shabby trick as this is not worth thinking of. How is your friend in Manchester?"

"Dead." (This in a tearful whisper.)

"Oh! . . . Well, my dear, I am very sorry to hear it. And Mr Hawkins will say the same when I tell him of it. Poor girl! – you have a sad homecoming."

That evening at supper (a very small amount of fried beef to a great deal of boiled turnip) Fanny told Mr Hawkins, "She has gone to bed – she says she has a shocking head ach. I dare say she was a great deal more attached to him than we believed. It was never very likely that she should have escaped whole-hearted from the attentions of such a man as Captain Fox. You may recall I said so at the time."

Mr Hawkins said nothing; the Hawkins' domestic affairs were arranged upon the principle that Fanny supplied the talk and he the silence.

"Well!" continued Fanny. "We must all live as cheaply as we can. I dare say there are more savings I can make." Fanny looked around the shabby parlour in search of any luxuries that had hitherto gone undiscovered. Not finding any, she merely re-marked that things lasted a great deal longer than those people supposed who always like to have every thing new; indeed it had been a very long time since Fanny had had any thing new; the worn stone flags of her parlour floor were bare, the chairs were hard and inconvenient, and the wallpaper was so ancient and faded that it appeared to shew withered garlands of dead flowers tied up with dry brown ribbons.

The next morning Fanny's thoughts ran upon the subject of her grievances against Captain Fox, and her anger against him was such that she found herself obliged to speak of it almost incessantly – while at the same time continually advising Venetia to think of Captain Fox no more. After half an hour Venetia said with a sigh that she thought she would walk in the fresh air for a while.

"Oh!" said Fanny. "Which way do you go?"

"I do not know."

"Well, if you were to go towards the village then there are several things I need."

So Venetia went along Church-lane to Kissingland and, though it would benefit the dignity of the Female Sex in general to report that she now despised and hated Captain Fox, Venetia was not so unnatural. Instead she indulged in many vain sighs and regrets, and tried to derive such consolation as she could from the reflection that it was better to be poor and forgotten in Kissingland, where there were green trees and sweet flowery meadows, than in Manchester where her friend, Mrs Whitsun, had died in a cold grey room at the top of a dismal lodging house.

Captain Fox was a tall Irishman of thirty-six or -seven who bore the reputation of having red hair. Indeed in some weathers and lights it did appear to have a little red in it, but it was more his name, his long ironical grin and a certain Irish wildness that made people believe they saw red hair. He also had a reputation for quite unheard-of bravery, for he had once contradicted the Duke of Wellington when all around were most energetically agreeing with that illustrious person.

It had been a question of boots. The boots (ten thousand pairs of them) had been proceeding east from Portugal upon the backs of seventy mules to where the British army, with boots entirely worn out, anxiously awaited them. Without the new boots the army was entirely unable to begin its long march north to re-take Spain from the French. The Duke of Wellington had been in a great passion about it, had talked a great deal about the nuisance of delay and what the British might lose by it, but in the end he had admitted that the soldiers could do nothing without new boots. Upon the contrary, Captain Fox had cried; it would be better by far for the boots to travel along a more northerly path to the city of S _____ where they could meet the army on its way north – which would mean that for the first part of the march the men would be coming ever closer to their new boots – a cheerful thought that would doubtless encourage them to go faster. The Duke of Wellington had thought for a while; "I believe," he had said at last, "that Captain Fox is right."

Upon turning the corner at Blewitt's yard Venetia came in sight of a substantial stone house. This was the residence of Mr Grout, a well-to-do lawyer. So vigorous were the roses in Mr Grout's garden that one of the walls of his house seemed to be nothing but a trembling cliff of pale pink; but this delightful sight only served to remind Venetia that Captain Fox had been excessively fond of pale pink roses, and had twice told her with significant glances that, when he married and had a garden of his own, he did not think he would have any other sort.

She determined upon thinking of something else for a while but was immediately thwarted in that resolve when the first person she saw in the High-street was Captain Fox's servant, Lucas Barley.

"Lucas!" she cried. "What! Is the Captain here?" She looked about her hastily, and only when quite certain that the Captain was not in sight did she attend properly to Lucas. She saw with some surprize that he had undergone a strange transformation. Gone was his smart brown coat, gone his shining top boots, gone his swaggering air – the air of someone with a proper consciousness of the fact that his master had once given the Duke of Wellington a flat contradiction. In place of these he wore a dirty green apron several sizes too big for him and wooden pattens on his feet. He was carrying two enormous pewter tankards that slopped beer into the mud. "What are you doing with those jugs, Lucas? Have you left the Captain's service?"

"I do not know, Miss."

"You do not know! What do you mean?"

"I mean, Miss, that should I ever lay eyes on Captain Fox

again I shall certainly ask him for his opinion on that point; and if he should ask me for my opinion on that point I shall certainly say to him that I do not care about it one way or the other. You may well look surprized, Miss – I myself am in a state of perpetual astonishment. But I am not alone in that – the Captain is parting with all his old friends."

And, having no hands disengaged to point with, Lucas indicated by a sort of straining expression of his face that Venetia should look behind her, to where a most beautiful brown-black mare was being led into Mr Grout's mews.

"Good Lord!" cried Venetia. "Belle-dame!"

"A message has come from Mrs Mabb's house that she is to be sold to Mr Grout, Miss."

"But is the Captain quitting the regiment?"

"I do not know, Miss. But what will such a little, round man as Mr Grout do with such a horse as that? He had better take care that she does not mistake him for a turnip and eat him."

Indeed the mare seemed to have some thoughts of her own in that direction; the disdainful light in her wild brown eye shewed that she was aware of having come down in the world, and thought someone ought to suffer for it, and was at this moment turning over in her mind whom exactly that someone ought to be.

"It happened like this, Miss," said Lucas. "The morning after you left, Mrs Mabb sent a message to the Captain to ask him if he would make a fourth at cards; and I went with him – for someone once told me that Mrs Mabb has a great number of aunts and nieces and female relations living with her, every one of them more beautiful than the last – and I hoped to make myself acquainted with any as was not too proud to speak to me. But when we got to the house I was made to wait in a little stone antechamber as cold as a tomb and furnished with nothing but a few bones in the hearth. I waited and I waited and I waited and then I waited some more; and I could hear the sound of the Captain talking and the sound of female laughter, high and loud. And after a while, Miss, I saw that my fingernails were getting longer and I felt that my chin was all bristles – which gave me quite a fright as you may suppose. So, the front door being open, I shot through it and ran all the way back to Kissingland, where I discovered that I had been standing in Mrs Mabb's little stone room for three days and three nights."

"Good Lord!" cried Venetia. She pondered this a moment. "Well," she said at last with a sigh, "if people discover they were mistaken in their affections or find that they like another person better . . . I suppose she is very beautiful?"

Lucas made a scornful sound as though he would like to say something very cutting about the beauty of Mrs Mabb and was only prevented by the fact of his never having seen her.

"I do not think that Mrs Mabb ought to be named with you in the same day, Miss. The Captain told me several times, Miss, that you and he would marry soon and that we would all go off to Exeter to live in a little white house with a garden and a trellis of pink roses; and I had made myself a solemn vow, one morning in church, to serve you very faithfully and honourably – for you were always very kind to me."

"Thank you, Lucas . . ." said Venetia, but she found she could get no further. This picture of what would never come to pass affected her too strongly and her eyes filled with tears.

She would have liked to have given Lucas a little money but there was nothing in her purse but what would pay for the bread that she had come out to buy for Fanny.

"It is of no consequence, Miss," said Lucas. "We are all of us a great deal worse off on account of Mrs Mabb." He paused. "I am sorry I made you cry, Miss."

Which remark, said with a great deal of kindness, was enough to make her glad to hurry away to the bakery where melancholy fancies of Captain Fox gaily abandoning his career for the sake of Mrs Mabb, and Mrs Mabb laughing loudly to see him do it, so took off her attention from what she was doing that when she got home and opened up the packages she found to her surprize that she had bought three dozen French milk-rolls and an apricot-jam tart – none of which were the things that Fanny had wanted.

"What in the world were you thinking of?" cried Fanny in great perplexity when she saw what Venetia had done. Fanny was quite appalled by the waste of money and under the baneful influence of the milk-rolls and the jam tart became snappish and cross, a mood that threatened to last all day until Venetia remembered that, just before she died, her friend, Mrs Whitsun, had given her some curtains as a wedding-present. Now that there was to be no wedding it seemed both proper and kind for Venetia to fetch the curtains down from her bedroom and make a present of them to Fanny. The material was very pretty – primrose-yellow with a fine white stripe. Fanny's good humour was restored upon the instant and with Venetia's help she set about altering the curtains for the parlour window and when they were settled at their work, "Fanny," asked Venetia, "who is Mrs Mabb?"

"A very wicked person, my dear," said Fanny happily brandishing her large black scissars.

"In what way is she wicked?"

But Fanny had no precise information to offer upon this point and all that Venetia could learn was that Mrs Mabb's wickedness chiefly consisted in being very rich and never doing any thing if she did not like it.

"What does she look like?" asked Venetia.

"Oh, Lord! I do not know. I never saw her."

"Then she is quite recently come into the neighbourhood?"

"Oh, yes! Quite recently . . . But then again, I am not quite sure. Now that I come to think of it I believe she has been here a great long while. She was certainly here when Mr Hawkins came here fifteen years ago."

"Where does she live?"

"A great way off! Beyond Knightswood."

"Near to Dunchurch, then?"

"No, my dear, not near Dunchurch. Nearer to Piper than any where, but not particularly near there either . . ." (These were all towns and villages in the neighbourhood of Kissingland.) ". . . If you leave the turnpike road just before Piper and go by an overgrown lane that descends very suddenly, you come to a lonely stretch of water full of reeds called Greypool, and above that − atop a little hill − there is a circle of ancient stones. Beyond the hill there is a little green valley and then an ancient wood. Mrs Mabb's house stands betwixt the stones and the wood, but nearer to the wood than the stones."

"Oh!" said Venetia.

The next day Fanny declined Venetia's offer to walk to the village again to buy bread and instead sent her off with a basket of vegetables and some soup to pay a charity visit to a destitute family in Piper. For, as Fanny said, mistakes in purchases came expensive but if Venetia were so inattentive as to give the soup to the wrong paupers it would not much signify.

Venetia delivered the basket to the destitute family in Piper, but on the way back she passed an opening in a hedge where a narrow, twisting lane descended steeply from the turnpike road. Massive ancient trees grew upon each side and their branches overarched the path and made of it a confusing, shadowy place where the broken sunlight illuminated a clump of violets here, three stalks of grass there.

Now all of English landscape contained nothing that could hold Venetia's gaze quite as rapt as that green lane for it was the very lane that Fanny had spoken of as leading to the house of

Mrs Mabb, and all of Venetia's thoughts ran upon that house and its inhabitants. "Perhaps," she thought, "I will just walk a little way along the lane. And perhaps, if it is not too far, I will just go and take a peep at the house. I should like to know that *he* is happy."

How she proposed to discover whether or not the Captain was happy by looking at the outside of a strange house, she did not consider too exactly, but down the lane she went and she passed the lonely pool and climbed up to the ancient stones and on and on, until she came to a place where round green hills shut out the world.

It was a quiet and empty place. The grass which covered the hills and the valley was as unbroken as any sheet of water – and, almost as if it were water, the sunshiny breeze made little waves in it. On the opposite hill stood an ancient-looking house of grey stone. It was a very tall house, something indeed between a house and a tower, and it was surrounded by a high stone wall in which no opening or gate could be discerned, nor did any path go up to the house.

Yet despite its great height the house was overtopped by the bright sunlit forest wall behind it and she could not rid herself of the idea that she was actually looking at a very small house – a house for a field mouse or a bee or a butterfly – a house which stood among tall grasses.

"It will not do to linger," she thought. "Suppose I should chance to meet the Captain and Mrs Mabb? Horrible thought!" She turned and walked away quickly, but had not gone far when she heard the drumming of hooves upon the turf behind her. "I shall not look behind me," she thought, "for, if it is Captain Fox then I am sure that he will be kind and let me go away undisturbed."

But the sound of hooves came on and was joined by many more, till it seemed that a whole army must have risen up out of the silent hills. Greatly amazed, she turned to see what in the world it could be.

Venetia wore a queer old-fashioned gown of fine blue wool. The bodice was embroidered with buttercups and daisies and the waist was low. It was none too long in the skirt but this was amply compensated for by a great number of linen petticoats. She mused upon this for a moment or two. "It appears to be," she thought, "a costume for a milkmaid or a shepherdess or some such other rustic person. How odd! I cannot recall ever having been a milkmaid or a shepherdess. I suppose I must be going to act in some play or other – well, I fear that I shall do it very ill for I do not remember my speeches or any thing about it."

"She has got a little more colour," said Fanny's anxious voice. "Do not you think so, Mr Hawkins?"

Venetia found that she was in Fanny's parlour and Mr Hawkins was kneeling on the flagstones before her chair. There was a basin of steaming water on the floor with a pair of ancient green silk dancing slippers beside it. Mr Hawkins was washing her feet and ancles with a cloath. This was odd too – she had never known him do such a thing before. When he had finished he began to bathe her face with an air of great concentration.

"Be careful, Mr Hawkins!" cried his wife. "You will get the soap in her eyes! Oh, my dear! I was never so frightened in my life as when they brought you home! I thought I should faint from the shock and Mr Hawkins says the same."

That Fanny had been seriously alarmed was apparent from her face; she was commonly hollow-eyed and hollow-cheeked – fifteen years' worrying about money had done that – but now fright had deepened all the hollows, made her eyes grow round and haunted-looking, and sharpened up her nose until it resembled the tip of a scissar blade.

Venetia gazed at Fanny a while and wondered what could have so distressed her. Then she looked down at her own hands and was surprized to find that they were all scratched to pieces. She put her hand up to her face and discovered tender places there.

She jumped up. There was a little scrap of a looking-glass hung upon the opposite wall and there she saw herself, face all bruises and hair pulled this way and that. The shock was so great that she cried out loud.

As she remembered nothing of what had happened to her it was left to Fanny to tell her – with many digressions and exclamations – that she had been found earlier in the day wandering in a lane two or three miles from Piper by a young man, a farmer called Purvis. She had been in a state of the utmost confusion and had answered Mr Purvis's concerned inquiries with queer rambling monologues about silver harness bells and green banners shutting out the sky. For some time Mr Purvis had been unable to discover even so much as her name. Her clothes were torn and dirty and she was barefoot. Mr Purvis had put her on his horse and taken her to his house where his mother had given her tea to drink and the queer old-fashioned gown and the dancing slippers to wear.

"Oh! but, my dear," said Fanny, "do not you remember any thing at all of what happened?"

"No, nothing," said Venetia. "I took the soup to the Peasons – just as you told me – and then what did I do? I believe I went somewhere. But where? Oh! Why can I not remember!"

Mr Hawkins, still on his knees before her, put his finger to his lips as a sign that she should not be agitated and began gently to stroke her forehead.

"You tumbled into a ditch, my dear," said Fanny, "that is all. Which is a nasty, disagreeable thing to happen and so naturally you don't wish to dwell upon it." She started to cry. "You always were a forgetful girl, Venetia."

Mr Hawkins put his finger to his lips as a sign that Fanny should not be agitated and somehow contrived to continue stroking Venetia's forehead while patting Fanny's hand.

"Fanny," said Venetia, "was there a procession today?"

"A procession?" said Fanny. She pushed Mr Hawkins' hand away and blew her nose loudly. "Whatever do you mean?"

"*That* is what I did today. I remember now. I watched the soldiers ride by."

"There was no procession today," said Fanny. "The soldiers are all in their lodgings I suppose."

"Oh! Then what was it that I saw today? Hundreds of riders with the sunlight winking on their harness and the sound of silver bells as they rode by . . ."

"Oh! Venetia," cried Fanny in great irritation of spirits, "do not talk so wildly or Mr Hawkins and I will be obliged to send for the physician – and then there will be his guinea fee and all sorts of medicines to buy no doubt . . ." Fanny launched upon a long monologue upon the expensiveness of doctors and little by little talked herself up into such paroxysms of worry that she seemed in grave danger of making herself more ill than Venetia had ever been. Venetia hastened to assure her that a physician was quite unnecessary and promised not to talk of processions again. Then she went up to her room and made a more detailed examination of her own person. She found no injuries other than scrapes and bruises. "I suppose," she thought, "I must have fainted but it is very odd for I never did so before." And when the household sat down to supper, which was rather late that evening, Venetia's strange adventure was not mentioned again, other than a few complaints from Fanny to the effect that the Purvises had still got Venetia's gown.

The next morning Venetia was stiff and aching from head to

toe. "I feel," she thought, "as if I had tumbled two or three times off a horse." It was a familiar sensation. Captain Fox had taught her to ride in the previous November. They had gone up to a high field that overlooked Kissingland and Captain Fox had lifted her up onto Belle-dame's back. Beneath them the village had been all a-glow with the ember colours of autumn trees and the candlelight in people's windows. Wisps of vivid blue smoke had drifted up from bonfires in Mr Grout's gardens.

"Oh! how happy we were! Except that Pen Harrington would always contrive to discover where we were going and insist on coming with us and she would always want the Captain to pay attention to her, which he – being all nobility – was obliged to do. She is a very tiresome girl. Oh! but now I am no better off than she is – or any of those other girls who liked the Captain and were scorned by him for the sake of Mrs Mabb. It would be far more natural in me to hate the Captain and to feel sisterly affection towards poor Pen. . . ."

She sat a while trying to arrange her feelings upon this model, but at the end of five minutes found she liked Pen no better and loved the Captain no less. "I suppose the truth is that one cannot feel much pity for a girl who wears a buttercup-yellow gown with lavender trimmings – buttercup-yellow and lavender look so extremely horrid together. But as for what happened yesterday the most likely explanation is that I fainted in the lane and Mr Purvis found me, picked me up and put me on his horse, but subsequently dropped me – which would account for the bruises and the holes in my clothes. And I suppose that he now is too embarrassed to tell any one – which I can well understand. The Captain," she thought with a sigh, "would not have dropped me."

That morning as the sisters worked together in the kitchen (Venetia shelling peas, Fanny making pastry) they heard the unexpected sounds of a horse and carriage.

Fanny looked out of the window. "It is the Purvises," she said.

Mrs Purvis proved to be a fat, cheerful woman who, the moment she set eyes upon Venetia, gave a delighted cry and embraced her very heartily. She smelt of sweet milk, new bread and freshly turned earth, as if she had spent the morning in the dairy, the kitchen and the vegetable-garden – as indeed she had.

"I dare say, ma'am," said Mrs Purvis to Fanny, "you are surprized at my warmth but if you had seen Miss Moore when John first brought her in, all white and shaking, then I think you would excuse me. And I know that Miss Moore will excuse me for she and I got to be great friends when she was in my kitchen."

"Did we, though?" thought Venetia.

"And you see, my dear," continued Mrs Purvis, delving in a great canvas bag, "I have brought you my little china shepherdess that you liked so much. Oh! do not thank me. I have half a dozen other such that I scarcely look at. And here, ma'am . . ." She addressed Fanny respectfully, ". . . are asparagus and strawberries and six beautiful goose eggs. I dare say you will agree with me that it is scarcely any wonder that our young ladies faint dead away when they let themselves get so thin."

Fanny always liked visitors and Mrs Purvis was precisely the sort to please her – full of harmless gossip, and deferring to Fanny as a farmer's widow should defer to a curate's wife. Indeed so pleased was Fanny that she was moved to give each of the Purvises a small biscuit. "I did have a bottle of very good madeira-wine," she told them, "but I fear it is all drunk." Which was true – Mr Hawkins had finished it at Christmas eight years before.

Of the queer, old-fashioned gown Mrs Purvis had this to say: "It was my sister's, Miss Moore. She died when she was about your age and she was almost as pretty as you are. You are welcome to keep it, but I expect you like to have everything of the new fashion like other young ladies."

The visit ended with Mrs Purvis nodding and making signs to her son that he should say something. He stammered out his great pleasure in seeing Miss Moore looking so much better and hoped that she and Mrs Hawkins would not object to his calling upon them again in a day or two. Poor man, his blushing countenance seemed to shew that Venetia had not been alone in sustaining some hurt from the previous day's adventures; her rescuer also appeared to have received a blow – in his case to the heart.

When they were gone Fanny said, "She seems a very worthy sort of woman. It is however extremely provoking that she has not brought back your clothes. I was several times upon the point of asking her about it, but each time I opened my mouth she began to talk of something else. I cannot understand what she means by keeping them so long. Perhaps she thinks of selling them. We have only her word for it that the clothes are spoiled."

Fanny had a great deal of useless speculation of this sort of get through but she had scarcely begun when she discovered that she had left her huswife in her bedroom and sent Venetia upstairs to fetch it.

In the lane beneath Fanny's bedroom window Mrs Purvis and her son were making ready to drive away. As Venetia watched, John Purvis took a big wooden pail out of the back of the ancient gig and placed it upside-down on the ground as an extra step for his mother to mount up to the driver's seat.

Venetia heard Mrs Purvis say, "Well, my mind is much eased to see her looking so much better. It is a great blessing that she remembers nothing about it."

Here Purvis said something, but his face was still turned away and Venetia could not hear what it was.

"It was soldiers, John, I am sure of it. Those great slashes in her gown were made by swords and sabres. It would have frightened them both into fits – as much as it frightened me, I am sure – to see how cut about her clothes were when you found her. It is my belief that this Captain Fox – the same I told you of, John – must have set on some of his men to frighten her off. For all that he has treated her so cruel she may still love him. With such a sweet nature as she has got it is the likeliest thing in the world . . ."

"Good God!" whispered Venetia in great astonishment.

At first the horror which she ought to have felt was quite overtaken by her indignation on the Captain's behalf; "I dare say she was very kind to take me in, but she is a very stupid woman to invent such lies about Captain Fox who is every thing that is honourable and would never do harm to any one – always excepting, of course, in pursuit of his military duties." But then, as images of her poor, ill-treated gown rose up before her fancy, the disagreeable impression which Mrs Purvis's words had created grew until Venetia was thoroughly frightened. "What in the world can have happened to me?" she wondered.

But she had no satisfactory answer.

On the following day after dinner, Venetia felt in need of fresh air and told Fanny that she thought she would walk out for a while. She went down Church-lane and turned the corner at Blewitt's yard; looking up she saw something behind the walls of Mr Grout's kitchen garden – Oh! the most terrible thing in all the world! – and the fright of it was so great that her legs gave way beneath her and she fell to the ground.

"Young lady! Young lady! What is the matter?" cried a voice. Mr Grout appeared with his housekeeper, Mrs Baines. They were very shocked to find Venetia crawling on the ground and she was scarcely less shocked to be found. "Young lady!" cried Mr Grout. "What in the world has happened to you?".

"I thought I saw a strange procession coming towards me," said Venetia, "but now I see that what I took for pale green banners a-fluttering in the breeze are only the tops of some birch trees."

Mr Grout looked as if he did not very well understand this.

Mrs Baines said, "Well, my dear, whatever it was a glass of marsala-wine is sure to put it right." – and, though Venetia assured them that she was quite well and was certain to stop shaking in a moment, they helped her into the house where they made her sit down by the fire and gave her marsala-wine to drink.

Mr Grout was an attorney who had been settled many years in Kissingland where he had lived quietly and inexpensively. He had always appeared friendly and was generally well thought of, until he had suddenly got very rich and bought two farms in Knightswood parish. This was all quite recent, yet long enough for Mr Grout to have acquired a reputation as a most unreasonable landlord who bullied the farmers who worked his land and who increased their rents just as it suited him.

"You will eat something, perhaps?" said Mr Grout to Venetia. "My excellent Mrs Baines has been baking this morning if I am not mistaken. I smell apple tarts!"

"I want nothing, sir. Thank you," said Venetia and then, because she could not think of any thing else to say, she added, "I do not think I was in your house, sir, since I was a little girl."

"Indeed?" said Mr Grout. "Then you will see a great many improvements! It is a curious thing, young lady, but wealth don't suit everybody. The mere notion of great quantities of money is enough to make some people uneasy. Happily I can bear the thought of any amount with equanimity. Money, my dear, does more than provide mere material comforts; it lifts the burden of cares from one's shoulders, it imparts vigour and decisiveness to all one's actions and a delicate clearness to the complexion. It puts one in good humour with oneself and all the world. When I was poor I was not fit to be seen."

Money did indeed seem to have worked some curious changes in Mr Grout: his lawyer's stoop had vanished overnight taking with it all his wrinkles; his silver hair shone so much that, in certain lights, he appeared to be sanctified, and his eyes and skin had a queer sparkle to them, not entirely pleasant to behold. He was known to be more than a little vain of all these new graces and he smiled at Venetia as though inviting her to fall in love with him on the spot.

"Well, sir," she said, "I am sure that no one could deserve good fortune more. You made some cunning investments no doubt?"

"No, indeed. All my good fortune has sprung from the same noble source, a great lady who has employed me as her man of business – for which I may say I have been very handsomely rewarded. *Mrs Mabb* is the lady's name."

"Oh!" said Venetia. "She is someone I have a great curiosity to see."

"I do not doubt it, young lady," said Mr Grout laughing pleasantly, "for she has got your sweetheart, the bold Captain Fox, has she not? Oh! there is no need to pretend that it is not so, for, as you see, I know all about it. There is no shame in being seen from the field by such a rival as Mrs Mabb. Mrs Mabb is a pearl beyond price and praise. The soul delights in the smallest motion of her hand. Her smile is like the sunshine – No! it is better than sunshine! One would gladly live in darkness all the days of one's life for the sake of Mrs Mabb's smile. Oh, young lady! The curve of Mrs Mabb's neck! Her eye-brow! Her smallest fingernail! Perfection every one!"

Venetia sighed. "Well," she said and then, not knowing very well how to continue, she sighed again.

"In her youth, I believe," continued Mr Grout, "she was most industrious in managing her estates and ordering the affairs of her relations and dependants – who are very numerous and who all live with her – but at length the follies of the world began to disgust her and for many years she has lived a very retired life. She stays at home where she is very busy with her needle. I myself have been privileged to examine yard upon yard of the most exquisite embroidery, all of Mrs Mabb's production. And all her spinster cousins and maiden aunts and other such inferior females as she condescends to keep about her embroider a great deal too, for Mrs Mabb will not tolerate idleness."

"She lives near Piper, does she not?" said Venetia.

"Piper!" cried Mr Grout. "Oh no! Whatever gave you that idea? Mrs Mabb's house is not half so far and in quite another direction. It is reached by the little path that crosses the churchyard and goes out by the ivy-covered arch. The path, which is somewhat overgrown with cow parsley and foxgloves, passes a little pool full of reeds and then climbs a smooth green hill. At the top of the hill the visitor must climb through a gap in a ruined wall of ancient stones – whereupon he finds himself in Mrs Mabb's garden."

"Oh!" said Venetia. "How strange! For I am sure that some-one told me that she lived near Piper. But, sir, I promised my sister that I would not be gone long and she is sure to grow anxious if I do not return soon."

"Oh!" said Mr Grout. "But we are just beginning to get acquainted! My dear, I hope you are not one of those prim young misses who are afraid to be alone with an old friend. An old friend, after all, is what I am, for all I look so young."

In Church-lane Venetia climbed up and looked over the churchyard-wall. "So that is the path that leads to Mrs Mabb's house and there is the ivy-covered arch!"

She could not remember ever having observed either of them before. "Well! I do not think it can do any harm to go up very quietly and privately to look at her house."

And so, quite forgetting that she had told Mr Grout that

Fanny would worry if she did not return home soon, she slipped into the churchyard and beneath the ivy-covered arch, and passed the pool and climbed the hill and came at last to the broken wall.

"I wonder that such a great lady should have no better entrance to her house than this inconvenient gap in an ancient wall!"

She passed through.

Majestic trees of great age and height stood about a great expanse of velvety green lawn. The trees had all been clipped into smooth rounded shapes, each one taller than Kissingland church tower, each one a separate mystery, and each one provided by the evening sun with a long shadow as mysterious as itself. Far, far above, a tiny moon hung in the blue sky like its own insubstantial ghost.

"Oh! How quiet and empty it is! Now I am quite certain that I ought not to have come for I was never in so private a place in my life. Any moment now I shall hear silver bells and hooves upon the turf, I know I shall! And as for the house I do not see one."

Yet there was something; at the one end of the lawn stood a round tower built of ancient-looking, grey stones, with battlements at the top and three dark slits for windows very high up. It was quite a tall tower, but in spite of its height it was overtopped by a monstrous hedge of pale roses that stood behind it and she could not rid herself of the idea that the tower was actually very tiny – a tower for an ant or a bee or a bird.

"I suppose it is that monstrous hedge that confuses one. It must be a summerhouse. I wonder how you get inside – I do not see a door. Oh! Someone is playing a pipe! Yet there is no one here. And now a drum! How odd it is that I cannot see who is playing! I wonder if . . . Two steps forward, curtsey and turn . . ."

The words came from nowhere into her head and the steps came from nowhere into her feet. She began to dance and was not at all surprized to find that, at the appropriate moment, someone took her outstretched hand.

Someone was crying very quietly and, just as before, Mr Hawkins knelt by Venetia's chair and washed her feet.

"And yet," she thought, "they will never be clean if he washes them in blood."

The water in the basin was bright red.

"Fanny," said Venetia.

The crying stopt and a small sound – something between a squeak and a sniff – seemed to shew that Fanny was nearby.

"Fanny, is it evening?"

"It is dawn," said Fanny.

"Oh!"

The curtains in Fanny's parlour were drawn back, but in the grey light of early dawn they had lost all their primrose colour. And everything outside the window – Fanny's vegetable-garden, Robin Tolliday's barn, John Harker's field, God's sky, England's clouds – all could be seen with perfect clarity but all had lost their colour as if all were made of grey water. Fanny began to cry again. "Perhaps she is in pain," thought Venetia, "for there is certainly a pain somewhere."

"Fanny?" she said.

"Yes, my love?"

"I am very tired, Fanny."

Then Fanny said something which Venetia did not hear and Venetia turned her head and when she opened her eyes she was in bed and Fanny was sitting in the wicker-chair, mending a hole in Mr Hawkins' shirt, and the curtains were drawn against the bright sunshine.

"Oh, Venetia!" said Fanny with a sigh and a despairing shake of her head. "Where in the world have you been? And what in the world have you been doing?"

It was not the sort of question that expected an answer but Venetia attempted one anyway; "I remember that I drank a glass of wine at Mr Grout's house, but I told him very plainly that I must come home, for I knew you were waiting for me. Did I not come home, Fanny?"

"No, Venetia," said Fanny, "you did not." And Fanny told Venetia how she and Mr Hawkins and their neighbours had searched through the night, and how, just before dawn, John Harker and George Buttery had looked into the churchyard and seen the pale shape of Venetia's gown billowing out in the darkness. She had been under the big yew tree, turning and turning and turning, with her arms spread wide. It had taken both of them holding tight on to her to make her stop.

"Two pairs of shoes," sighed Fanny, "one entirely gone and the other in tatters. Oh, Venetia! Whatever were you thinking of?"

Venetia must have fallen asleep again for when she woke it seemed to be late evening. She could hear the clatter of plates as Fanny got the supper ready downstairs; and as Fanny went back and forth between parlour and kitchen she talked to Mr Hawkins: ". . . and if it should come to that, she shall not be sent to the madhouse – I could not bear that she should go to one of those horrid places and be ill-treated. No, indeed! Take warning, Mr Hawkins, that I expressly forbid it . . ."

"As if he would suggest such a thing!" thought Venetia. "So good as he is to me."

". . . I dare say that mad people are no more expensive to keep than sane ones – except perhaps in the articles of medicines and restraining chairs."

Early next morning Fanny, Venetia and Mr Hawkins were at breakfast in the parlour when there was a loud knocking at the door. Fanny went to the door and returned in a moment with Mr Grout, who wasted no time upon apologies or explanations but immediately addressed Venetia in accents of great displeasure.

"Young lady! I am expressly sent to you by Mrs Mabb who has bid me tell you that she will not have you creeping around and around her house!"

"Ha!" cried Venetia, so loudly that Fanny started.

"Mrs Mabb's relations and dependants," continued Mr Grout with a severe look at Venetia's exulting expression, "have all been frightened out of their wits by your odd behaviour. You have given her aged uncles bad dreams, made the children afraid to go asleep at night and caused the maids to drop the china upon the floor. Mrs Mabb says that there is not one complete dinner service left in the house! She says that the butter will not come in the churns because you have given her cows malicious looks – Miss Moore, will you stop tormenting this lady?"

"Let her give up Captain Fox to me," said Venetia, "and she shall never hear of me again."

"Oh, Venetia!" cried Fanny.

"But young lady!" cried Mr Grout. "It is Mrs Mabb that the Captain loves. As I think I have explained to you before, Mrs Mabb is as fair as the apple-blossom that hangs upon the bough. One glance of Mrs Mabb's eyes . . ."

"Yes, yes! I know!" cried Venetia impatiently. "You told me all that before! But it is just so much nonsense! It is *me* the Captain loves. Had it been otherwise he would have told me so himself – or at least sent me a letter – but I have neither seen nor heard any thing of him since I returned from Manchester. Oh! Do not tell me that Mrs Mabb forbade him to come or some such other foolishness – Captain Fox is not the man to be dissuaded from doing his duty by any body. No, depend upon it, this is another trick of Mrs Mabb's."

"Young lady!" cried Mr Grout, very much appalled. "It ill becomes a young person of no consequence, such as yourself, to go about slandering great people in all the dignity of their property!"

"Mr Grout!" cried Fanny, unable to keep silent a moment longer. "Do not speak to her so! Use milder language to her, sir, I beg you! Can you not see that she is ill? I am, of course, extremely sorry that Mrs Mabb should have been put to any inconvenience by Venetia's going to the house – though I must say you make a great piece of work of it – and merely remark, in justice to Venetia, that all these cows and uncles must be extraordinarily nervous creatures to have been put in such a pickle by a poor, sick girl looking at them! But I tell you what I shall do. To keep her from wandering abroad and causing further nuisance to our neighbours I shall hide the green slippers the Purvises gave her – which are the only shoes she has – where she cannot find them and then, you know," Fanny concluded triumphantly, "she must remain at home!"

Mr Grout looked at Venetia as though hopeful that she would admit defeat.

But Venetia only said sweetly, "You have my answer, sir, and I advise you to go and deliver it. I dare say Mrs Mabb does not tolerate procrastination."

For the next two days Venetia waited for an opportunity to go in search of Mrs Mabb but in all this time Fanny neither left her alone nor answered any of her inquiries about Mrs Mabb. But on the third day Fanny was called away after dinner to take some elderflower tea and peppermint cordial and other remedies to John Harker's maid who had a bad cold. As Fanny went up Church-lane to Harker's farm it seemed probable that among the things her basket contained were the green silk dancing slippers, for when Venetia came to look for them she could not find them anywhere.

So she wrapped her feet up in rags and went anyway.

In a golden light, by what the inhabitants of Kissingland were pleased to call a river and which other, less partial people would probably have called a stream, in a fresh green meadow, beneath blossoming May-trees, some children were playing. One boy with a tin whistle was the Duke of Wellington, another boy with a drum was the entire British army and four little girls in grass-stained gowns of blossom-coloured muslin gave a lively portrayal of the ferocity and indomitable spirit of Napoleon and his French generals.

By the time Venetia passed by in the lane in search of Mrs Mabb her feet were very sore. She thought she would stop and bathe them; but as she went down to the river the two boys began to play a melancholy air upon the whistle and the drum.

Upon the instant Venetia was seized by a terror so blind that she scarcely knew what she did. When she recovered herself she found that she was holding fast to the hand of a most surprised little girl of eight or nine years of age.

"Oh! I beg your pardon. It was only the music that frightened me," she said; and then, as the girl continued to stare at her in astonishment, she added, "I used to be so fond of music you see, but now I do not care for it at all. Whenever I hear a pipe and drum I am certain that I shall be compelled to dance for ever and ever without stopping. Does not it strike you that way sometimes?"

The little girls looked very much amazed but did not answer her. Their names were Hebe, Marjory, Joan and Nan, but as to which was which Venetia had not the least idea in the world. She bathed her feet and lay down to rest – for she was still very weak – in the sweet green grass. She heard Hebe, Marjory, Joan or Nan observe to the others that Miss Moore had, as was well known, run mad for the love of handsome Captain Fox.

The little girls had got some daisies to pull apart and as they did so they made wishes. One wished for a sky-blue carriage spotted with silver, another to see a dolphin in Kissingland river, one to marry the Archbishop of Canterbury and wear a diamond-spangled mitre (which she insisted she would be entitled to do as an Archbishop's wife though the others were more doubtful), and one that there would be bread and beef dripping for her supper.

"I wish to know where I may find Mrs Mabb's house," said Venetia.

There was a silence for a moment and then either Hebe, Marjory, Joan or Nan remarked contemptuously that every one knew that.

"Every one, it seems, but me," said Venetia to the blue sky and the sailing clouds.

"Mrs Mabb lives at the bottom of Billy Little's garden," said another child.

"Behind a great heap of cabbage leaves," said a third.

"Then I doubt that we can mean the same person," said Venetia, "Mrs Mabb is a very fine lady as I understand."

"Indeed, she is," agreed the first, "the finest lady that ever there was. She has a coachman . . ."

". . . a footman . . ."

". . . a dancing master . . ."

". . . and a hundred ladies-in-waiting . . ."

". . . and one of the ladies-in-waiting has to eat the dull parts of Mrs Mabb's dinner so that Mrs Mabb only ever has to eat roast pork, plum-cake and strawberry jam . . ."

"I see," said Venetia.

". . . and they all live together at the bottom of Billy Little's garden."

"Do not they find that rather inconvenient?" asked Venetia, sitting up.

But Hebe, Marjory, Joan and Nan could not suppose that

there would be any particular inconvenience attached to a residence at the bottom of Billy Little's garden. However, they were able to provide Venetia with the further information that Mrs Mabb drank her breakfast coffee out of an acorn-cup, that her chamberlain was a thrush and her coachman a blackbird and that she herself was "about the size of a pepper-pot".

"Well," said Venetia, "what you tell me is very strange, but no stranger than many of the things that have happened to me recently. Indeed it seems to me to be all of a piece with them – and so perhaps you will have the goodness to shew me where I may find this curious house."

"Oh!" said one child, clapping her hand to her mouth in alarm.

"You had much better not," said another kindly.

"She could turn you into butter," said a third.

"Which might melt," observed the fourth.

"Or a pudding."

"Which might get eaten."

"Or a drawing of yourself on white paper."

"Which someone might set fire to, you know, without meaning to."

But Venetia insisted upon their taking her to Mrs Mabb's house straight away, which at length they agreed to do.

Billy Little was an ancient farm labourer of uncertain temper who lived in a tumbledown cottage in Shilling-lane. He was at war with all the children of Kissingland and all the children of Kissingland were at war with him. His garden was at the back of the cottage and Venetia and Hebe, Marjory, Joan and Nan were obliged to bend low to creep past his uncurtained window.

Someone was standing on the window-sill. She wore a brightly coloured gown, and had a cross expression upon her face.

"There you are, at last!" said Venetia. She straightened herself and addressed this lady in the following words: "Now, madam! If I might trouble you to answer one or two questions . . ."

"Where are you going?" hissed Hebe, Marjory, Joan or Nan and took hold of Venetia by her gown and pulled her down again.

"Oh! Do you not see?" said Venetia. "Mrs Mabb is just above us, on the window-sill."

"*That* is not Mrs Mabb!" whispered Hebe, Marjory, Joan or Nan. "*That* is only Billy Little's Betsy-jug, with his Toby-jug beside it."

Venetia popped her head back up, and this time she observed the china lady's china husband. The couple were indeed jugs for they had large handles sticking out of their backs.

"Oh! very well," said Venetia, crossly.

"But," she thought to herself, "I have half a mind to push her off the window-sill anyway – for it is my opinion that, where Mrs Mabb is concerned, you never can tell."

Beyond the heap of cabbage leaves and other dark, decaying matter, the path led past a sad-looking pond and up a steep bank. At the top of the bank was a smooth expanse of bright green grass, at one end of which a dozen or so tall stones and slates were piled together. It was possible they were intended for a bee-hive, but it was equally possible that they were simply left over from some ancient wall. Tall flowers grew behind them – meadowsweet, cow parsley and buttercups – so that it was the easiest thing in the world to fancy one was looking at a tower or castle-keep on the edge of an ancient wood.

"Now this is odd," said Venetia, "for I have seen this place before. I know I have."

"There she is!" cried one of the children.

Venetia looked round and thought she saw a quivering in the air. "A moth," she thought. She approached and the shadow of her gown fell across the stones. A dark, damp chill hung about them, which the sunlight had no power to dissipate. She stretched out her hands to break apart Mrs Mabb's house, but upon the instant a pale-green something – or a pale-green someone – flew out of a gap in the stones and sprang up into the sunlight – and then another, and another – and more, and more, until the air seemed crowded with people, and there was a strange glitter all around, which Venetia associated with the sight of sunlight glinting on a thousand swords. So rapid was the manner in which they darted about that it was entirely impossible to hold any of them in one's gaze for more than a moment, but it seemed to Venetia that they rushed upon her like soldiers who had planned an ambush.

"Oh!" she cried. "Oh! You wicked creatures! You wicked, wicked creatures!"; and she snatched them out of the sparkling air and crushed them in her hands. Then it seemed to Venetia that they were dancing, and that the steps of their dance were the most complicated ever invented and had been devised on purpose to make her mad; so she took great pleasure in knocking them to the ground and treading upon their pale green clothes. But, though she was certain that some were killed and dozens of others were sent away injured, there never appeared to be any diminution in their number. Gradually the strength of her own passion began to exhaust her; she was sure she must sink to the ground. At that moment she looked up and saw, just beyond the battle's fray, the pale, heart-shaped face of a little girl and Venetia heard her say in a puzzled tone, "'Tis only butterflies, Miss Moore."

Butterflies? she thought.

"It was only butterflies, my love," said Fanny, smoothing Venetia's cheek.

She was in her own room, laid upon her own bed.

"A cloud of pale-green butterflies," said Fanny. "Hebe,

Marjory, Joan and Nan said that you were crying out at them and beating them down with your fists and tearing them apart with your fingers until you fell down in a faint." Fanny sighed. "But I dare say you remember nothing about it."

"Oh! But I remember perfectly well!" said Venetia. "Hebe, Marjory, Joan and Nan took me to Mrs Mabb's house, which as you may know is at the bottom of Billy Little's garden, and Captain Fox was inside it – or at least so I suppose – and had Mrs Mabb not sent the butterflies to prevent me, I would have fetched him out, and . . ."

"Oh, Venetia!" cried Fanny in exasperation.

Venetia opened her hand and found several fragments of a pale-green colour, like torn paper yet not half the thickness of paper and of no weight whatsoever: the broken remains of two or three butterflies.

"Now I have you, Mrs Mabb," she whispered.

She took a scrap of paper and folded the broken butterflies up inside it. Upon the outside she wrote, "For Mrs Mabb".

It was not difficult for Venetia to prevail upon Mr Hawkins (who loved her dearly and who was particularly anxious about her at this period) to deliver the folded paper to Mr Grout.

Next morning Venetia waited hopefully for the return of Captain Fox. When he did not appear she determined to go in search of him again – which both Fanny and Mr Hawkins seemed to have expected, for Fanny had hidden Venetia's dancing slippers in an empty rabbit-hutch in the garden and Mr Hawkins had fetched them out again half an hour later. Mr Hawkins had placed them upon Venetia's bed, where Venetia found them at three o'clock, together with a page torn from Mr Hawkins's memorandum book upon which was drawn a map of Kissingland and the surrounding woods – and deep within those woods, the house of Mrs Mabb.

Downstairs in the kitchen Mr Hawkins was blacking Fanny's

boots and – what was very strange – doing it very ill, so that Fanny was obliged to stand over him and scold him about it. She never heard Venetia slip out of the front door and run down the lane.

The map shewed Mrs Mabb's house to be much deeper in the woods than Venetia had ever gone before. She had walked for an hour or so – and was still some way off from Mrs Mabb's house – when she came to a wide glade surrounded by great oaks, beeches, elders and other sweet English trees. At the furthest end of this glade a cloud of insects rose up suddenly against the sunlit wood and a man appeared. But whether he had stepped out of the wood or out of the cloud of insects would have been impossible to say. His hair had the appearance of being a sort of reddish-brown, and he wore the blue coat and white britches of General _____'s regiment.

"Venetia!" he cried the moment he saw her. "But I thought you had gone to Manchester!"

"And so I did, my dear, dear Captain Fox," said she, running towards him in great delight, "and am now returned."

"That is impossible," said Captain Fox, "for we parted only yesterday and I gave you my watch-chain to wear as keepsake."

They argued about this for some time and Venetia said several times how almost four months had passed since last they met and Captain Fox said how it was nothing of the sort. "It is very odd," thought Venetia, "his virtues are all exactly as I remember them, but I had entirely forgot how very exasperating he is!"

"Well, my love," she said, "I dare say you are right – you always are – but perhaps you will explain to me how the trees in this wood got so heavy with leaves and blossoms and buds? I know they were bare when I went away. And where did all these roses come from? And all this sweet fresh grass?"

At which Captain Fox crossed his arms and looked about him and frowned very hard at the trees. "I cannot explain it," he said at last. "But, Venetia," he said more cheerfully, "you will never guess where I have been all this time – with Mrs Mabb! She sent me a message asking me to make a fourth at Casino but when I arrived I found that all she wanted was to talk love and all sorts of nonsense to me. I bore with it as long as I could, but I confess that she began to try my patience. I tell you, Venetia, she is a very odd woman. There was scarcely a stick of furniture in the place – just one chair for her to sit on and then everybody else must prop himself up against the wall. And the house is very queer. One goes through a door – thinking perhaps to fetch a cup from the kitchen or a book from the library – and suddenly one finds oneself in a little wood, or upon some blasted heath, or being drenched by the waves of some melancholy ocean. Oh! And someone – I have not the least idea who – came several times to the house. Which put all the family and servants in a great uproar, for it was a person whom Mrs Mabb most emphatically did not wish to see. So they were at great pains to get rid of this unwelcome visitor. And what a piece of work they made of it! The third time several of them were killed outright. Two bloody corpses were brought home not more than an hour ago – wrapped in paper – which was a little odd, I thought – with 'For Mrs Mabb' written on the top. I observed that Mrs Mabb grew pale at the sight of them and declared that the game was not worth the candle and that, much as she detested yielding to any body, she could not allow any more noble spirits to be destroyed in this cause. I was glad to hear her say so, for I fancy she can be obstinate at times. A little while afterwards she asked me if I should like to go home."

"And what did you do, my love, while Mrs Mabb's servants were removing this troublesome person?" asked Venetia sweetly.

"Oh! I dozed quietly in the back-parlour and let them all rampage about me if that was what they wished. A soldier – as I think I have told you before, Venetia – must be able to sleep any where. But you see how it is: if the head of a household is governed by passion instead of by reason – as is the case here – then confusion and lack of discipline are quickly communicated to the lower orders. It is the sort of thing one sees very often in the army . . ." And as Captain Fox expounded upon the different generals he had known and their various merits and defects, Venetia took his arm and led him back to Kissingland.

They walked for some time and had a great deal to say to each other and when twilight fell it brought with it a sweet-smelling rain; and birds sang on every side. There were two lights ahead – at the sight of which Venetia was at first inclined to feel some alarm – but they were immediately discovered to be lanterns – only lanterns, the most commonplace articles in the world; and almost as quickly one of the lanterns swung up to reveal Fanny's thin face and; "Oh, Mr Hawkins!" came her glad cry. "Here she is! I have found her!"

The DUKE of WELLINGTON

MISPLACES HIS HORSE

This story is set in the world created by Neil Gaiman and Charles Vess in Stardust. *It concerns Wall, a village in England where there is an actual wall that divides our world and Faerie. If you can evade the burly villagers with big sticks who guard the opening in the wall, then you can cross over. But really you had much better not.*

T HE PEOPLE OF the village of Wall in _____ shire are celebrated for their independent spirit. It is not their way to bow down before great men. An aristocratic title makes no impression upon them and any thing in the nature of pride and haughtiness they detest.

In 1819 the proudest man in all of England was, without a doubt, the Duke of Wellington. This was not particularly surprising; when a man has twice defeated the armies of the wicked French Emperor, Napoleon Bonaparte, it is only natural that he should have a rather high opinion of himself.

In late September of that year the Duke happened to spend one night at The Seventh Magpie in Wall and, though it was only one night, Duke and village soon quarrelled. It began with a general dissatisfaction on both sides at the other side's insolent behaviour, but it soon resolved itself into a skirmish over Mrs Pumphrey's embroidery scissars.

The Duke's visit occurred when Mr Bromios was away from Wall. He had gone somewhere to buy wine, as he did from time to time. Some people said that when he came back from one of these expeditions he smelt faintly of the sea, but other people said it was more like aniseed. Mr Bromios had left The Seventh Magpie in the care of Mr and Mrs Pumphrey.

Mrs Pumphrey sent her husband to fetch her scissars from the upstairs parlour where the Duke was at dinner, but the Duke sent Mr Pumphrey away again because he did not like to be disturbed while he was eating. Consequently when Mrs Pumphrey took in the roast pork she banged it upon the table and gave the Duke a look to shew him what she thought of him. This so enraged the Duke that he hid her scissars in his breeches pocket (though he fully intended to return them in the morning when he left).

That night a poor clergyman called Duzamour arrived at the inn. At first Mr Pumphrey told him that they had no room but, on discovering that Mr Duzamour had a horse, Mr Pumphrey changed his mind, for he thought he saw a way to vent some of his anger against the Duke. He told John Cockcroft, the stableman, to remove the Duke's noble chestnut stallion from the warm, comfortable stable and install Mr Duzamour's ancient grey mare in his place.

"But what shall I do with the Duke's horse?" asked John.

"Oh!" said Mr Pumphrey spitefully. "There is a perfectly good meadow over the road with not so much as a goat grazing in it. Put it there!"

The next morning the Duke rose and looked out of the window. He saw his favourite horse, Copenhagen, contentedly eating grass in a large green meadow. After breakfast the Duke took a stroll in that direction to give Copenhagen a bit of white bread. For some reason two men with cudgels stood, one upon either side of the entrance to the meadow. One of them spoke to the Duke, but the Duke had no attention to spare for whatever the fellow might be saying (it was something about a bull), because at that precise moment he saw Copenhagen walk between the trees on the far side of the meadow and disappear from view. The Duke looked round and discovered that one of the men had raised his staff as though intending to strike him!

The Duke stared at him in amazement.

The man hesitated, as though asking himself if he really intended to strike the Duke who was, after all, Europe's Defender and the Nation's Hero. It was only a moment's hesitation, but it was enough: the Duke strode forward into Faerie in pursuit of Copenhagen.

Beyond the trees the Duke found himself upon a little white path in a pleasant country of round, plump hills. Scattered among the hills were ancient woods of oak and ash which were so overgrown with ivy, dog-roses and honeysuckle that each wood was a solid mass of greenery.

The Duke had only gone a mile or so when he came to a stone house surrounded by a dark moat. The moat was spanned by a bridge so thick with moss that it appeared to have been built out of green velvet cushions. The stone-tiled roof of the house was supported by crumbling stone giants who were bowed and bent by its weight.

Thinking that one of the inhabitants of the house might have seen Copenhagen, the Duke went up to the door and knocked. He waited a while and then began to look in at all the windows. The rooms were bare. The sunlight made golden stripes upon their dusty floors. One room contained a battered pewter goblet but that seemed to be the full stretch of the house's furnishings until, that is, the Duke came to the last window.

In the last room a young woman in a gown of deepest garnet-red was seated upon a wooden stool with her back to the window. She was sewing. Spread out around her was a vast and magnificent piece of embroidery. Reflections of its rich hues danced upon the walls and ceiling. If she had held a molten stained-glass window in her lap the effect could not have been more wonderful.

The room contained only one other thing: a shabby birdcage that hung from the ceiling with a sad-looking bird inside it.

"I wonder, my dear," said the Duke leaning in through the open window, "if you might have seen my charger?"

"No," said the young lady, continuing to sew.

"A pity," said the Duke. "Poor Copenhagen. He was with me at Waterloo and I shall be sorry to lose him. I hope who ever finds him is kind to him. Poor fellow."

There was a silence while the Duke contemplated the elegant curve of the young lady's white neck.

"My dear," he said, "might I come in and have a few moments' conversation with you?"

"As you wish," said the young lady.

Inside, the Duke was pleased to find that the young lady was every bit as good-looking as his first glimpse of her had suggested. "This is a remarkably pretty spot, my dear," he said, "although it seems a little lonely. If you have no objection I shall keep you company for an hour or two."

"I have no objection," said the lady, "but you must promise not disturb me at my work."

"And for whom are you doing such a monstrous quantity of embroidery, my dear?"

The lady smiled ever so slightly. "Why, for you, of course!" she said.

The Duke was surprized to hear this. "And might I be permitted to look?" he asked.

"Certainly," said the lady.

The Duke went round and peered over her shoulder at her work. It consisted of thousands upon thousands of the most exquisite embroidered pictures, some of which seemed very odd and some of which seemed quite familiar.

Three in particular struck the Duke as extraordinary. Here was a chestnut horse, remarkably like Copenhagen, running in a meadow with the village of Wall behind him; then came a picture of the Duke himself walking along a little white path among round green hills; and then came a picture of the Duke here in this very room, looking down over the lady's shoulder at the embroidery! It was complete in every detail – even the sad-looking bird in the cage was there.

At that moment a large brindled rat ran out a hole in the wainscotting and began to gnaw on a corner of the embroidery. It happened to be the part which depicted the birdcage. But what was most extraordinary was that the instant the stitches were broken, the cage in the room disappeared. With a joyous burst of song the bird flew out of the window.

"Well, that is very odd to be sure!" thought the Duke. "But now that I come to think of it, she could not possibly have worked those pictures since I arrived. She must have embroidered those scenes *before the events happened!* It seems that whatever this lady sews into her pictures is sure to come to pass. What comes next, I wonder?"

He looked again.

The next picture was of a knight in silver armour arriving at the house. The one after that shewed the Duke and the knight engaged in a violent quarrel and the last picture (which the lady was just finishing) shewed the knight plunging his sword into the Duke.

"But this is most unfair!" he cried indignantly. "This fellow has a sword, a spear, a dagger and a what-you-may-call-it with a spiked ball on the end of a chain! Whereas I have no weapon whatsoever!"

The lady shrugged as if that were no concern of hers.

"But could you not embroider me a little sword? Or a pistol perhaps?" asked the Duke.

"No," said the lady. She finished her sewing and, securing the last thread with a stout knot, she rose and left the room.

The Duke looked out of the window and saw upon the brow of the hill a sparkle, such as might be produced by sunlight striking silver armour, and a dancing speck of brilliant colour, which might have been a scarlet feather on top of a helmet.

The Duke made a rapid search through the house for some sort of weapon, but found nothing but the battered pewter cup. He returned to the room which contained the embroidery.

"I have it!" He was suddenly struck with a most original idea. "I will not quarrel with him! Then he will not kill me!" He looked down at the embroidery. "Oh, but he has such a conceited expression! Who could help but quarrel with such a ninny!"

Gloomily the Duke plunged his hands into his breeches pocket and found something cold and metallic: Mrs Pumphrey's needlework scissars.

"A weapon at last, by God! Oh! But what is the use? I doubt very much that he will be so obliging as to stand still while I poke these little blades through the chinks in his armour."

The knight in silver armour was crossing the moss-covered bridge. The clatter of his horse's hooves and the clank-clank-clank of his armour sounded throughout the house. His scarlet plume passed by the window.

"Wait!" cried the Duke. "I do believe that this is not a military problem at all. It is a problem of *needlework*!"

He took Mrs Pumphrey's scissars and snipped all the threads in the pictures which shewed the knight arriving at the house; their quarrel; and his own death. When he had finished he looked out of the window; the knight was nowhere to be seen.

"Excellent!" he cried. "Now, for the rest!"

With a great deal of concentration, muttering and pricking of his fingers he added some pictures of his own to the lady's embroidery, all in the largest, ugliest stitches imaginable. The Duke's first picture shewed a stick figure (himself) leaving the house, the next was of his joyful reunion with a stick horse (Copenhagen) and the third and last shewed their safe return through the gap in the wall.

He would have liked to embroider some horrible disaster befalling the village of Wall. Indeed he got so far as to pick out some violent-coloured red and orange silks for the purpose, but in the end he was obliged to give it up, his skills in embroidery being in no way equal to the task.

He picked up his hat and walked out of the ancient stone house. Outside, he found Copenhagen waiting for him – precisely where his large stitches had shewn the horse would be – and great was their rejoicing at the sight of one another. Then the Duke of Wellington mounted upon his horse's back and rode back to Wall.

The Duke believed that he had suffered no ill effects from his short sojourn in the moated house. In later life he was at different times a Diplomat, a Statesman and Prime Minister of Great Britain, but he came more and more to believe that all his exertions were in vain. He told Mrs Arbuthnot (a close friend) that: "On the battlefields of Europe I was master of my own destiny, but as a politician there are so many other people I must please, so many compromises I must make, that I am at best a stick figure."

Mrs Arbuthnot wondered why the Duke suddenly looked so alarmed and turned pale.

Allhope Rectory, Derbyshire
To Mrs Gathercole Dec. 20th., 1811.

Madam,

I shall not try your patience by a repetition of those arguments with which I earlier tried to convince you of my innocence. When I left you this afternoon I told you that it was in my power to place in your hands *written evidence* that would absolve me from every charge which you have seen fit to heap upon my head and in fulfilment of that promise I enclose my journal. And should you discover, madam, in perusing these pages, that I have been so bold as to attempt a sketch of *your own character*, and should that portrayal prove *not entirely flattering*, then I beg you to remember that it was written as a private account and never intended for another's eyes.

You will hear no entreaties from me, madam. Write to the Bishop by all means. I would not stay your hand from any course of action which you felt proper. But one accusation I must answer: that I have acted without due respect for members of your family. It is, madam, my all too lively regard for your family that has brought me to my present curious situation.

I remain, madam, yr. most obedient & very humble Sert.

The Reverend Alessandro Simonelli

From the Journals of Alessandro Simonelli

Aug. 10th., 1811.   Corpus Christi College, Cambridge.
I am beginning to think that I must marry. I have no money, no prospects of advancement and no friends to help me. This queer face of mine is my only capital now and must, I fear, be made to pay; John Windle has told me privately that the bookseller's widow in Jesus-lane is quite desperately in love with me and it is common knowledge that her husband left her nearly £15 thousand. As for the lady herself, I never heard any thing but praise of her. Her youth, virtue, beauty and charity make her universally loved. But still I cannot quite make up my mind to it. I have been too long accustomed to the rigours of scholarly debate to feel much enthusiasm for *female* conversation – no more to refresh my soul in the company of Aquinas, Aristophanes, Euclid, and Avicenna, but instead to pass my hours attending to a discourse upon the merits of a bonnet trimmed with coquelicot ribbons.

Aug. 11th., 1811.
Dr Prothero came smiling to my rooms this morning. "You are surprized to see me, Mr Simonelli," he said. "We have not been such good friends lately as to wait upon each other in our rooms."

True, but whose fault is that? Prothero is the very worst sort of Cambridge scholar: loves horses and hunting more than books and scholarship; has never once given a lecture since he was made Professor though obliged to do so by the deed of foundation every other week in term; once ate 5 roast mackerel at a sitting (which very nearly killed him); is drunk most mornings and *every* evening; dribbles upon his waistcoat as he nods in his chair. I believe I have made my opinion of him pretty widely known and, though I have done myself no good by my honesty, I am pleased to say that I have done him some harm.

He continued, "I bring you good news, Mr Simonelli! You should offer me a glass of wine – indeed you should! When you hear what excellent news I have got for you, I am sure you will wish to offer me a glass of wine!" And he swung his head around like an ugly old tortoise, to see if he could catch sight of a bottle. But I have no wine and so he went on, "I have been asked by a family in Derbyshire – friends of mine, you understand – to find them some learned gentleman to be Rector of their village. Immediately I thought of you, Mr Simonelli! The duties of a country parson in that part of the world are not onerous. And you may judge for yourself of the health of the place, what fine air it is blessed with, when I tell you that Mr Whitmore, the last clergyman, was ninety-three when he died. A good, kind soul, much loved by his parish, but not a scholar. Come, Mr Simonelli! If it is agreeable to you to have a house of your own – with garden, orchard and farm all complete – then I shall write tonight to the Gathercoles and relieve them of all their anxiety by telling them of your acceptance!"

But, though he pressed me very hard, I would not give him my answer immediately. I believe I know what he is about. He has a nephew whom he hopes to steer into my place if I leave Corpus Christi. Yet it would be wrong, I think, to refuse such an opportunity merely for the sake of spiting him.

I believe it must be either the parish or matrimony.

Sept. 9th., 1811.
I was this day ordained as a priest of the Church of England. I have no doubts that my modest behaviour, studiousness and extraordinary mildness of temper make me peculiarly fitted for the life.

Sept. 15th., 1811.   The George, Derby.

Today I travelled by stage coach as far as Derby. I sat outside –
which cost me ten shillings and sixpence – but since it rained
steadily I was at some trouble to keep my books and papers dry.
My room at The George is better aired than rooms in inns
generally are. I dined upon some roast woodcocks, a fricassee of
turnips and apple dumplings. All excellent but not cheap and so
I complained.

Sept. 16th., 1811.

My first impressions were *not* encouraging. It continued to rain
and the country surrounding Allhope appeared very wild and
almost uninhabited. There were steep, wooded valleys, rivers of
white spurting water, outcrops of barren rock surmounted by
withered oaks, bleak windswept moorland. It was, I dare say,
remarkably picturesque, and might have provided an excellent
model for a descriptive passage in a novel, but to me who must
now live here it spoke very eloquently of extreme seclusion and
scarce society characterized by ignorant minds and uncouth
manners. In two hours' walking I saw only one human habitation – a grim farmhouse with rain-darkened walls set among
dark, dripping trees.

   I had begun to think I must be very near to the village when I
turned a corner and saw, a little way ahead of me in the rain, two
figures on horseback. They had stopped by a poor cottage to
speak to someone who stood just within the bounds of the
garden. Now I am no judge of horses but these were quite
remarkable; tall, well-formed and shining. They tossed their
heads and stamped their hooves upon the ground as if they
scorned to be stood upon so base an element. One was black and
one was chestnut. The chestnut, in particular, appeared to be the
only bright thing in the whole of Derbyshire; it glowed like a
bonfire in the grey, rainy air.

The person whom the riders addressed was an old bent man. As I drew near I heard shouts and a curse, and I saw one of the riders reach up and make a sign with his hand above the old man's head. This gesture was entirely new to me and must, I suppose, be peculiar to the natives of Derbyshire. I do not think that I ever before saw any thing so expressive of contempt and as it may be of some interest to study the customs and quaint beliefs of the people here I append a sort of diagram or drawing to shew precisely the gesture the man made.

I concluded that the riders were going away dissatisfied from their interview with the old cottager. It further occurred to me that, since I was now so close to the village, this ancient person was certainly one of my parishioners. I determined to lose no time in bringing peace where there was strife, harmony where there was discord. I quickened my steps, hailed the old man, informed him that I was the new Rector and asked him his name, which was Jemmy.

"Well, Jemmy," said I, assuming a cordial manner and accommodating my language to his uneducated condition, "what has happened here? What have you done to make the gentlemen so angry?"

He told me that the rider of the chestnut horse had a wife who had that morning been brought to bed. He and his servant had come to inquire for Jemmy's wife, Joan, who for many years had attended all the women in the neighbourhood.

"Indeed?" said I in accents of mild reproof. "Then why do you keep the gentleman waiting? Where is your wife?"

He pointed to where the lane wound up the opposite hillside, to where I could just discern through the rain an ancient church and a graveyard.

"Who takes care of the women in their childbeds now?" I asked.

There were, it seemed, two executors of that office: Mr Stubb, the apothecary in Bakewell, or Mr Horrocks, the physician in Buxton. But both these places were two, three hours' hard ride away on bad roads and the lady was already, in Jemmy's words, "proper poorly".

To own the truth I was a little annoyed with the gentleman on the chestnut horse who had not troubled until today to provide an attendant for his wife: an obligation which, presumably, he might have discharged at any time within the last nine months. Nevertheless I hurried after the two men and, addressing the rider of the chestnut horse, said, "Sir, my name is Simonelli. I have studied a great variety of subjects – law, divinity, medicine – at the University at Cambridge and I have for many years maintained a correspondence with one of the most eminent physicians of the age, Mr Matthew Baillie of Great Windmill-street in London. If it is not disagreeable to you, I shall be happy to attend your wife."

He bent upon me a countenance thin, dark, eager. His eyes were exceptionally fine and bright and their expression unusually intelligent. His black hair was his own, quite long, and tied with a black ribbon in a pigtail, rather in the manner of an old-fashioned queue wig. His age, I thought, might be between forty and fifty.

"And are you an adherent of Galenus or Paracelsus?" he said.

"Sir?" I said (for I thought he must intend the question as a joke). But then, since he continued to look at me, I said, "The ancient medical authorities whom you mention, sir, are quite outdated. All that Galen knew of anatomy he got from observing the dissections of pigs, goats and apes. Paracelsus believed in the efficacy of magic spells and all sorts of nonsense. Indeed, sir," I said with a burst of laughter, "you might as well inquire whose cause I espoused in the Trojan War as ask me to chuse between those illustrious, but thoroughly discredited, gentlemen!"

Perhaps it was wrong to laugh at him. I felt it was wrong immediately. I remembered how many enemies my superior abilities had won me at Cambridge, and I recalled my resolution to do things differently in Allhope and to bear patiently with ignorance and misinformation wherever I found it. But the gentleman only said, "Well, Dando, we have had better fortune than we looked for. A scholar, an eminent physician to attend my lady." He smiled a long thin smile which went up just one side of his dark face. "She will be full of gratitude, I have no doubt."

While he spoke I made some discoveries: to wit that both he and his servant were amazingly dirty – I had not observed it at first because the rain had washed their faces clean. His coat, which I had taken to be of brown drugget or some such material, was revealed upon closer inspection to be of red velvet, much discoloured, worn and matted with dirt and grease.

"I had intended to hoist the old woman up behind Dando," he said, "but that will scarcely do for you." He was silent a moment and then suddenly cried, "Well, what do you wait for, you sour-faced rogue?" (This startled me, but a moment later I understood that he addressed Dando.) "Dismount! Help the learned doctor to the horse."

I was about to protest that I knew nothing of horses or riding but Dando had already jumped down and had somehow tipped me on to the horse's back; my feet were in the stirrups and the reins were in my hands before I knew where I was.

Now a great deal is talked in Cambridge of horses and the riding of horses and the managing of horses. A great number of the more ignorant undergraduates pride themselves upon their understanding of the subject. But I find there is nothing to it. One has merely to hold on as tight as one can: the horse, I find, does *all*.

Immense speed! Godlike speed! We turned from the highway immediately and raced through ancient woods of oak and ash and holly; dead leaves flew up, rain flew down, and the gentleman and I – like spirits of the sad, grey air – flew between! Then up, up we climbed to where the ragged grey clouds tore themselves apart like great doors opening in Heaven to let us through! By moorland pools of slate-grey water, by lonely wind-shaped hawthorn trees, by broken walls of grey stones – a ruined chapel – a stream – over the hills, to a house that stood quite alone in a rain-misted valley.

It was a very ancient-looking place, the different parts of which had been built at many different times and of a great variety of materials. There were flints and stones, old silvery-grey timbers, and rose-red brick that glowed very cheerfully in the gloom. But as we drew nearer I saw that it was in a state of the utmost neglect. Doors had lost their hinges and were propped into place with stones and stuffed round with faded brown rags; windows were cracked and broken and pasted over with old paper; the roof, which was of stone tiles, shewed many gaping black holes; dry, dead grasses poked up between the paving stones. It gave the house a melancholy air, particularly since it was surrounded by a moat of dark, still water that reproduced all this desolation as faithfully as any mirror.

We jumped off our horses, entered the house and passed rapidly through a great number of rooms. I observed that the gentleman's servants (of which he appeared to have a most extraordinary number) did not come forward to welcome their master or give him news of his wife but lurked about in the shadows in the most stupid fashion imaginable.

The gentleman conducted me to the chamber where his wife lay, her only attendant a tiny old woman. This person was remarkable for several things, but chiefly for a great number of long, coarse hairs that grew upon her cheeks and resembled nothing so much in the world as porcupine quills.

The room had been darkened and the fire stoked up in accordance with the old-fashioned belief that women in child-birth require to be heated. It was abominably hot. My first action upon entering the room was to pull back the curtains and throw open the windows but when I looked around I rather regretted having done any such thing, for the squalor of that room is not to be described.

The sheets, upon which the gentleman's wife lay, were crawling with vermin of all sorts. Pewter plates lay scattered about with rotting food upon them. And yet it was not the wretchedness of poverty. There was a most extraordinary muddle everywhere one looked. Over here a greasy apron embraced a volume of Diderot's *Encyclopédie*; over there a jewelled red-velvet slipper was trapped by the lid of a warming-pan; under the bed a silver diadem was caught on the prongs of a garden-fork; on the window-ledge the dried-out corpse of some animal (I think a cat) rested its powdery head against a china-jug. A bronze-coloured velvet garment (which rather resembled the robe of a Coptic pope) had been cast down on the floor in lieu of a carpet. It was embroidered all over with gold and pearls, but the threads had broken and the pearls lay scattered in the dirt. It was altogether such an extraordinary blending of magnificence and filth as I could never have conceived of, and left me entirely astonished that any one should tolerate such slothfulness and neglect on the part of their servants.

As for the lady, poor thing, she was very young – perhaps no more than fifteen – and very thin. Her bones shewed through an almost translucent skin which was stretched, tight as a drum, over her swollen belly. Although I have read a great deal upon the subject, I found it more difficult than I had imagined to make the lady attend to what I was saying. My instructions were exceptionally clear and precise, but she was weak and in pain and I could not persuade her to listen to me.

I soon discovered that the baby was lodged in a most unfortunate position. Having no forceps I tried several times to turn it with my hand and at the fourth attempt I succeeded. Between the hours of four and five a male child was born. I did not at first like his colour. Mr Baillie told me that newborn children are generally the colour of claret; sometimes, he said, they may be as dark as port-wine but this child was, to all intents and purposes, black. He was, however, quite remarkably strong. He gave me a great kick as I passed him to the old woman. A bruise upon my arm marks the place.

But I could not save the mother. At the end she was like a house through which a great wind rushes making all the doors bang at their frames: death was rushing through her and her wits came loose and banged about inside her head. She appeared to believe that she had been taken by force to a place where she was watched night and day by a hideous jailoress.

"Hush," said I, "these are very wild imaginings. Look about you. Here is good, kind . . ." I indicated the old woman with the porcupine face, ". . . who takes such excellent care of you. You are surrounded by friends. Be comforted." But she would not listen to me and called out wildly for her mother to come and take her home.

I would have given a great deal to save her. For what in the end was the result of all my exertions? One person came into this world and another left it – it seemed no very great achievement.

I began a prayer of commendation, but had not said above a dozen words when I heard a sort of squeal. Opening one eye, I saw the old woman snatch up the baby and run from the room as fast as her legs could carry her.

I finished my prayer and, with a sigh, went to find the lady's husband. I discovered him in his library where, with an admirable shew of masculine unconcern, he was reading a book. It was then about seven or eight o'clock.

I thought that it became me as a clergyman to offer some comfort and to say something of the wife he had lost, but I was prevented by my complete ignorance of everything that concerned her. Of her virtue I could say nothing at all. Of her beauty I knew little enough; I had only ever seen her with features contorted in the agonies of childbirth and of death. So I told him in plain words what had happened and finished with a short speech that sounded, even to my own ears, uncommonly like an apology for having killed his wife.

"Oh!" he said. "I dare say you did what you could."

I admired his philosophy though I confess it surprised me a little. Then I recalled that, in speaking to me, she had made several errors of grammar and had employed some dialect words and expressions. I concluded that perhaps, like many gentlemen before him, he had been enticed into an unequal marriage by blue eyes and fair hair, and that he had later come to regret it.

"A son, you say?" he said in perfect good humour. "Excellent!" And he stuck his head out of the door and called for the baby to be brought to him. A moment later Dando and the porcupine-faced nurse appeared with the child. The gentleman examined his son very minutely and declared himself delighted. Then he held the baby up and said the following words to it: "On to the shovel you must go, sir!" He gave the child a hearty shake; "And into the fire you must go, sir!" Another shake; "And under the burning coals you must go, sir!" And another shake.

I found his humour a little odd.

Then the nurse brought out a cloath and seemed to be about to wrap the baby in it.

"Oh, but I must protest, sir!" I cried, "Indeed I must! Have you nothing cleaner to wrap the child in?"

They all looked at me in some amazement. Then the gentleman smiled and said, "What excellent eyesight you must have, Mr Simonelli! Does not this cloath appear to you to be made of the finest, whitest linen imaginable?"

"No," said I in some irritation, "it appears to me to be a dirty rag that I would scarcely use to clean my boots!"

"Indeed?" said the gentleman in some surprize. "And Dando? Tell me, how does he strike you? Do you see the ruby buckles on his shoes? No? What of his yellow velvet coat and shining sword?"

I shook my head. (Dando, I may say, was dressed in the same quaint, old-fashioned style as his master, and looked every inch what he no doubt was – a tattered, swaggering scoundrel. He wore jack-boots up to his thighs, a bunch of ragged dirty lace at his throat and an ancient tricorne hat on his head.)

The gentleman gazed thoughtfully at me for a minute or two. "Mr Simonelli," he said at last, "I am quite struck by your face! Those lustrous eyes! Those fine dark eye-lashes! Those noble eye-brows! Every feature proclaims your close connexion with my own family! Do me the kindnes, if you will, of stepping before this mirror and standing at my side."

I did as he asked and, leaving aside some difference in our complexions (his as brown as beechmast, mine as white as hot-pressed paper), the resemblance was, I confess, remarkable. Everything which is odd or unsettling in my own face, I saw repeated in his: the same long eye-brows like black pen-strokes terminating in an upward flourish; the same curious slant to the eye-lid which bestows upon the face an expression of sleepy arrogance; the same little black mole just below the right eye.

"Oh!" he cried. "There can be no doubt about it! What was your father's name?"

"Simonelli," I said with a smile, "evidently."

"And his place of birth?"

I hesitated. "Genoa," I said.

"What was your mother's name?"

"Frances Simon."

"And her place of birth?"

"York."

He took a scrap of paper from the table and wrote it all down. "Simon and Simonelli," he said, "that is odd." He seemed to wait for some further illumination upon the matter of my parentage. He was disappointed. "Well, no matter," he said. "Whatever the connexion between us, Mr Simonelli, I shall discover it. You have done me a great service and I had intended to pay you liberally for it, but I have no notion of relations paying for services that ought to be given freely as part of the duty that family members owe one another." He smiled his long, knowing smile, "And so I must examine the question further," he said.

So all his much-vaunted interest in my face and family came to this: he would not pay me! It made me very angry to think I could have been so taken in by him! I informed him briefly that I was the new Rector of Allhope and said that I hoped to see him in church on Sunday.

But he only smiled and said, "We are not in your parish here. This house is Allhope House and according to ancient agreement I am the Lord of Allhope Manor, but over the years the house and village have become separated and now stand, as you see, at some distance from each other."

I had not the least idea what he was talking about. I turned to go with Dando who was to accompany me back to the village, but at the library door I looked back and said, "It is a curious thing, sir, but you never told me your name."

"I am John Hollyshoes," said he with a smile.

Just as the door closed I could have sworn I heard the sound of a shovel being pushed into the fire and the sound of coals being raked over.

The ride back to the village was considerably less pleasant than the ride to Allhope House had been. The moonlight was all shut out by the clouds and it continued to rain, yet Dando rode as swiftly as his master and at every moment I expected our headlong rush to end in broken necks.

A few lights appeared – the lights of a village. I got down from the black horse and turned to say something to Dando, whereupon I discovered that in that same instant of my dismounting he had caught up the reins of the black horse and was gone. I took one step and immediately fell over my trunk and parcels of books – which I presume had been left for me by Dando and which I had entirely forgot until that moment.

There seemed to be nothing close at hand but a few miserable cottages. Some distance off to the right, half a dozen windows blazed with light and their large size and regular appearance impressed me with ideas of warm rooms, supper tables and comfortable sofas. In short they suggested the abode of a *gentleman*.

My knock was answered by a neat maidservant. I inquired whether this was Mr Gathercole's house. She replied that *Admiral* Gathercole had drowned six years ago. Was I the new Rector?

The neat maidservant left me in the hall to go and announce me to someone or other and I had time to look about me. The floor was of ancient stone flags, very well swept, and the bright gleam upon every oak cabinet, every walnut chest of drawers, every little table, plainly spoke of the plentiful application of beeswax and of pleasant female industry. All was cleanliness, delicacy, elegance – which was more, I discovered, than could be said for me. I was well provided with all the various stains, smears and general dishevelments that may be acquired by walking for hours through heavy rain, galloping through thickly wooded countryside and then toiling long and hard at a childbed and a deathbed; and in addition I had acquired a sort of veneer of black grease – the inevitable result, I fancy, of a sojourn in John Hollyshoes's house.

The neat maidservant led me to a drawing-room where two ladies waited to see what sort of clergyman they had got. One rose with ponderous majesty and announced herself to be Mrs Gathercole, the Admiral's relict. The other lady was Mrs Edmond, the Admiral's sister.

An old-fashioned Pembroke-table had been spread with a white linen cloath for supper. And the supper was a good one. There was a dish of fricasseed chicken and another of scalloped oysters, there was apple tart, Wensleydale cheese, and a decanter of wine and glasses.

Mrs Gathercole had my own letter and another upon which I discerned the unappetising scrawl of Dr Prothero. "Simonelli is an Italian name, is it not?" asked Mrs Gathercole.

"It is, madam, but the bearer of the name whom you see before you is an Englishman." She pressed me no further upon this point and I was glad not to be obliged to repeat the one or two falsehoods I had already uttered that day.

She took up Dr Prothero's letter, read aloud one or two compliments upon my learning in a somewhat doubting tone and began to speak of the house where I was to live. She said that when a house was for many years in the care of an ancient gentleman – as was the case here – it was liable to fall into a state of some dilapidation – she feared I would have a good many repairs to make and the expense would be very great, but as I was a gentleman of independent property, she supposed I would not mind it. She ran on in this manner and I stared into the fire. I was tired to death. But as I sat there I became conscious of something having been said which was not quite right, which it was my duty to correct as soon as possible. I stirred myself to speak. "Madam," I said, "you labour under a misapprehension. I have no property."

"Money, then," she said, "Government bonds."

"No, madam. Nothing."

There was a short silence.

"Mr Simonelli," said Mrs Gathercole, "this is a small parish and, for the most part, poor. The living yields no more than £50 a year. It is very far from providing an income to support a gentleman. You will not have enough money to live on."

Too late I saw the perfidious Prothero's design to immure me in poverty and obscurity. But what could I do? I had no money and no illusions that my numerous enemies at Cambridge, having once got rid of me, would ever allow me to return. I sighed and said something of my modest needs.

Mrs Gathercole gave a short, uncheerful laugh. "You may think so, Mr Simonelli, but your wife will think very differently when she understands how little she is to have for her house-keeping expences.

"My wife, madam?" said I in some astonishment.

"You are a married man, are not you, Mr Simonelli?"

"I, madam? No, madam!"

A silence of much longer duration.

"Well!" she said at last. "I do not know what to say. My instructions were clear enough, I think! A respectable, married man of private fortune. I cannot imagine what Prothero is thinking of. I have already refused the living of Allhope to one young man on the grounds of his unmarried state, but he at least has six hundred pounds a year."

The other lady, Mrs Edmond, now spoke for the first time. "What troubles *me* rather more," she said, "is that Dr Prothero appears to have sent us a scholar. Upperstone House is the only gentleman's house in the parish. With the exception of Mrs Gathercole's own family your parishioners will all be hill-farmers, shepherds and tradesmen of the meanest sort. Your learning, Mr Simonelli, will all be wasted here."

I had nothing to say and some of the despair I felt must have shewed in my face for both ladies became a little kinder. They told me that a room had been got ready for me at the Rectory and Mrs Edmond asked how long it had been since I had eaten. I confessed that I had had nothing since the night before. They invited me to share their supper and then watched as everything I touched — dainty china, white linen napkins — became covered with dark, greasy marks.

As the door closed behind me I heard Mrs Edmond say, "Well, well. So that is Italian beauty! Quite remarkable. I do not think I ever saw an example of it before."

10 o'clock, Sept. 17th., 1811.
Last night complete despair! This morning perfect hope and cheerfulness! New plans constantly bubbling up in my brain! What could be more calculated to raise the spirits than a bright autumn morning with a heavy dew? Everything is rich colour, intoxicating freshness, and sparkle!

I am excessively pleased with the Rectory — and hope that I may be allowed to keep it. It is an old stone house. The ceilings are low, the floor of every room is either higher or lower than the floors of neighbouring rooms and there are more gables than chimneys. It has fourteen rooms! What in the world will I do with fourteen rooms?

I discovered Mr Whitmore's clothes in a cupboard. I had not, I confess, spared many thoughts for this old gentleman, but his clothes brought him vividly before me. Every bump and bulge of his ancient shoes betray their firm conviction that they still enclose his feet. His half-unravelled wig has not yet noticed that his poor old head is gone. The cloath of his long, pale coat is stretched and bagged, *here* to accomodate his sharp elbows, *there* to take account of the stoop of his shoulders. It was almost as if I had opened the cupboard and discovered Mr Whitmore.

Someone calls me from the garden . . .

4 o'clock, the same day.

Jemmy – the old man I spoke to yesterday – is dead. He was found this morning outside his cottage, struck clean in two from the crown of his head to his groin. Is it possible to conceive of any thing more horrible? Curiously, in all the rain we had yesterday, no one remembers seeing any lightning. The funeral will be tomorrow. He was the first person I spoke to in Allhope and my first duty will be to bury him.

The second, and to my mind *lesser*, misfortune to have befallen the parish is that a young woman has disappeared. Dido Puddifer has not been seen since early this morning when her mother, Mrs Glossop, went to a neighbour's house to borrow a nutmeg grater. Mrs Glossop left Dido walking up and down in the orchard with her baby at her breast, but when she returned the baby was lying in the wet grass and Dido was gone.

I accompanied Mrs Edmond to the cottage to pay a visit of sympathy to the family and as we were coming back Mrs Edmond said, "The worst of it is that she is a very pretty girl, all golden curls and soft blue eyes. I cannot help but suppose some passing scoundrel has taken a fancy to her and made her go along with him."

"But does it not seem more likely," said I, "that she went with him of her own accord? She is uneducated, illiterate, and probably never thought seriously upon ethical questions in her life."

"I do not think you quite understand," said Mrs Edmond. "No girl ever loved home and husband more than Dido. No girl was more delighted to have a baby of her own. Dido Puddifer is a silly, giddy sort of girl, but she is also as good as gold."

"Oh!" said I, with a smile. "I dare say she was very good until today, but then, you know, temptation might never have come her way before."

But Mrs Edmond proved quite immoveable in her prejudice in favour of Dido Puddifer and so I said no more. Besides she soon began to speak of a much more interesting subject – my own future.

"My sister-in-law's wealth, Mr Simonelli, causes her to overrate the needs of other people. She imagines that no one can exist upon less than seven hundred pounds a year, but you will do well enough. The living is 50 pounds a year, but the farm could be made to yield twice, thrice that amount. The first four or five years you must be frugal. I will see to it that you are supplied with milk and butter from Upperstone-farm, but by midsummer, Mr Simonelli, you must buy a milch-cow of your own." She thought a moment. "I dare say Marjory Hollinsclough will let me have a hen or two for you."

Sept. 20th., 1811.

This morning Rectory-lane was knee-deep in yellow and brown leaves. A silver rain like smoke blew across the churchyard. A dozen crows in their clerical dress of decent black were idling among the graves. They rose up to flap about me as I came down the lane like a host of winged curates all ready to do my bidding.

There was a whisper of sounds at my back, stifled laughter, a genteel cough, and then: "Oh! Mr Simonelli!" spoken very sweetly and rather low.

I turned.

Five young ladies; on each face I saw the same laughing eyes, the same knowing smiles, the same rain-speckled brown curls, like a strain of music taken up and repeated many different ways. There were even to my befuddled senses the same bonnets, umbrellas, muslins, ribbons, repeated in a bewildering variety of colours but all sweetly blending together, all harmonious. All that I could have asserted with any assurance at that moment was that they were all as beautiful as angels. They were grouped most fetchingly, sheltering each other from the rain with their umbrellas, and the composure and dignity of the two eldest were in no way compromised by the giggles of the two youngest.

The tallest – she who had called my name – begged my pardon. To call out to someone in the lane was very shocking, she hoped I would forgive her but, ". . . Mama has entirely neglected to introduce us and Aunt Edmond is so taken up with the business about poor Dido that . . . well, in short, Mr Simonelli, we thought it best to lay ceremony aside and introduce ourselves. We are made bold to do it by the thought that you are to be our clergyman. The lambs ought not to fear the shepherd, ought they, Mr Simonelli? Oh, but I have no patience with that stupid Dr Prothero! Why did he not send you to us earlier? I hope, Mr Simonelli, that you will not judge Allhope by this dull season!" And she dismissed with a wave of her hand the sweetest, most tranquil prospect imaginable; woods, hills, moors and streams were all deemed entirely unworthy of my attention. "If only you had come in July or August then we might have shewn you all the beauties of Derbyshire, but now I fear you will find it very dull." But her smile defied me to find any place dull where *she* was to be found. "Yet," she said, brightening, "perhaps I shall persuade mama to give a ball. Do you like dancing, Mr Simonelli?"

"But Aunt Edmond says that Mr Simonelli is a scholar," said one of her sisters with the same sly smile. "Perhaps he only cares for books."

"Which books do you like best, Mr Simonelli?" demanded a Miss Gathercole of the middle size.

"Do you sing, Mr Simonelli?" asked the tallest Miss Gathercole.

"Do you shoot, Mr Simonelli?" asked the smallest Miss Gathercole, only to be silenced by an older sister. "Be quiet, Kitty, or he may shoot *you*."

Then the two eldest Miss Gathercoles each took one of my arms and walked with me and introduced me to my parish. And every remark they uttered upon the village and its inhabitants betrayed their happy conviction that it contained nothing half so interesting or delightful as *themselves*.

Sept. 27th., 1811.
I dined this evening at Upperstone House. Two courses. Eighteen dishes in each. Brown Soup. Mackerel. Haricot of mutton. Boiled chicken particularly good. Some excellent apple tarts. I was the only gentleman present.

Mrs Edmond was advising me upon my farm. ". . . and when you go to buy your sheep, Mr Simonelli, I shall accompany you. I am generally allowed to be an excellent judge of livestock."

"Indeed, madam," said I, "that is most kind, but in the meantime I have been thinking that there is no doctor nearer than Buxton and it seems to me that I could not do better than advertise my services as a physician. I dare say you have heard reports that I attended Mrs Hollyshoes."

"Who is Mrs Hollyshoes?" asked Mrs Edmond.

"The wife of the gentleman who owns Allhope House."

"I do not understand you, Mr Simonelli. There is no Allhope House here."

"Whom do you mean, Mr Simonelli?" asked the eldest Miss Gathercole.

I was vexed at their extraordinary ignorance but, with great patience, I gave them an account of my meeting with John Hollyshoes and my visit to Allhope House. But the more particulars I gave, the more obstinately they declared that no such person and no such house existed.

"Perhaps I have mistaken the name," I said – though I knew that I had not.

"Oh! You have certainly done that, Mr Simonelli!" said Mrs Gathercole.

"Perhaps it is Mr Shaw he means," said the eldest Miss Gathercole, doubtfully.

"Or John Wheston," said Miss Marianne.

They began to discuss whom I might mean, but one by one every candidate was rejected. *This* one was too old, *that* one too young. Every gentleman for miles around was pronounced entirely incapable of fathering a child and each suggestion only provided further dismal proofs of the general decay of the male sex in this particular part of Derbyshire.

Sept. 29th., 1811.

I have discovered why Mrs Gathercole was so anxious to have a rich, married clergyman. She fears that a poor, unmarried one would soon discover that the quickest way to improve his fortune is to marry one of the Miss Gathercoles. Robert Yorke (the clergyman whom Mrs Gathercole mentioned on my first evening in Allhope as having £600 a year) was refused the living because he had already shewn signs of being in love with the eldest Miss Gathercole. It must therefore be particularly galling to Mrs Gathercole that I am such a favourite with all her daughters. Each has something she is dying to learn and naturally I am to tutor all of them: French conversation for the eldest Miss Gathercole, advanced Italian grammar for Miss Marianne, the romantic parts of British History for Henrietta, the bloodthirsty parts for Kitty, Mathematics and Poetry for Jane.

Oct. 9th., 1811.

On my return from Upperstone House this morning I found Dando at the Rectory door with the two horses. He told me that his master had something of great importance and urgency to communicate to me.

John Hollyshoes was in his library as before, reading a book. Upon a dirty little table at his side there was wine in a dirty glass. "Ah! Mr Simonelli!" he cried, jumping up. "I am very glad to see you! It seems, sir, that you have the family failing as well as the family face!"

"And what would that be?" said I.

"Why! Lying, of course! Oh, come, Mr Simonelli! Do not look so shocked. You are found out, sir. Your father's name was *not* Simonelli – and, to my certain knowledge, he was never at Genoa!"

A silence of some moments' duration.

"Did you know my father, sir?" said I, in some confusion.

"Oh, yes! He was my cousin."

"That is entirely impossible," said I.

"Upon the contrary," said he. "If you will take a moment to peruse this letter you will see that it is exactly as I say." And he handed me some yellowing sheets of paper.

"What your aim may be in insulting me," I cried, "I cannot pretend to guess, but I hope, sir, that you will take back those words or we shall be obliged to settle the matter *some other way*." With the utmost impatience I thrust his letter back at him, when my eye was caught by the words, "the third daughter of a York linen-draper". "Wait!" I cried and snatched it back again. "My mother was the third daughter of a York linen-draper!"

"Indeed, Mr Simonelli," said John Hollyshoes, with his long sideways smile.

The letter was addressed to John Hollyshoes and had been written at The Old Starre Inn in Stonegate, York. The writer of the letter mentioned that he was in the middle of a hasty breakfast and there were some stains as of preserves and butter. It seemed that the writer had been on his way to Allhope House to pay John Hollyshoes a visit when he had been delayed in York by a sudden passion for the third daughter of a York linen-draper. His charmer was most minutely described. I read of "a slight plumpness", "light silvery-gold curls", "eyes of a forget-me-not blue".

By all that I have ever been told by my friends, by all that I have ever seen in sketches and watercolour portraits, this was my mother! But if nothing else proved the truth of John Holly-shoes's assertion, there was the date – January 19th., 1778 – nine months to the day before my own birth. The writer signed himself, "Your loving cousin, Thomas Fairwood".

"So much love," I said, reading the letter, "and yet he deserted her the very next day!"

"Oh! You must not blame him," said John Hollyshoes. "A person cannot help his disposition, you know."

"And yet," said I, "one thing puzzles me still. My mother was extremely vague upon all points concerning her seducer – she did not even know his name – yet one thing she was quite clear about. He was a foreign gentleman."

"Oh! That is easily explained," he said. "For though we have lived in this island a very long time – many thousands of years longer than its other inhabitants – yet still we hold ourselves apart and pride ourselves on being of quite other blood."

"You are Jews perhaps, sir?" said I.

"Jews?" said he. "No, indeed!"

I thought a moment. "You say my father is dead?"

"Alas, yes. After he parted from your mother, he did not in fact come to Allhope House, but was drawn away by horse races at *this* place and cock-fighting at *that* place. But some years later he wrote to me again telling me to expect him at midsummer and promising to stay with me for a good long while. This time he got no further than a village near Carlisle where he fell in love with two young women . . ."

"Two young women!" I cried in astonishment.

"Well," said John Hollyshoes. "Each was as beautiful as the other. He did not know how to chuse between them. One was the daughter of a miller and the other was the daughter of a baker. He hoped to persuade them to go with him to his house in the Eildon Hills where he intended that both should live for ever and have all their hearts' desire. But, alas, it did not suit these ungrateful young women to go and the next news I had of him was that he was dead. I discovered later that the miller's daughter had sent him a message which led him to believe that she at least was on the point of relenting, and so he went to her father's mill, where the fast-running water was shaded by a rowan tree – and I pause here merely to observe that of all the trees in the greenwood the rowan is the most detestable. Both young women were waiting for him. The miller's daughter jangled a bunch of horrid rowan-berries in his face. The baker's daughter was then able to tumble him into the stream whereupon both women rolled the millstone on top of him, pinning him to the floor of the stream. He was exceedingly strong. All my family – *our* family I should say – are exceedingly strong, exceedingly hard to kill, but the millstone lay on his chest. He was unable to rise and so, in time, he drowned."

"Good God!" I cried. "But this is dreadful! As a clergyman I cannot approve his habit of seducing young women, but as a son I must observe that in this particular instance the revenge extracted by the young women seems out of all proportion to his offence. And were these bloodthirsty young women never brought to justice?"

"Alas, no," said John Hollyshoes. "And now I must beg that we cease to speak of a subject so very unpleasant to my family feelings. Tell me instead why you fixed upon this odd notion of being Italian."

I told him how it had been my grandfather's idea. From my

own dark looks and what his daughter had told him he thought I might be Italian or Spanish. A fondness for Italian music caused him to prefer that country. Then he had taken his own name, George Alexander Simon, and fashioned out of it a name for me, Giorgio Alessandro Simonelli. I told how that excellent old gentleman had *not* cast off his daughter when she fell but had taken good care of her, provided money for attendants and a place for her to live and how, when she died of sorrow and shame shortly after my birth, he had brought me up and had me educated.

"But what is most remarkable," said John Hollyshoes, "is that you fixed upon that city which – had Thomas Fairwood ever gone to Italy – was precisely the place to have pleased him most. Not gaudy Venice, not trumpeting Rome, not haughty Florence, but Genoa, all dark shadows and sinister echoes tumbling down to the shining sea!"

"Oh! But I chose it quite at random, I assure you."

"That," said John Hollyshoes, "has nothing to do with it. In choosing Genoa you exhibited the extraordinary penetration which has always distinguished our family. But it was your eyesight that betrayed you. Really, I was never so astonished in my life as I was when you remarked upon the one or two specks of dust which clung to the baby's wrapper."

I asked after the health of his son.

"Oh! He is well. Thank you. We have got an excellent wet-nurse – from your own parish – whose milk agrees wonderfully well with the child."

Oct. 20th., 1811.

In the stable-yard at Upperstone House this morning the Miss Gathercoles were preparing for their ride. Naturally I was invited to accompany them.

"But, my dear," said Mrs Edmond to the eldest Miss

Gathercole, "you must consider that Mr Simonelli may not ride. Not everyone rides." And she gave me a questioning look as if she would help me out of a difficulty.

"Oh!" said I. "I can ride a horse. It is of all kinds of exercise the most pleasing to me." I approached a conceited-looking grey mare but instead of standing submissively for me to mount, this ill-mannered beast shuffled off a pace or two. I followed it – it moved away. This continued for some three or four minutes, while all the ladies of Upperstone silently observed us. Then the horse stopt suddenly and I tried to mount it, but its sides were of the most curious construction and instead of finding myself upon its back in a twinkling – as invariably happens with John Hollyshoes's horses – I got stuck halfway up.

Of course the Upperstone ladies chose to find fault with me instead of their own malformed beast and I do not know what was more mortifying, the surprized looks of Miss Gathercole and Miss Marianne, or the undisguised merriment of Kitty.

I have considered the matter carefully and am forced to conclude that it will be a great advantage to me in such a retired spot to be able to ride whatever horses come to hand. Perhaps I can prevail upon Joseph, Mrs Gathercole's groom, to teach me.

Nov. 4th., 1811.
Today I went for a long walk in company with the five Miss Gathercoles. Sky as blue as paint, russet woods, fat white clouds like cushions – and that is the sum of all that I discovered of the landscape, for my attention was constantly being called away to the ladies themselves. "Oh! Mr Simonelli! Would you be so kind as to do *this*?"; or "Mr Simonelli, might I trouble you to do *that*?"; or "Mr Simonelli! What is your opinion of such and such?" I was required to carry picnic-baskets, discipline unruly sketching easels, advise upon perspective, give an opinion on Mr Coleridge's poetry, eat sweet-cake and dispense wine.

I have been reading over what I have written since my arrival here and one thing I find quite astonishing – that I ever could have supposed that there was a strong likeness between the Miss Gathercoles. There never were five sisters so different in tastes, characters, persons and countenances. Isabella, the eldest, is also the prettiest, the tallest and the most elegant. Henrietta is the most romantic, Kitty the most light-hearted and Jane is the quietest; she will sit hour after hour, dreaming over a book. Sisters come and go, battles are fought, she that is victorious sweeps from the room with a smile, she that is defeated sighs and takes up her embroidery. But Jane knows nothing of any of this – and then, quite suddenly, she will look up at me with a slow mysterious smile and I will smile back at her until I quite believe that I have joined with her in unfathomable secrets.

Marianne, the second eldest, has copper-coloured hair, the exact shade of dry beech leaves, and is certainly the most exasperating of the sisters. She and I can never be in the same room for more than a quarter of an hour without beginning to quarrel about something or other.

Nov. 16th., 1811.
John Windle has written me a letter to say that at High Table at Corpus Christi College on Thursday last Dr Prothero told Dr Considine that he pictured me in ten years' time with a worn-out slip of a wife and a long train of broken-shoed, dribble-nosed children, and that Dr Considine had laughed so much at this that he had swallowed a great mouthful of scalding-hot giblet soup, and returned it through his nose.

Nov. 26th., 1811.
No paths or roads go down to John Hollyshoes' house. His servants do not go out to farm his lands; there *is* no farm that I

know of. How they all live I do not know. Today I saw a small creature – I think it was a rat – roasting over the fire in one of the rooms. Several of the servants bent over it eagerly, with pewter plates and ancient knives in their hands. Their faces were all in shadow. (It is an odd thing but, apart from Dando and the porcupine-faced nurse, I have yet to observe *any* of John Hollyshoes's servants at close quarters: they all scuttle away when ever I approach.)

John Hollyshoes is excellent company, his conversation instructive, his learning quite remarkable. He told me today that Judas Iscariot was a most skilful beekeeper and his honey superior to any that had been produced in all the last two thousand years. I was much interested by this information, having never read or heard of it before and I questioned him closely about it. He said that he believed he had a jar of Judas Iscariot's honey somewhere and if he could lay his hand upon it he would give it to me.

Then he began to speak of how my father's affairs had been left in great confusion at his death and how, since that time, the various rival claimants to his estate had been constantly fighting and quarrelling among themselves.

"Two duels have been fought to my certain knowledge," he said, "and as a natural consequence of this two claimants are dead. Another – whose passion to possess your father's estate was exceeded only by his passion for string quartets – was found three years ago hanging from a tree by his long silver hair, his body pierced through and through with the bows of violins, violoncellos, and violas like a musical Saint Sebastian. And only last winter an entire houseful of people was poisoned. The claimant had already run out of the house into the blizzard in her nightgown and it was only her servants that died. Since I have made no claim upon the estate, I have escaped most of their malice – though, to own the truth, I have a better right to the property than any of them. But naturally the person with the best claim of all would be Thomas Fairwood's son. All dissension would be at an end, should a *son* arise to claim the estate." And he looked at me.

"Oh!" said I, much surprized. "But might not the fact of my illegitimacy . . .?"

"We pay no attention to such things. Indeed with us it is more common than not. Your father's lands, both in England and elsewhere, are scarcely less extensive than my own and it would cost you very little trouble to procure them. Once it was known that you had *my* support, then I dare say we would have you settled at Rattle-heart House by next Quarter-day."

Such a stroke of good fortune, as I never dreamt of! Yet I dare not depend upon it. But I cannot help thinking of it *constantly*! No one would enjoy vast wealth more than I; and my feelings are not entirely selfish, for I honestly believe that I am exactly the sort of person who *ought* to have the direction of large estates. If I inherit then I shall improve my lands scientifically and increase its yields three or fourfold (as I have read of other gentlemen doing). I shall observe closely the lives of my tenants and servants and teach them to be happy. Or perhaps I shall sell my father's estates and purchase land in Derbyshire and marry Marianne or Isabella so that I may ride over every week to Allhope for the purpose of inquiring most minutely into Mrs Gathercole's affairs, and advising her and Mrs Edmond upon every point.

7 o'clock in the morning, Dec. 8th., 1811.
We have had no news of Dido Puddifer. I begin to think that Mrs Edmond and I were mistaken in fancying that she had run off with a tinker or gypsy. We have closely questioned farm-labourers, shepherds and innkeepers, but no gypsies have been seen in the neighbourhood since midsummer. I

intend this morning to pay a visit to Mrs Glossop, Dido's mother.

8 o'clock in the evening, the same day.

What a revolution in all my hopes! From perfect happiness to perfect misery in scarcely twelve hours. What a fool I was to dream of inheriting my father's estate! – I might as well have contemplated taking a leasehold of a property in Hell! And I wish that I might go to Hell now, for it would be no more than I deserve. I have failed in my duty! I have imperilled the lives and souls of my parishioners. My parishioners! – the very people whose preservation from all harm ought to have been my first concern.

I paid my visit to Mrs Glossop. I found her, poor woman, with her head in her apron, weeping for Dido. I told her of the plan Mrs Edmond and I had devised to advertise in the Derby and Sheffield papers to see if we could discover any one who had seen or spoken to Dido.

"Oh!" said she, with a sigh. " 'Twill do no good, sir, for I know very well where she is."

"Indeed?" said I in some confusion. "Then why do you not fetch her home?"

"And so I would this instant," cried the woman, "did I not know that John Hollyshoes has got her!"

"John Hollyshoes?" I cried in amazement.

"Yes, sir," said she, "I dare say you will not have heard of John Hollyshoes for Mrs Edmond does not like such things to be spoken of and scolds us for our ignorant, superstitious ways. But we country people know John Hollyshoes very well. He is a very powerful fairy that has lived hereabouts – oh! since the world began, for all I know – and claims all sorts of rights over us. It is my belief that he has got some little fairy baby at End-Of-All-Hope House – which is where he lives – and that he needs a strong lass with plenty of good human milk to suckle it."

I cannot say that I believed her. Nor can I say that I did not. I do know that I sat in a state of the utmost shock for some time without speaking, until the poor woman forgot her own distress and grew concerned about *me*, shaking me by the shoulder and hurrying out to fetch brandy from Mrs Edmond. When she came back with the brandy I drank it down at one gulp and then went straight to Mrs Gathercole's stable and asked Joseph to saddle Quaker for me. Just as I was leaving, Mrs Edmond came out of the house to see what was the matter with me.

"No time, Mrs Edmond! No time!" I cried and rode away.

At John Hollyshoes' house Dando answered my knock and told me that his master was away from home.

"No matter," said I, with a confident smile, "for it is not John Hollyshoes that I have come to see, but my little cousin, the dear little sprite . . ." – I used the word "sprite" and Dando did not contradict me – ". . . whom I delivered seven weeks ago." Dando told me that I would find the child in a room at the end of a long hallway.

It was a great bare room that smelt of rotting wood and plaster. The walls were stained with damp and full of holes that the rats had made. In the middle of the floor was a queer-shaped wooden chair where sat a young woman. A bar of iron was fixed before her so that she could not rise and her legs and feet were confined by manacles and rusty chains. She was holding John Hollyshoes's infant son to her breast.

"Dido?" I said.

How my heart fell when she answered me with a broad smile. "Yes, sir?"

"I am the new Rector of Allhope, Dido."

"Oh, sir! I am very glad to see you. I wish that I could rise and make you a curtsey, but you will excuse me, I am sure. The little gentleman has such an appetite this morning!"

She kissed the horrid creature and called it her angel, her doodle and her dearie-darling-pet.

"How did you come here, Dido?" I asked.

"Oh! Mr Hollyshoes' servants came and fetched me away one morning. And weren't they set upon my coming?" – she laughed merrily – "All that a-pulling of me uphill and a-putting of me in carts! And I told them plainly that there was no need for any such nonsense. As soon as I heard of the poor little gentleman's plight," – here she shook the baby and kissed it again – "I was more than willing to give him suck. No, my only misfortune, sir, in this heavenly place, is that Mr Hollyshoes declares I must keep apart from my own sweet babe while I nurse his, and if all the angels in Heaven went down upon their shining knees and begged him he would not think any differently. Which is a pity, sir, for you know I might very easily feed two."

In proof of this point she, without the slightest embarrassment, uncovered her breasts which to my inexperienced eye did indeed appear astonishingly replete.

She was anxious to learn who suckled her own baby. Anne Hargreaves, I told her. She was pleased at this and remarked approvingly that Nan had always had a good appetite. "Indeed, sir, I never knew a lass who loved a pudding better. Her milk is sure to be sweet and strong, do not you think so, sir?"

"Well, certainly Mrs Edmond says that little Horatio Arthur thrives upon it. Dido, how do they treat you here?"

"Oh! sir. How can you ask such a question? Do you not see this golden chair set with diamonds and pearls? And this room with pillars of crystal and rose-coloured velvet curtains? At night – you will not believe it, sir, for I did not believe it myself – I sleep on a bed with six feather mattress one atop the other and six silken pillows to my head."

I said it sounded most pleasant. And was she given enough to eat and drink?

Roast pork, plum pudding, toasted cheese, bread and dripping: there was, according to Dido Puddifer, no end to the good things to be had at End-Of-All-Hope House – and I dare say each and every one of them was in truth nothing more than the mouldy crusts of bread that I saw set upon a cracked dish at her feet.

She also believed that they had given her a gown of sky-blue velvet with diamond buttons to wear and she asked me, with a conscious smile, how I liked it.

"You look very pretty, Dido," I said and she looked pleased. But what I really saw was the same russet-coloured gown she had been wearing when they took her. It was all torn and dirty. Her hair was matted with the fairy-child's puke and her left eye was crusted with blood from a gash in her forehead. She was altogether such a sorry sight that my heart was filled with pity for her and, without thinking what I did, I licked my fingertips and cleaned her eye with my spittle.

I opened my mouth to ask if she were ever allowed out of the golden chair encrusted with diamonds and pearls, but I was prevented by the sound of a door opening behind me. I turned and saw John Hollyshoes walk in. I quite expected him to ask me what I did there, but he seemed to suspect no mischief and instead bent down to test the chains and the shackles. These were, like everything else in the house, somewhat decayed and he was right to doubt their strength. When he had finished he rose and smiled at me.

"Will you stay and take a glass of wine with me?" he said. "I have something of a rather particular nature to ask you."

We went to the library where he poured two glasses of wine. He said, "Cousin, I have been meaning to ask you about that family of women who live upon my English estates and make themselves so important at my expense. I have forgot their name."

"Gathercole?" said I.

"Gathercole. Exactly," said he and fell silent for a moment with a kind of thoughtful half-smile upon his dark face. "I have been a widower seven weeks now," he said, "and I do not believe I was ever so long without a wife before – not since there were women in England to be made wives of. To speak plainly, the sweets of courtship grew stale with me a long time ago and I wondered if you would be so kind as to spare me the trouble and advise me which of these women would suit me best."

"Oh!" said I. "I am quite certain that you would heartily dislike all of them!"

He laughed and put his arm around my shoulders. "Cousin," he said, "I am not so hard to please as you suppose."

"But really," said I, "I cannot advise you in the way you suggest. You must excuse me – indeed I cannot!"

"Oh? And why is that?"

"Because . . . Because I intend to marry one of them myself!" I cried.

"I congratulate you, cousin. Which?"

I stared at him. 'What?" I said.

"Tell me which you intend to marry and I will take another."

"Marianne!" I said, 'No, wait! Isabella! That is . . ." It struck me very forcibly at that moment that I could not chuse one without endangering all the others.

He laughed at that and affectionately patted my arm. 'Your enthusiasm to possess Englishwomen is no more than I should have expected of Thomas Fairwood's son. But my own appetites are more moderate. One will suffice for me. I shall ride over to Allhope in a day or two and chuse one young lady, which will leave four for you."

The thought of Isabella or Marianne or any of them doomed to live for ever in the degradation of End-Of-All-Hope House! Oh! it is too horrible to be borne.

I have been staring in the mirror for an hour or more. I was always amazed at Cambridge how quickly people appeared to take offence at everything I said, but now I see plainly that it was not my words they hated − it was this fairy face. The dark alchemy of this face turns all my gentle human emotions into fierce fairy vices. Inside I am all despair but this face shews only fairy scorn. My remorse becomes fairy fury and my pensiveness is turned to fairy cunning.

Dec. 9th., 1811.

This morning at half past ten I made my proposals to Isabella Gathercole. She − sweet, compliant creature! − assured me that I had made her the happiest of women. But she could not at first be made to agree to a secret engagement.

"Oh!" she said. "Certainly mama and Aunt Edmond will make all sorts of difficulties, but what will secrecy achieve? You do not know them as I do. Alas, they cannot be reasoned into an understanding of your excellent qualities. But they can be worn down. An unending stream of arguments and pleas must be employed and the sooner it is begun, the sooner it will bring forth the happy resolution we wish for. I must be tearful; you must be heartbroken. I must get up a little illness − which will take time as I am just now in the most excellent good looks and health."

What could the mean-spirited scholars of Cambridge not learn from such a charming instructress? She argued so sweetly that I almost forgot what I was about and agreed to all her most reasonable demands. In the end I was obliged to tell her a little truth. I said that I had recently discovered that I was related to someone very rich who lived nearby and who had taken a great liking to me. I said that I hoped to inherit a great property very soon; surely it was not unreasonable to suppose that Mrs Gathercole would look with more favour upon my suit when I was as wealthy as she?

Isabella saw the sense of this immediately and would, I think, have begun to speak again of love and so forth, only I was obliged to hurry away as I had just observed Marianne going into the breakfast-room.

Marianne was inclined to be quarrelsome at first. It was not, she said, that she did not wish to marry me. After all, she said, she must marry someone and she believed that she and I might do very well together. But why must our engagement be a secret? That, she said, seemed almost dishonourable.

"As you wish," said I. "I had thought that your affection for me might make you glad to indulge me in this one point. And besides, you know, a *secret engagement* will oblige us to speak Italian to each other constantly."

Marianne is passionately fond of Italian, particularly since none of her sisters understand a word. "Oh! Very well," she said.

In the garden at half past eleven Jane accepted my proposals by leaning up to whisper in my ear: "His face is fair as heav'n when springing buds unfold." She looked up at me with her soft secret smile and took both my hands in hers.

In the morning-room a little before midday I encountered a problem of a different sort. Henrietta assured me that a secret engagement was the very thing to please her most, but begged to be allowed to write of it to her cousin in Aberdeen. It seems that this cousin, Miss Mary Macdonald, is Henrietta's dearest friend and most regular correspondent, their ages – fifteen and a half – being exactly the same.

It was the most curious thing, she said, but the very week she had first beheld me (and instantly fallen in love with me) she had had a letter from Mary Macdonald full of *her* love for a sandy-haired Minister of the Kirk, the Reverend John McKenzie, who appeared from Mary Macdonald's many detailed descriptions of him to be almost as handsome as myself! Did I not agree with her that it was the strangest thing in the

world, this curious resemblance in their situations? Her eagerness to inform Mary Macdonald immediately on all points
concerning our engagement was not, I fear, unmixed with a
certain rivalry, for I suspected that she was not quite sincere in
hoping that Mary Macdonald's love for Mr McKenzie might
enjoy the same happy resolution as her own for me. But since I
could not prevent her writing, I was obliged to agree.

In the drawing-room at three o'clock I finally came upon
Kitty who would not at first listen to any thing that I had to say,
but whirled around the room full of a plan to astound all the
village by putting on a play in the barn at Christmas.

"You are not attending to me," said I. "Did not you hear me
ask you to marry me?"

"Yes," said she, "and I have already said that I would. It is
you who are not attending to *me*. You must advise us upon a
play. Isabella wishes to be someone very beautiful who is
vindicated in the last act, Marianne will not act unless she can
say something in Italian, Jane cannot be made to understand
any thing about it so it will be best if she does not have to
speak at all, Henrietta will do whatever I tell her, and, oh! I
long to be a bear! The dearest, wisest old talking bear! Who
must dance – like this! And you may be either a sailor or a
coachman – it does not matter which, as we have the hat for
one and the boots for the other. Now tell me, Mr Simonelli,
what plays would suit us?"

Two o'clock, Dec. 10th., 1811.   In the woods
between End-Of-All-Hope House and the village of Allhope.
I take out my pen, my inkpot and this book.

"What are you doing?" whimpers Dido, all afraid.

"Writing my journal," I say.

"Now?" says she in amazement. Poor Dido! As I write she
keeps up a continual lament that it will soon be dark and that the

snow falls more heavily – which is I admit a great nuisance for the flakes fall upon the page and spoil the letters.

This morning my vigilant watch upon the village was rewarded. As I stood in the church-porch, hidden from all eyes by the thick growth of ivy, I saw Isabella coming down Upperstone-lane. A bitter wind passed over the village, loosening the last leaves from the trees and bringing with it a few light flakes of snow. Suddenly a spinning storm of leaves and snowflakes seemed to take possession of Upperstone-lane and John Hollyshoes was there, bowing low and smiling.

It is a measure of my firm resolution that I was able to leave her then, to leave all of them. Everything about John Hollyshoes struck fear into my heart, from the insinuating tilt of his head to the enigmatic gesture of his hands, but I had urgent business to attend to elsewhere and must trust that the Miss Gathercoles' regard for me will be strong enough to protect them.

I went straight to End-Of-All-Hope House and the moment I appeared in the bare room at the end of the corridor, Dido cried out, "Oh, sir! Have you come to release me from this horrid place?"

"Why, Dido!" said I, much surprized. "What has happened? I thought you were quite contented."

"And so I was, sir, until you licked your finger and touched my eye. When you did that the sight of my eye was changed. Now if I look through this eye," – she closed her left eye and looked through her right – "I am wearing a golden dress in a wonderful palace and cradling the sweetest babe that ever I beheld. But if I look through *this* eye," – she closed the right and opened her left – "I seem to be chained up in a dirty, nasty room with an ugly goblin child to nurse. But," she said hurriedly (for I was about to speak), "whichever it is I no longer care, for I am very unhappy here and should very much like to go home."

"I am pleased to hear you say so, Dido," said I. Then, warning her not to express any surprize at any thing I said or did, I put my head out of the door and called for Dando.

He was with me in an instant, bowing low.

"I have a message from your master," I said, "whom I met just now in the woods with his new bride. But, like most English-women, the lady is of a somewhat nervous disposition and she has taken it into her head that End-Of-All-Hope House is a dreadful place full of horrors. So your master and I have put our heads together and concluded that the quickest way to soothe her fears is to fetch this woman . . ." – I indicated Dido – ". . . whom she knows well, to meet her. A familiar face is sure to put her at her ease."

I stopped and gazed, as though in expectation of something, at Dando's dark, twisted face. And he gazed back at me, perplexed.

"Well?" I cried. "What are you waiting for, blockhead? Do as I bid you! Loose the nurse's bonds so that I may quickly convey her to your master!" And then, in a fine counterfeit of one of John Hollyshoes' own fits of temper, I threatened him with everything I could think of: beatings, incarcerations and en-chantments! I swore to tell his master of his surliness. I promised that he should be put to work to untangle all the twigs in the woods and comb smooth all the grass in the meadows for insulting me and setting my authority at nought.

Dando is a clever sprite, but I am a cleverer. My story was so convincing that he soon went and fetched the key to unlock Dido's fetters, but not before he had quite worn me out with apologies and explanations and pleas for forgiveness.

When the other servants heard the news that their master's English cousin was taking the English nurse away, it seemed to stir something in their strange clouded minds and they all came out of their hiding places to crowd around us. For the first time I saw them clearly. This was most unpleasant for me, but for Dido it was far worse. She told me afterwards that through her right eye she had seen a company of ladies and gentlemen who bent upon her looks of such kindness that it made her wretched to think she was deceiving them, while through her other eye she had seen the goblin forms and faces of John Hollyshoes' servants.

There were horned heads, antlered heads, heads carapaced like insects' heads, heads as puckered and soft as a mouldy orange; there were mouths pulled wide by tusks, mouths stretched out into trumpets, mouths that grinned, mouths that gaped, mouths that dribbled; there were bats' ears, cats' ears, rats' whiskers; there were ancient eyes in young faces, large, dewy eyes in old worn faces, there were eyes that winked and blinked in parts of anatomy where I had never before expected to see any eyes at all. The goblins were lodged in every part of the house: there was scarcely a crack in the wainscotting which did not harbour a staring eye, scarcely a gap in the banisters without a nose or snout poking through it. They prodded us with their horny fingers, they pulled our hair and they pinched us black and blue. Dido and I ran out of End-Of-All-Hope House, jumped up upon Quaker's back and rode away into the winter woods.

Snow fell thick and fast from a sea-green sky. The only sounds were Quaker's hooves and the jingle of Quaker's harness as he shook himself.

At first we made good progress, but then a thin mist came up and the path through the woods no longer led where it was supposed to. We rode so long and so far that – unless the woods had grown to be the size of Derbyshire and Nottinghamshire together – we must have come to the end of them, but we never did. And whichever path I chose we were for ever riding past a white gate with a smooth, dry lane beyond it – a remarkably dry lane considering the amount of snow which had fallen – and Dido asked me several times why we did not go down it. But I did not care for it. It was the most commonplace lane in the world, but a wind blew along it – a hot wind like the breath of an oven, and there was a smell as of burning flesh mixed with sulphur.

When it became clear that riding did no more than wear out ourselves and our horse I told Dido that we must tie Quaker to a tree – which we did. Then we climbed up into the branches to await the arrival of John Hollyshoes.

Seven o'clock, the same day.
Dido told me how she had always heard from her mother that red berries, such as rowan-berries, are excellent protection against fairy magic.

"There are some over there in that thicket," she said.

But she must have been looking with her enchanted eye for I saw, not red berries at all, but the chestnut-coloured flanks of Pandemonium, John Hollyshoes' horse.

Then the two fairies on their fairy-horses were standing before us with the white snow tumbling across them.

"Ah, cousin!" cried John Hollyshoes. "How do you do? I would shake hands with you, but you are a little out of reach up there." He looked highly delighted and as full of malice as a pudding is of plums. "I have had a very exasperating morning. It seems that the young gentlewomen have all contracted themselves to someone else – yet none will say to whom. Is that not a most extraordinary thing?"

"Most," said I.

"And now the nurse has run away." He eyed Dido sourly. "I never was so thwarted, and were I to discover the author of all my misfortunes – well, cousin, what do you suppose that I would do?"

"I have not the least idea," said I.

"I would kill him," said he. "No matter how dearly I loved him."

The ivy that grew about our tree began to shake itself and to ripple like water. At first I thought that something was trying to escape from beneath it, but then I saw that the ivy itself was moving. Strands of ivy like questing snakes rose up and wrapped themselves around my ancles and legs.

"Oh!" cried Dido in a fright and tried to pull them off me.

The ivy did not only move; it grew. Soon my legs were lashed to the tree by fresh, young strands; they coiled around my chest and wound around the upper part of my right arm. They threatened to engulf my journal but I was careful to keep *that* out of harm's way. They did not stop until they caressed my neck, leaving me uncertain as to whether John Hollyshoes intended to strangle me or merely to pin me to the tree until I froze to death.

John Hollyshoes turned to Dando. "Are you deaf, Ironbrains? Did you never hear me say that he is as accomplished a liar as you and I?" He paused to box Dando's ear. "Are you blind? Look at him! Can you not perceive the fierce fairy heart that might commit murder with indifference? Come here, Unseelie elf! Let me poke some new holes in your face! Perhaps you will see better out of those!"

I waited patiently until my cousin had stopped jabbing at his servant's face with the blunt end of his whip and until Dando had ceased howling. "I am not sure," I said, "whether I could commit murder with indifference, but I am perfectly willing to try." With my free arm I turned to the page in my journal where I have described my arrival in Allhope. I leant out of the tree as far as I could (this was very easily accomplished as the ivy held me snug against the trunk) and above John Hollyshoes' head I made the curious gesture that I had seen him make over the old man's head.

We were all as still as the frozen trees, as silent as the birds in the thickets and the beasts in their holes. Suddenly John Hollyshoes burst out, "Cousin . . .!"

It was the last word he ever spoke. Pandemonium, who appeared to know very well what was about to happen, reared up and shook his master from his back, as though terrified that he too might be caught up in my spell. There was a horrible rending sound; trees shook; birds sprang, cawing, into the air. Any one would have supposed that it was the whole world, and not merely some worthless fairy, that was being torn apart. I looked down and John Hollyshoes lay in two neat halves upon the snow.

"Ha!" said I.

"Oh!" cried Dido.

Dando gave a scream which if I were to try to reproduce it by means of the English alphabet would possess more syllables than any word hitherto seen. Then he caught up Pandemonium's reins and rode off with that extraordinary speed of which I know him to be capable.

The death of John Hollyshoes had weakened the spell he had cast on the ivy and Dido and I were able quite easily to tear it away. We rode back to Allhope where I restored her to joyful parent, loving husband, and hungry child. My parishioners came to the cottage to load me with praises, grateful thanks, promises of future aid, etc., etc. I however was tired to death and, after making a short speech advising them to benefit from the example I had given them of courage and selflessness, I pleaded the excuse of a head ach to come home.

One thing, however, has vexed me *very much* and that is there was no time to conduct a proper examination of John Hollyshoes' body. For it occurs to me that just as Reason is seated in the brain of Man, so we Fairies may contain within ourselves some *organ of Magic*. Certainly the fairy's bisected corpse had some curious features. I append here a rough sketch and a few notes describing the ways in which Fairy anatomy appears to depart from Human anatomy. I intend to be in the woods at first light to examine the corpse more closely.

Dec. 11th., 1811.
The body is gone. Dando, I suppose, has spirited it away. This is most vexatious as I had hoped to have it sent to Mr Baillie's anatomy school in Great Windmill-street in London. I suppose that the baby in the bare room at the end of the corridor will inherit End-Of-All-Hope House and all John Hollyshoes' estates, but perhaps the loss of Dido's milk at this significant period in its life will prevent its growing up as strong in wickedness as its parent.

I have not abandoned my own hopes of inheriting my father's estate and may very well pursue my claim when I have the time. I have never heard that the possession of an extensive property in Faerie was incompatible with the duties of a priest of the Church of England – indeed I do not believe that I ever heard the subject mentioned.

Dec. 17th., 1811.
I have been most villainously betrayed by the Reverend John McKenzie! I take it particularly hard since he is the person from whom – as a fellow clergyman – I might most reasonably have expected support. It appears that he is to marry the heiress to a castle and several hundred miles of bleak Scottish wilderness in Caithness. I hope there may be bogs and that John McKenzie may drown in them. Disappointed love has, I regret to say, screwed Miss Mary Macdonald up to such a pitch of anger that she has turned upon Henrietta and me. She writes to Henrietta that she is certain I am not be trusted and she threatens to write to Mrs Gathercole and Mrs Edmond. Henrietta is not afraid; rather she exults in the coming storm.

"You will protect me!" she cried, her eyes flashing with strange brilliance and her face flushed with excitement.

"My dear girl," said I, "I will be *dead*."

Dec. 20th., 1811.

George Hollinsclough was here a moment ago with a message that I am to wait upon Mrs Gathercole and Mrs Edmond *immediately*. I take one last fond look around this room . . .

THE FRIENDSHIP BETWEEN the eighteenth-century Jewish physician, David Montefiore, and the fairy, Tom Brightwind, is remarkably well documented. In addition to Montefiore's own journals and family papers, we have numerous descriptions of encounters with Montefiore and Brightwind by eighteenth- and early-nineteenth-century letter-writers, diarists and essayists. Montefiore and Brightwind seem, at one time or another, to have met most of the great men of the period. They discussed slavery with Boswell and Johnson, played dominoes with Diderot, got drunk with Richard Brinsley Sheridan and, upon one famous occasion, surprized Thomas Jefferson in his garden at Monticello.[1]

---

1 Poor David Montefiore was entirely mortified to be discovered trespassing upon another gentleman's property and could scarcely apologise enough. He told Thomas Jefferson that they had heard so much of the beauty of Monticello that they had been entirely unable to resist coming to see it for themselves. This polite explanation went a good way towards pacifying the President (who was inclined to be angry). Unfortunately Tom Brightwind immediately began to describe the many ways in which his own gardens were superior to Thomas Jefferson's. Thomas Jefferson promptly had them both turned off his property.

Yet, fascinating as these contemporary accounts are, our most vivid portrait of this unusual friendship comes from the plays, stories and songs which it inspired. In the early nineteenth century "Tom and David" stories were immensely popular both here and in Faerie Minor, but in the latter half of the century they fell out of favour in Europe and the United States. It became fashionable among Europeans and Americans to picture fairies as small, defenceless creatures. Tom Brightwind – loud, egotistical and six feet tall – was most emphatically not the sort of fairy that Arthur Conan Doyle and Charles Dodgson hoped to find at the bottom of their gardens.

The following story first appeared in *Blackwood's Magazine* (Edinburgh: September, 1820) and was reprinted in *Silenus's Review* (Faerie Minor: April, 1821). Considered as literature it is deeply unremarkable. It suffers from all the usual defects of second-rate early-nineteenth-century writing. Nevertheless, if read with proper attention, it uncovers a great many facts about this enigmatic race and is particularly enlightening on the troublesome relationship between fairies and their children.

Professor James Sutherland
Research Institute of Sidhe Studies
University of Aberdeen
October 1999

For most of its length Shoe-lane in the City of London follows a gentle curve and it never occurs to most people to wonder why. Yet if they were only to look up (and they never do) they would see the ancient wall of an immense round tower and it would immediately become apparent how the lane curves to accommodate the tower.

This is only one of the towers that guard Tom Brightwind's

house. From his earliest youth Tom was fond of travelling about and seeing everything and, in order that he might do this more conveniently, he placed each tower in a different part of the world. From one tower you step out into Shoe-lane; another occupies the greater part of a small island in the middle of a Scottish loch; a third looks out upon the dismal beauty of an Algerian desert; a fourth stands upon Drying-Green-street in a city in Faerie Minor; and so on. With characteristic exuberance Tom named this curiously constructed house *Castel des Tours saunz Nowmbre*, which means the Castle of Innumerable Towers. David Montefiore had counted the innumerable towers in 1764. There were fourteen of them.

On a morning in June in 1780 David Montefiore knocked upon the door of the Shoe-lane tower. He inquired of the porter where Tom might be found and was told that the master was in his library.

As David walked along dim, echoing corridors and trotted up immense stone staircases, he bade a cheerful "Good Morning! Good Morning!" to everyone he passed. But the only answer that he got was doubtful nods and curious stares, for no matter how often he visited the house, the inhabitants could never get used to him. His face was neither dazzlingly handsome nor twisted and repulsive. His figure was similarly undistinguished. His countenance expressed neither withering scorn, nor irresistible fascination, but only good humour and a disposition to think well of everyone. It was a mystery to the fairy inhabitants of *Castel des Tours Saunz Nowmbre* why any one should wish to wear such an expression upon his face.

Tom was not in the library. The room was occupied by nine fairy princesses. Nine exquisite heads turned in perfect unison to stare at David. Nine silk gowns bewildered the eye with their different colours. Nine different perfumes mingled in the air and made thinking difficult.

They were a few of Tom Brightwind's grand-daughters. Princess Caritas, Princess Bellona, Princess Alba Perfecta, Princess Lachrima and Princess Flammifera were one set of sisters; Princess Honey-of-the-Wild-Bees, Princess Lament-from-across-the-Water, Princess Kiss-upon-a-True-Love's-Grave and Princess Bird-in-the-Hand were another.

"O David ben Israel!" said Princess Caritas. "How completely charming!" and offered him her hand.

"You are busy, Highnesses," he said, "I fear I disturb you."

"Not really," said Princess Caritas. "We are writing letters to our cousins. Duty letters, that is all. Be seated, O David ben Israel."

"You did not say that they are our female cousins," said Princess Honey-of-the-Wild-Bees. "You did not make that plain. I should not like the Jewish doctor to run away with the idea that we write to any other sort of cousin."

"To our female cousins *naturally*," said Princess Caritas.

"We do not know our male cousins," Princess Flammifera informed David.

"We do not even know their names," added Princess Lament-from-across-the-Water.

"And even if we did, we would not *dream* of writing to them," remarked Princess Alba Perfecta.

"Though we are told they are very handsome," said Princess Lachrima.

"Handsome?" said Princess Caritas. "Whatever gave you that idea? I am sure I do not know whether they are handsome or not. I do not care to know. I never think of such things."

"Oh now, *really* my sweet!" replied Princess Lachrima with a brittle laugh. "Tell the truth, do! You scarcely ever think of any thing else."

Princess Caritas gave her sister a vicious look.

"And to which of your cousins are you writing?" asked David quickly.

"To Igraine . . ."

"Nimue . . ."

"Elaine . . ."

"And Morgana."

"Ugly girls," remarked Princess Caritas.

"Not their fault," said Princess Honey-of-the-Wild-Bees generously.

"And will they be away long?" asked David.

"Oh!" said Princess Flammifera.

"Oh!" said Princess Caritas.

"Oh!" said Princess Honey-of-the-Wild-Bees.

"They have been sent away," said Princess Bellona.

"For ever . . ." said Princess Lament-from-across-the-Water.

". . . and a day," added Princess Flammifera.

"We thought everybody knew that," said Princess Alba Perfecta.

"Grandfather sent them away," said Princess Kiss-upon-a-True-Love's-Grave.

"They offended Grandfather," said Princess Bird-in-the-Hand.

"Grandfather is most displeased with them," said Princess Lament-from-across-the-Water.

"They have been sent to live in a house," said Princess Caritas.

"Not a nice house," warned Princess Alba Perfecta.

"A nasty house!" said Princess Lachrima, with sparkling eyes. "With nothing but male servants! Nasty, dirty male servants with thick ugly fingers and hair on the knuckles! Male servants who will doubtless shew them no respect!" Lachrima put on a knowing, amused look. "Though perhaps they may shew them something else!" she said.

Caritas laughed. David blushed.

"The house is in a wood," continued Princess Bird-in-the-Hand.

"Not a nice wood," added Princess Bellona.

"A nasty wood!" said Princess Lachrima excitedly. "A thoroughly damp and dark wood, full of spiders and creepy, slimy, foul-smelling . . ."

"And why did your grandfather send them to this wood?" asked David quickly.

"Oh! Igraine got married," said Princess Caritas.

"Secretly," said Princess Lament-from-across-the-Water.

"We thought everyone knew that," said Princess Kiss-upon-a-True-Love's-Grave.

"She married a Christian man," explained Princess Caritas.

"Her harpsichord master!" said Princess Bellona, beginning to giggle.

"He played such beautiful concertos," said Princess Alba Perfecta.

"He had such beautiful . . ." began Princess Lachrima.

"Rima! Will you desist?" said Princess Caritas.

"Cousins," said Princess Honey-of-the-Wild-Bees sweetly, "when you are banished to a dark, damp wood, we will write to *you*."

"I did wonder, you know," said Princess Kiss-upon-a-True-Love's-Grave, "when she began to take harpsichord lessons every day. For she was never so fond of music till Mr Cartwright came. Then they took to shutting the door – which, I may say, I was very sorry for, the harpsichord being a particular favourite of mine. And so, you know, I used to creep to the door to listen, but a quarter of an hour might go by and I would not hear a single note – except perhaps the odd discordant plink as if one of them had accidentally leant upon the instrument. Once I thought I would go in to see what they were doing, but when I tried the handle of the door I discovered that they had turned the key in the lock. . ."

"Be quiet, Kiss!" said Princess Lament-from-across-the-Water.

"She's only called Kiss," explained Princess Lachrima to David helpfully. "She's never *actually* kissed any one."

"But I do not quite understand," said David. "If Princess Igraine married without her grandfather's permission, then that of course is very bad. Upon important matters children ought always to consult their parents, or those who stand in the place of parents. Likewise parents – or as we have in this case, grandparents – ought to consider not only the financial aspects of a marriage and the rank of the prospective bride or bridegroom, but also the child's character and likely chances of happiness with that person. The inclinations of the child's heart ought to be of paramount importance . . ."

As David continued meditating out loud upon the various reciprocal duties and responsibilities of parents and children, Princess Honey-of-the-Wild-Bees stared at him with an expression of mingled disbelief and distaste, Princess Caritas yawned loudly and Princess Lachrima mimed someone fainting with boredom.

". . . But even if Princess Igraine offended her grandfather in this way," said David, "why were her sisters punished with her?"

"Because they did not stop her of course," said Princess Alba Perfecta.

"Because they did not tell Grandfather what she was about," said Princess Lament-from-across-the-Water.

"We thought everybody knew that," said Princess Bird-in-the-Hand.

"What happened to the harpsichord master?" asked David.

Princess Lachrima opened her large violet-blue eyes and leant forward with great eagerness, but at that moment a voice was heard in the corridor.

". . . but when I had shot the third crow and plucked and skinned it, I discovered that it had a heart of solid diamond –

just as the old woman had said – so, as you see, the afternoon was not entirely wasted."

Tom Brightwind had a bad habit of beginning to talk long before he entered a room, so that the people whom he addressed only ever heard the end of what he wished to say to them.

"What?" said David.

"Not entirely wasted," repeated Tom.

Tom was about six feet tall and unusually handsome even for a fairy prince (for it must be said that in fairy society the upper ranks generally make it their business to be better-looking than the commoners). His complexion gleamed with such extraordinary good health that it seemed to possess a faint opalescence, slightly unnerving to behold. He had recently put off his wig and taken to wearing his natural hair which was long and straight and a vivid chestnut-brown colour. His eyes were blue, and he looked (as he had looked for the last three or four thousand years) about thirty years of age. He glanced about him, raised one perfect fairy eye-brow and muttered sourly, "Oak and Ash, but there are a lot of women in this room!"

There was a rustle of nine silk gowns, the slight click of door, a final exhalation of perfume, and suddenly there were no princesses at all.

"So where have you been?" said Tom, throwing himself into a chair and taking up a newspaper. "I expected you yesterday. Did you not get my message?"

"I could not come. I had to attend to my patients. Indeed I cannot stay long this morning. I am on my way to see Mr Monkton."

Mr Monkton was a rich old gentleman who lived in Lincoln. He wrote David letters describing a curious pain in his left side and David wrote back with advice upon medicines and treatments.

"Not that he places any faith in what I tell him," said David cheerfully. "He also corresponds with a physician in Edinburgh and a sort of sorcerer in Dublin. Then there is the apothecary in Lincoln who visits him. We all contradict one another but it does not matter because he trusts none of us. Now he has written to say he is dying and at this crisis we are summoned to attend him in person. The Scottish physician, the Irish wizard, the English apothecary and me! I am quite looking forward to it! Nothing is so pleasant or instructive as the society and conversation of one's peers. Do not you agree?"

Tom shrugged.[2] "Is the old man really ill?" he asked.

"I do not know. I never saw him."

Tom glanced at his newspaper again, put it down again in irritation, yawned and said, "I believe I shall come with you." He waited for David to express his rapture at this news.

What in the world, wondered David, did Tom think there would be at Lincoln to amuse him? Long medical conversations in which he could take no part, a querulous sick old gentleman and the putrid airs and hush of a sick-room! David was upon the point of saying something to this effect, when it occurred to him that, actually, it would be no bad thing for Tom to come to Lincoln. David was the son of a famous Venetian rabbi. From his youth he had been accustomed to debate good principles and right conduct with all sorts of grave Jewish persons. These conversations had formed his own character and he naturally supposed that a small measure of the same could not help but improve other people's. In short he had come to believe that if only one talks long enough and expresses oneself properly, it is

---

2 Fairy princes do not often trouble to seek out other fairy princes, and on the rare occasions that they do meet, it is surprising with what regularity one of them will die – suddenly, mysteriously, and in great pain.

perfectly possible to argue people into being good and happy. With this aim he generally took it upon himself to quarrel with Tom Brightwind several times a week – all without noticeable effect. But just now he had a great deal to say about the unhappy fate of the harpsichord master's bride and her sisters, and a long ride north was the perfect opportunity to say it.

So the horses were fetched from the stables, and David and Tom got on them. They had not gone far before David began.

"Who?" asked Tom, not much interested.

"The Princesses Igraine, Nimue, Elaine and Morgana."

"Oh! Yes, I sent them to live in . . . What do you call that wood on the far side of Pity-Me? What is the name that you put upon it? No, it escapes me. Anyway, there."

"But eternal banishment!" cried David in horror. "Those poor girls! How can you bear the thought of them in such torment?"

"I bear it very well, as you see," said Tom. "But thank you for your concern. To own the truth, I am thankful for any measure that reduces the number of women in my house. David, I tell you, those girls talk *constantly*. Obviously I talk a great deal too. But then I am always doing things. I have my library. I am the patron of three theatres, two orchestras and a university. I have numerous interests in Faerie Major. I have seneschals, magistrates and proctors in all the various lands of which I am sovereign, who are obliged to consult my pleasure constantly. I am involved in . . ." Tom counted quickly on his long, white fingers. ". . . thirteen wars which are being prosecuted in Faerie Major. In one particularly complicated case I have allied myself with the Millstone Beast and with his enemy, La Dame d'Aprigny, and sent armies to both of them . . ." Tom paused here and frowned at his horse's ears. "Which means I suppose that I am at war with myself. Now why did I do that?" He seemed to consider a moment or two, but making no progress he shook his head and continued. "What was I saying? Oh, yes! So *naturally* I have a great deal to say. But those girls do nothing. Absolutely nothing! A little embroidery, a few music lessons. Oh! and they read English novels! David! Did you ever look into an English novel? Well, do not trouble yourself. It is nothing but a lot of nonsense about girls with fanciful names getting married."

"But this is precisely the point I wish to make," said David. "Your children lack proper occupation. Of course they will find some mischief to get up to. What do you expect?"

David often lectured Tom upon the responsibilities of parenthood which annoyed Tom who considered himself to be a quite exemplary fairy parent. He provided generously for his children and grandchildren and only in exceptional circumstances had any of them put to death.[3]

"Young women must stay at home quietly until they marry," said Tom. "What else would you have?"

---

3 Fairies exceed even Christians and Jews in their enthusiasm for babies and young children, and think nothing of adding to their brood by stealing a pretty Christian child or two.

Yet in this, as in so many things, fairies rarely give much thought to the consequences of their actions. They procreate or steal other people's children, and twenty years later they are amazed to discover that they have a house full of grown men and women. The problem is how to provide for them all. Unlike the sons and daughters of Christians and Jews, fairy children do not live in confident expectation of one day inheriting all their parents' wealth, lands and power, since their parents are very unlikely ever to die.

It is a puzzle that few fairies manage to solve satisfactorily and it is unsurprizing that many of their children eventually rebel. For over seven centuries Tom Brightwind had been involved in a vicious and bloody war against his own firstborn son, a person called Prince Rialobran.

"I admit that I cannot imagine any other system for regulating the behaviour of young Christian and Jewish women. But in their case the interval between the schoolroom and marriage is only a few years. For fairy women it may stretch into centuries. Have you no other way of managing your female relations? Must you imitate Christians in everything you do? Why! You even dress as if you were a Christian!"

"As do you," countered Tom.

"And you have trimmed your long fairy eye-brows."

"At least I still have eye-brows," retorted Tom. 'Where is your beard, Jew? Did Moses wear a little grey wig?" He gave David's wig of neat curls a contemptuous flip. "I do not think so."

"You do not even speak your own language!" said David, straightening his wig.

"Neither do you," said Tom.

David immediately replied that Jews, unlike fairies, honoured their past, spoke Hebrew in their prayers and upon all sorts of ritual occasions. "But to return to the problem of your daughters and grand-daughters, what did you do when you were in the *brugh*?"

This was tactless. The word "*brugh*" was deeply offensive to Tom. No one who customarily dresses in spotless white linen and a midnight-blue coat, whose nails are exquisitely manicured, whose hair gleams like polished mahogany – in short no one of such refined tastes and delicate habits likes to be reminded that he spent the first two or three thousand years of his existence in a damp dark hole, wearing (when he took the trouble to wear any thing at all) a kilt of coarse, undyed wool and a mouldering rabbitskin cloak.[4]

---

4 The *brugh* was for countless centuries the common habitation of the fairy race. It is the original of all the fairy palaces one reads *cont'd over/*

"In the *brugh*," said Tom, lingering on the word with ironic emphasis to shew that it was a subject polite people did not mention, "the problem did not arise. Children were born and grew up in complete ignorance of their paternity. I have not the least idea who my father was. I never felt any curiosity on the matter."

By two o'clock Tom and David had reached Nottinghamshire,[5] a county which is famous for the greenwood which once spread over it. Of course at this late date the forest was no longer a hundredth part of what it once had been, but there were still a number of very ancient trees and Tom was determined to pay his respects to those he considered his particular friends and to shew his disdain of those who had not

---

4 *cont'd*   of in folktales. Indeed the tendency of Christian writers to glamorize the *brugh* seems to have increased with the centuries. It has been described as a "fairy palace of gold and crystal, in the heart of the hill" (Lady Wilde, *Ancient Legends, Mystic Charms and Superstitions of Ireland,* Ward & Downey, London, 1887). Another chronicler of fairy history wrote of "a steep-sided grassy hill, round as a pudding-basin . . . A small lake on its summit had a crystal floor, which served as a skylight." (Sylvia Townsend Warner, *The Kingdoms of Elfin,* Chatto & Windus, London, 1977).

The truth is that the *brugh* was a hole or series of interconnecting holes that was dug into a barrow, very like a rabbit's warren or badger's set. To paraphrase a writer of fanciful stories for children, this was not a comfortable hole, it was not even a dry, bare sandy hole; it was a nasty, dirty, wet hole.

Fairies, who are nothing if not resilient, were able to bear with equanimity the damp, the dark and the airlessness, but stolen Christian children brought to the *brugh* died, as often as not, of suffocation.

5 In the late eighteenth century a journey from London to Nottinghamshire might be expected to take two or three days. Tom and David seem to have arrived after a couple of hours: this presumably is one of the advantages of choosing as your travelling companion a powerful fairy prince.

behaved well towards him.[6] So long was Tom in greeting his friends, that David began to be concerned about Mr Monkton.

"But you said he was not really ill," said Tom.

"That was not what I said at all! But whether he is or not, I have a duty to reach him as soon as I can."

---

6 Fairies born in the last eight centuries or so – sophisticated, literate and consorting all their lives with Christians – have no more difficulty than Christians themselves in distinguishing between the animate and the inanimate. But to members of older generations (such as Tom) the distinction is quite unintelligible.

Several magical theorists and commentators have noted that fairies who retain this old belief in the souls of stones, doors, trees, fire, clouds etc., are more adept at magic than the younger generation and their magic is generally much stronger.

The following incident clearly shews how, given the right circumstances, fairies come to regard perfectly ordinary objects with a strange awe. In 1697 an attempt was made to kill the Old Man of the White Tower, one of the lesser princes of Faerie. The would-be assassin was a fairy called Broc (he had stripes of black and white fur upon his face). Broc had been greatly impressed by what he had heard of a wonderful new weapon which Christians had invented to kill each other. Consequently he forsook all magical means of killing the Old Man of the White Tower (which had some chance of success) and purchased instead a pistol and some shot (which had none). Poor Broc made his attempt, was captured and the Old Man of the White Tower locked him up in a windowless stone room deep in the earth. In the next room the Old Man imprisoned the pistol, and in a third room the shot. Broc died some time around the beginning of the twentieth century (after three centuries without a bite to eat, a drop to drink or a sight of the sun, even fairies grow weaker). The pistol and the shot, on the other hand, are still there, still considered by the Old Man as equally culpable, still deserving punishment for their wickedness. Several other fairies who wished to kill the Old Man of the White Tower have begun by devising   *cont'd over/*

"Very well! Very well! How cross you are!" said Tom. "Where are you going? The road is just over there."

"But we came from the other direction."

"No, we did not. Well, perhaps. I do not know. But both roads join up later on so it cannot matter in the least which we chuse."

Tom's road soon dwindled into a narrow and poorly marked track which led to the banks of a broad river. A small, desolate-looking town stood upon the opposite bank. The road reappeared on the other side of the town and it was odd to see how it grew broader and more confident as it left the town and travelled on to happier places.

"How peculiar!" said Tom. "Where is the bridge?"

"There does not seem to be one."

"Then how are we to get across?"

"There is a ferry," said David.

A long iron chain stretched between a stone pillar on this side of the river and another pillar on the opposite bank. Also on the other side of the river was an ancient flat-bottomed boat attached to the chain by two iron brackets. An ancient ferryman appeared and hauled the boat across the river by means of the chain. Then Tom and David led the horses on to the boat and the ancient ferryman hauled them back over.

David asked the ferryman what the town was called.

"Thoresby, sir," said the man.

---

6 *cont'd*   elaborate plans to steal the pistol and the shot, which have attained a strange significance in the minds of the Old Man's enemies. It is well known to fairies that metal, stone and wood have stubborn natures; the gun and shot were set upon killing the Old Man in 1697 and it is quite inconceivable to the fairy mind that they could have wavered in the intervening centuries. To the Old Man's enemies it is quite clear that one day the gun and the shot will achieve their purpose.

Thoresby proved to be nothing more than a few streets of shabby houses with soiled, dusty windows and broken roofs. An ancient cart was abandoned in the middle of what appeared to be the principal street. There was a market cross and a market-place of sorts – but weeds and thorns grew there in abundance, suggesting there had been no actual market for several years. There was only one gentleman's residence to be seen: a tall old-fashioned house built of grey limestone, with a great many tall gables and chimneys. This at least was a respectable-looking place though in a decidedly provincial style.

Thoresby's only inn was called The Wheel of Fortune. The sign shewed a number of people bound to a great wheel which was being turned by Fortune, represented here by a bright pink lady wearing nothing but a blindfold. In keeping with the town's dejected air the artist had chosen to omit the customary figures representing good fortune and had instead shewn all the people bound to Fortune's wheel in the process of being crushed to pieces or being hurled into the air to their deaths.

With such sights as these to encourage them, the Jew and the fairy rode through Thoresby at a smart trot. The open road was just in sight when David heard a cry of "Gentlemen! Gentle-men!" and the sound of rapid footsteps. So he halted his horse and turned to see what was the matter.

A man came running up.

He was a most odd-looking creature. His eyes were small and practically colourless. His nose was the shape of a small bread roll, and his ears – which were round and pink – might have been attractive on a baby, but in no way suited him. But what was most peculiar was the way in which eyes and nose huddled together at the top of his face, having presumably quarrelled with his mouth which had set up a separate establishment for itself halfway down his chin. He was very shabbily dressed and his bare head had a thin covering of pale stubble upon it.

"You have not paid the toll, sirs!" he cried.

"What toll?" asked David.

"Why! The ferry toll! The toll for crossing the river."

"Yes. Yes, we have," said David. "We paid the man who carried us across the river."

The odd-looking man smiled. "No, sir!" he said. "You paid the fee, the ferryman's penny! But the toll is quite another thing. The toll is levied upon everyone who crosses the river. It is owed to Mr Winstanley and I collect it. A man and a horse is sixpence. Two men and two horses is twelvepence."

"Do you mean to say," said David in astonishment, "that a person must pay *twice* to come to this miserable place?"

"There is no toll, David," said Tom airily. "This scoundrel merely wishes us to give him twelvepence."

The odd-looking man continued to smile, although the expression of his eyes had rather a malicious sparkle to it. "The gentleman may insult me if he wishes," he said. "Insults are free. But I beg leave to inform the gentleman that I am very far from being a scoundrel. I am a lawyer. Oh, yes! An attorney consulted by people as far afield as Southwell. But my chief occupation is as Mr Winstanley's land agent and man of business. My name, sir, is Pewley Witts!"

"A lawyer?" said David. "Oh, I do beg your pardon!"

"David!" cried Tom. "When did you ever see a lawyer that looked like that? Look at him! His rascally shoes are broken all to bits. There are great holes in his vagabond's coat and he has no wig! Of *course* he is a scoundrel!" He leant down from his tall horse. "We are leaving now, scoundrel. Goodbye!"

"These are my sloppy clothes," said Pewley Witts sullenly. "My wig and good coat are at home. I had no time to put them on when Peter Dawkins came and told me that two gentlemen had crossed by the ferry and were leaving Thoresby without paying the toll – which, by the bye, is still twelvepence, gentlemen, and I would be much obliged if you would pay it."

A devout Jew must discharge his debts promptly – however inadvertently those debts might have been incurred; a gentleman ought never to procrastinate in such matters; and, as David considered himself to be both those things, he was most anxious to pay Pewley Witts twelvepence. A fairy, on the other hand, sees things differently. Tom was determined not to pay. Tom would have endured years of torment rather than pay.

Pewley Witts watched them argue the point back and forth. Finally he shrugged. "Under the circumstances, gentlemen," he said, "I think you had better talk to Mr Winstanley."

He led them to the tall stone house they had noticed before. A high stone wall surrounded the house and there was a little stone yard which was quite bare except for two small stone lions. They were crudely made things, with round, surprized eyes, snarls full of triangular teeth, and fanciful manes that more resembled foliage than fur.

A pretty maidservant answered the door. She glanced briefly at Pewley Witts and David Montefiore, but finding nothing to interest her there, her gaze travelled on to Tom Brightwind who was staring down at the lions.

"Good morning, Lucy!" said Pewley Witts. "Is your master within?"

"Where else would he be?" said Lucy, still gazing at Tom.

"These two gentlemen object to paying the toll, and so I have brought them here to argue it out with Mr Winstanley. Go and tell him that we are here. And be quick about it, Lucy. I am wanted at home. We are killing the spotted pig today."

Despite Pewley Witts' urging, it seemed that Lucy did not immediately deliver the message to her master. A few moments later from an open window above his head, David heard a sort of interrogatory murmur followed by Lucy's voice exclaiming, "A

beautiful gentleman! Oh, madam! The most beautiful gentleman you ever saw in your life!"

"What is happening?" asked Tom, drifting back from his
examination of the lions.

"The maid is describing me to her mistress," said David.

"Oh," said Tom and drifted away again.

A face appeared briefly at the window.

"Oh, yes," came Lucy's voice again, "and Mr Witts and
another person are with him."

Lucy reappeared and conducted Tom, David and Pewley
Witts through a succession of remarkably empty chambers and
passageways to an apartment at the back of the house. It was odd
to see how, in contrast to the other rooms, this was comfortably
furnished with red carpets, gilded mirrors and blue-and-white
china. Yet it was still a little sombre. The walls were panelled in
dark wood and the curtains were half-drawn across two tall
windows to create a sort of twilight. The walls were hung with
engravings but, far from enlivening the gloom, they only added
to it. They were portraits of worthy and historical personages, all
of whom appeared to have been in an extremely bad temper
when they sat for their likenesses. Here were more scowls,
frowns and stares than David had seen in a long time.

At the far end of the room a gentleman lay upon a sopha piled
with cushions. He wore an elegant green-and-white chintz
morning gown and loose Turkish slippers upon his feet. A
lady, presumably Mrs Winstanley, sat in a chair at his side.

As there was no one else to do it for them, Tom and David were
obliged to introduce themselves (an awkward ceremony at the
best of times). David told Mr and Mrs Winstanley his profession,
and Tom was able to convey merely by his way of saying his name
that he was someone of quite unimaginable importance.

Mr Winstanley received them with great politeness, welcom-
ing them to his house (which he called Mickelgrave House).

They found it a little odd, however, that he did not trouble to rise from the sopha – or indeed move any of his limbs in the slightest degree. His voice was soft and his smile was gentle. He had pleasant, regular features and an unusually white complexion – the complexion of someone who hardly ever ventured out of doors.

Mrs Winstanley (who rose and curtsied) wore a plain gown of blackberry-coloured silk with the merest edging of white lace. She had dark hair and dark eyes. Had she only smiled a little, she would have been extremely lovely.

Pewley Witts explained that Mr Brightwind refused to pay the toll.

"Oh no, Witts! No!" cried Mr Winstanley upon the instant. "These gentlemen need pay no toll. The sublimity of their conversation will be payment enough, I am certain." He turned to Tom and David. "Gentlemen! For reasons which I will explain to you in a moment I rarely go abroad. Truth to own I do not often leave this room and consequently my daily society is confined to men of inferior rank and education, such as Witts. I can scarcely express my pleasure at seeing you here!" He regarded David's dark, un-English face with mild interest. "Montefiore is an Italian name, I think. You are Italian, sir?"

"My father was born in Venice," said David, "but that city, sadly, has hardened its heart towards the Jews. My family is now settled in London. We hope in time to be English."

Mr Winstanley nodded gently. There was, after all, nothing in the world so natural as people wishing to be English. "You are welcome too, sir. I am glad to say that I am completely indifferent to a man's having a different religion from mine."

Mrs Winstanley leant over and murmured something in her husband's ear.

"No," answered Mr Winstanley softly, "I will not get dressed today."

"You are ill, sir?" asked David. "If there is any thing I can . . ."

Mr Winstanley laughed as if this were highly amusing. "No, no, physician! You cannot earn your fee quite as easily as that. You cannot persuade me that I feel unwell when I do not." He turned to Tom Brightwind with a smile. "The foreigner can never quite comprehend that there are more important considerations than money. He can never quite understand that there is a time to leave off doing business."

"I did not mean . . ." began David, colouring.

Mr Winstanley smiled and waved his hand to indicate that whatever David might have meant was of very little significance. "I am not offended in the least. I make allowances for you, *Dottore*." He leant back delicately against the cushions. "Gentlemen, I am a man who might achieve remarkable things. I have within me a capacity for greatness. But I am prevented from accomplishing even the least of my ambitions by the peculiar circumstances of this town. You have seen Thoresby. I dare say you are shocked at its wretched appearance and the astonishing idleness of the townspeople. Why, look at Witts! In other towns lawyers are respectable people. A lawyer in another town would not slaughter his own pig. A lawyer in another town would wear a velvet coat. His shirt would not be stained with gravy."

"Precisely," said Tom, looking with great disdain at the lawyer.

David was quite disgusted that any one should speak to his inferiors in so rude a manner and he looked at Witts to see how he bore with this treatment. But Witts only smiled and David could almost have fancied he was simple, had it not been for the malice in his eyes.

"And yet," continued Mr Winstanley, "I would not have you think that Witts is solely to blame for his slovenly appearance and lack of industry. Witts' life is blighted by Thoresby's difficulties, which are caused by what? Why, the lack of a bridge!"

Pewley Witts nudged Mr Winstanley with his elbow. "Tell them about Julius Caesar."

"Oh!" said Mrs Winstanley, looking up in alarm. "I do not think these gentlemen wish to be troubled with Julius Caesar. I dare say they heard enough of him in their schoolrooms."

"On the contrary, madam," said Tom, in accents of mild reproach, "I for one can never grow tired of hearing of that illustrious and courageous gentleman. Pray go on, sir." [7] Tom sat back, his head supported on his hand and his eyes fixed upon Mrs Winstanley's elegant form and sweet face.

"You should know, gentlemen," began Mr Winstanley, "that I have looked into the history of this town and it seems our difficulties began with the Romans – whom you may see represented in this room by Julius Caesar. His portrait hangs between the door and that pot of hyacinths. The Romans, as I dare say you know, built roads in England that were remarkable for both their excellence and their straightness. A Roman road passes very close to Thoresby. Indeed, had the Romans followed their own self-imposed principle of straightness, they ought by rights to have crossed the river here, at Thoresby. But they allowed themselves to be deterred. There was some problem – a certain marshyness of the land, I believe – and so they deviated from their course and crossed the river at Newark. At Newark they built a town with temples and markets and I do not know what else, while Thoresby remained a desolate marsh. This was the first of many occasions upon which Thoresby suffered for other people's moral failings."

"Lady Anne Lutterell," prompted Pewley Witts.

---

7 Tom Brightwind was not the only member of his race who was passionately devoted to the memory of Julius Caesar. Many fairies claim descent from him and there was a medieval Christian legend that Oberon (the wholly fictitious king of the fairies) was Julius Caesar's son.

"Oh, Mr Winstanley!" said his wife, with a little forced laugh. "I must protest. Indeed I must. Mr Brightwind and Mr Montefiore do not wish to concern themselves with Lady Anne. I feel certain that they do not care for history at all."

"Oh! quite, madam!" said Tom. "What passes for history these days is extraordinary. Kings who are remembered more for their long dull speeches than for any thing they did upon the battlefield, governments full of fat old men with grey hair, all looking the same – who cares about such stuff? But if you are speaking of real history, true history – by which of course I mean the spirited description of heroic personages of ancient times – Why! there is nothing which delights me more!"

"Lady Anne Lutterell," said Mr Winstanley, taking no notice of either of them, "was a rich widow who lived at Ossington." (Mrs Winstanley looked down at her folded hands in her lap.) "There is a picture of her ladyship between that little writing table and the longcase clock. It was widely known that she intended to leave a large sum of money as an act of piety to build a bridge in this exact spot. The bridge was promised and in anticipation of this promise the town of Thoresby was built. But at the last moment she changed her mind and built a chantry instead. I dare say, Mr Montefiore, you will not know what that is. A chantry is a sort of chapel where priests say mass for the dead. Such – though I am ashamed to admit it – were the superstitious practices of our ancestors."

"Queen Elizabeth," said Pewley Witts, winking at David and Tom. It was becoming clear how he revenged himself for all the slights and insults which he received from Mr Winstanley. It seemed unlikely that Mr Winstanley would have made quite so many foolish speeches without Witts to encourage him.

"Queen Elizabeth indeed, Witts," said Mr Winstanley pleasantly.

"Queen Elizabeth!" cried Mrs Winstanley in alarm. "Oh! But

she was a most disagreeable person! If we must talk of queens, there are several more respectable examples. What do you say to Matilda? Or Anne?"

Tom leant as closely as he conveniently could to Mrs Winstanley. His face shewed that he had a great many opinions upon Queen Matilda and Queen Anne which he wished to communicate to her immediately, but before he could begin, Mr Winstanley said, "You will find Elizabeth, Mr Brightwind, between the window and the looking-glass. In Elizabeth's time the people of Thoresby earned their living by making playing-cards. But the Queen granted a Royal Patent for a monopoly for the manufacture of playing-cards to a young man. He had written a poem praising her beauty. She was, I believe, about sixty-five years old at the time. As a consequence no one in England was allowed to make playing-cards except for this young man. He became rich and the people of Thoresby became destitute."

Mr Winstanley continued his little history of people who might have built a bridge at Thoresby and had not done so, or who had injured the town in some other way. His wife tried to hide his foolishness as much as was in her power by protesting vigorously at the introduction of each fresh character, but he paid her not the slightest attention.

His special contempt was reserved for Oliver Cromwell whose picture hung in pride of place over the mantelpiece. Oliver Cromwell had contemplated fighting an important battle at Thoresby but had eventually decided against it, thereby denying Thoresby the distinction of being blown up and laid to waste by two opposing armies.

"But surely," said David at last, "your best course is to build the bridge yourself."

"Ah!" smiled Mr Winstanley. "You would think so, wouldn't you? And I have spoken to two gentlemen who are in the habit of lending money to other gentlemen for their enterprises. A Mr Blackwell of London and a Mr Crumfield of Bath. Mr Witts and I described to both men the benefits that would accrue to them were they to build my bridge, the quite extraordinary amounts of money they would make. But both ended by declining to lend me the money." Mr Winstanley glanced up at an empty space on the wall as if he would have liked to see it graced by portraits of Mr Blackwell and Mr Crumfield and so complete his museum of failure.

"But it was a very great sum," said Mrs Winstanley. "You do not tell Mr Brightwind and Mr Montefiore what a very great sum it was. I do not believe I ever heard such a large figure named in my life before."

"Bridges are expensive," agreed David.

Then Mrs Winstanley, who seemed to think that the subject of bridges had been exhausted among them, asked David several questions about himself. Where had he studied medicine? How many patients had he? Did he attend ladies as well as gentlemen? From speaking of professional matters David was soon led to talk of his domestic happiness – of his wife and four little children.

"And are you married, sir?" Mrs Winstanley asked Tom.

"Oh no, madam!" said Tom.

"Yes," David reminded him. "You are, you know."

Tom made a motion with his hand to suggest that it was a situation susceptible to different interpretations.

The truth was that he had a Christian wife. At fifteen she had had a wicked little face, almond-shaped eyes and a most capricious nature. Tom had constantly compared her to a kitten. In her twenties she had been a swan; in her thirties a vixen; and then in rapid succession a bitch, a viper, a cockatrice and, finally, a pig. What animals he might have compared her to now no one knew. She was well past ninety now and for forty years or more she had been confined to a set of apartments in a distant part of the *Castel des Tours saunz Nowmbre* under strict instructions not to shew herself, while her husband waited impatiently for someone to come and tell him she was dead.

By now Tom and David had given the half hour to the Winstanleys which politeness demanded and David began to think of Mr Monkton in Lincoln and of his anxiousness to reach him. But Mr Winstanley could not quite bring himself to accept that his two new friends were about to leave him and he made several speeches urging them to stay for a week or two. It was left to Mrs Winstanley to bid them farewell in a more rational manner.

They were not, however, able to leave immediately. There was some delay about fetching the horses and while they were waiting in the yard Lucy came out and looked nervously from one to the other. "If you please, sir, Mrs Winstanley wishes to speak to you privately!"

"Ah ha!" said Tom, as if he half-expected such a summons.

"No, sir! Not you, sir!" Lucy curtsied her apologies. "It is the Jewish doctor that is wanted."

Mrs Winstanley was waiting in her bed-chamber. The room was large, but somewhat sparsely furnished. It contained nothing but a chair, a chest and a large four-poster bed with green brocade hangings. Mrs Winstanley stood by the bed. Everything about her – rigid bearing, strained look, the way in which she continually twisted her hands together – betrayed the greatest uneasiness.

She apologised for troubling him.

"It is no trouble," said David, "not the least in the world. There is something you wish to ask me?"

She looked down. "Mr Winstanley and I have been married for four years, but as yet we have no children."

"Oh!" He thought for a moment. "And there is no dislike upon either side to the conjugal act?"

"No." Mrs Winstanley sighed. "No. That is one duty at least that my husband does not shirk."

So David asked all the usual questions that a physician generally asks in such a situation and she answered without any false shame.

"There is nothing wrong as far as I can see," David told her. "There is no reason why you should not bear a child. Be in good health, Mrs Winstanley. That is my advice to you. Be cheerful and then . . ."

"Oh! But I had hoped that . . ." she hesitated. "I had hoped that, as a foreign gentleman, you might know something our English doctors do not. I am not the least afraid of any thing you might suggest. I can bear any pain for the sake of a child. It is all I ever think of. Lucy thinks that I ought to eat carrots and parsnips that have odd shapes, and that I ought to persuade Mr Winstanley to eat them too."

"Why?"

"Because they look like little people."

"Oh! Yes, of course. I see. Well, I suppose it can do no harm."

David took as affectionate a leave of Mrs Winstanley as was consistent with so brief an acquaintance. He pressed her hand warmly and told her how sincerely he hoped she might soon have everything she wished for. He was sure that no one could deserve it more.

Tom was seated upon his horse. David's horse stood at his side. "Well?" said Tom. "What did she want?"

"It is a lack of children," said David.

"What is?"

"That afflicts the lady. The reason she never smiles."

"Children are a great nuisance," said Tom, reverting immediately to his own concerns.

"To you, perhaps. But a human woman feels differently. Children are our posterity. Besides, all women, fairy, Christian or Jew, crave a proper object to love. And I do not think she can love her husband."

David was in the act of mounting his horse as he said this, an operation which invariably cost him a little trouble. He was somewhat surprised, on arriving upon the horse's back, to discover that Tom was nowhere to be seen.

"Now wherever has he gone?" he wondered. "Well, if he expects me to wait for him, he will be disappointed! I have told him half a dozen times today that I must go to Lincoln!"

David set off in the direction of Lincoln, but just as he reached the end of the town he heard a sound behind him and he looked round, expecting to see Tom.

It was Pewley Witts mounted on a horse which seemed to have been chosen for its great resemblance to himself in point of gauntness, paleness and ugliness. "Mr Montefiore!" he said. "Mr Winstanley is most anxious that you and Mr Brightwind should see his property and he has appointed me your guide. I have just spoken to Mr Brightwind, but he has something important to do in Thoresby and cannot spare the time. He says that you will go for both!"

"Oh, does he indeed?" said David.

Pewley Witts smiled confidentially. "Mr Winstanley thinks that you will build his bridge for him!"

"Why in the world should he think that?"

"Come, come! What sort of fools do you take us for in Thoresby? An English lord and a Jew travelling about the country together! Two of the richest devils in all creation! What can you be doing, but seeking opportunities to lengthen your long purses?"

"Well, I fear you will be disappointed. He is not an English lord and I am the wrong sort of Jew. And I am not travelling about the country, as you put it. I am going to Lincoln."

"As you wish. But it so happens that Mr Winstanley's

property lies on either side of the Lincoln road. You cannot help but see it, if you go that way." He grinned and said helpfully, "I will come with you and point out the places of interest."

In Mr Winstanley's fields the weeds stood as thick as the corn. A number of thin, sad-looking men, women and children were scaring the birds away.

"Poor wretches!" thought David. "They do indeed suffer for other people's moral failings. How I wish that I could persuade Tom to build the bridge for their sakes! But what hope is there of that? I cannot even persuade him into loving his own children."

While David indulged these gloomy reflections, Pewley Witts named the yields of Mr Winstanley's lands (so many bushels per acre) and described how those yields would be doubled and tripled should Mr Winstanley ever trouble to drain his waterlogged fields or enrich his soil with manure.

A little further on Pewley Witts pointed out some grassy hillocks beneath which, he said, was a thick layer of clay. He described how Mr Winstanley could, if he wished, establish a manufactory to make pots and vases out of the clay.

"I believe," said Pewley Witts, "that earthenware pots and vases are quite the thing nowadays and that some gentlemen make a great deal of money from their manufacture."

"Yes," said David with a sigh, "I have heard that."

In another place they looked at a thin wood of birch trees on a windblown, sunny hillside. Pewley Witts said that there was a rich seam of coal beneath the wood, and Mr Winstanley could, if he felt at all inclined to it, mine the coal and sell it in Nottingham or London.

"Answer me this then!" cried David in exasperation. "Why does he not do these things? Sell the coal! Make the pots! Grow more corn! Why does he do nothing?"

"Oh!" said Pewley Witts with his malicious smile. "I have

advised him against it. I have advised him that until the bridge is built he ought not to attempt any thing. For how would he carry the corn or pots or coal to the people who wanted them? He would lose half his profit to carriers and barge-owners."

The more David saw of Mr Winstanley's neglected lands, the more he began to doubt the propriety of going to Lincoln.

"After all," he thought, "Mr Monkton already has two doctors to attend him – not counting the Irish wizard. Whereas the poor souls of Thoresby have no one at all to be their friend. Do I not perhaps have a superior duty to stay and help them if I can by convincing Tom to build the bridge? But what in the world could I say to make him do it?"

To this last question he had no answer just at present, but in the meantime: "Mr Witts!" he cried. "We must go back. I too have something important to do in Thoresby!"

As soon as they arrived at Mickelgrave House David jumped off his horse and set about looking for Tom. He was walking down one of the empty stone passageways, when he happened to notice, through an open door, Mrs Winstanley and Lucy in the garden. They appeared to be in a state of some excitement and were exclaiming to each other in tones of amazement. David, wondering what in the world the matter could be, went out into the garden, and arrived there just as Lucy was climbing up upon a stone bench in order to look over the wall.

"It has reached Mr Witts' house!" she said.

"What is it? What is wrong?" cried David.

"We have just had a visit from three little boys!" said Mrs Winstanley, in a wondering tone.

"They were singing," said Lucy.

"Oh! Boys like to sing," said David. "My own two little sons – Ishmael and Jonah – know a comic song about a milkmaid and a cow which . . ."

"Yes, I dare say," interrupted Mrs Winstanley. "But this was quite different! These boys had wings growing out of their backs. They were sailing through the air in a tiny gilded ship rigged with silken ribbons and they were casting out rose petals on either hand."

David climbed up beside Lucy and looked over the wall. Far off in a bright blue sky, a small golden ship was just sailing out of sight behind the church tower. David made out three little figures with lutes in their hands; their heads were thrown back in song.

"What were they singing?" he asked.

"I do not know," said Mrs Winstanley, in perplexity. "It was in a language I did not know. Italian I think."

In the drawing-room the curtains had been pulled across the windows to shut out the golden light of early evening. Mr Winstanley was lying upon the sopha, with his hand thrown across his eyes.

"Mr Winstanley!" cried his wife. "The most extraordinary thing . . ."

Mr Winstanley opened his eyes and smiled to see David before him. "Ah! Mr Montefiore!" he said.

"Lucy and I were in the garden when . . ."

"My love," said Mr Winstanley in tones of mild reproach, "I am trying to speak to Mr Montefiore." He smiled at David. "And how did you enjoy your ride? I confess that I think our surroundings not unattractive. Witts said he believed you were mightily entertained."

"It was most . . . enlightening. Where is Mr Brightwind?"

The door was suddenly flung open and Tom walked in.

"Mr Winstanley," he said, "I have decided to build your bridge!"

Tom was always fond of amazing a roomful of people and of having everyone stare at him in speechless wonder, and upon this particular occasion he must have been peculiarly gratified.

Then Mr Winstanley began to speak his joy and his gratitude. "I have looked into the matter," he said, "or rather Mr Witts has done it on my account – and I believe that you can expect a return on your investment of so many per cent – that is to say, Mr Witts can tell you all about it . . ." He began to leaf rapidly through some papers which David was quite certain he had never looked at before.

"You may spare yourself the trouble," said Tom. "I have no thought of any reward. Mr Montefiore has been lecturing me today upon the necessity of providing useful employment for one's children and it occurs to me, Mr Winstanley, that unless this bridge is built your descendants will have nothing to do. They will be idle. They will never achieve that greatness of spirit, that decisiveness of action which ought to have been theirs."

"Oh, Indeed! Quite so!" said Mr Winstanley. "Then all that remains is to draw up plans for the bridge. I have made sketches of my ideas. I have them somewhere in this room. Witts estimates that two years should be enough to complete the work – perhaps less!"

"Oh!" said Tom. "I have no patience for a long undertaking. I shall build the bridge tonight between midnight and sunrise. I have just one condition." He held up a long finger. "One. Mr Winstanley, you and all your servants, and Mr Montefiore too, must go and stand upon the riverbank tonight and witness the building of my bridge."

Mr Winstanley eagerly assured him that not only he and Mrs Winstanley and all their servants would be there, but the entire population of the town.

As soon Mr Winstanley had stopped talking, David took the opportunity to tell Tom of how glad he was that Tom was going to build the bridge, but Tom (who was generally very fond of being thanked for things) did not seem greatly interested. He left the room almost immediately, pausing only to speak to Mrs Winstanley. David heard him say in a low voice, "I hope, madam, that you liked the Italian music!"

As David was now obliged to stay in Thoresby until the following morning, Mr Winstanley sent one of his servants to Lincoln to tell Mr Monkton that Mr Montefiore was on his way and would be at his house the next day.

Just before midnight the people of Thoresby gathered at The Wheel of Fortune. In honour of the occasion Mr Winstanley had got dressed. Oddly enough he was somehow less impressive in his clothes. The air of tragedy and romance which he commonly possessed, seemed to have disappeared entirely when he put his coat and breeches on. He stood upon a three-legged stool and told the wretched, ragged crowd how grateful they should be to the great, good and generous gentleman who was going to build them a bridge. This gentleman, said Mr Winstanley, would soon appear among them to receive their thanks.

But Tom did not appear. Nor was Mrs Winstanley present, which made her husband very angry and so he sent Lucy back to Mickelgrave House to fetch her.

Mr Winstanley said to David, "I am greatly intrigued by Mr Brightwind's proposal of building the bridge in one night. Is it to be an *iron* bridge, I wonder? I believe that someone has recently built an iron bridge in Shropshire. Quite astonishing. Perhaps an iron bridge can be erected very quickly. Or a wooden bridge? There is a wooden bridge at Cambridge . . ."

Just then Lucy appeared, white-faced and frightened.

"Oh, there you are!" said Mr Winstanley. "Where is your mistress?"

"What is the matter, Lucy?" asked David. "What in the world has happened to you?"

"Oh, sir!" cried Lucy. "I ran up the high street to find my mistress, but when I reached the gate of the house two lions came out and roared at me!"

"Lions?" said David.

"Yes, sir! They were running about beneath my feet and snapping at me with their sharp teeth. I thought that if they did not bite me to death they were sure to trip me up!"

"What nonsense this is!" cried Mr Winstanley. "There are no lions in Thoresby. If your mistress chuses to absent herself from tonight's proceedings then that is her concern. Though frankly I am not at all pleased at her behaviour. This is, after all, probably the most important event in Thoresby's history." He walked off.

"Lucy, how big were these lions?" asked David.

"A little larger than a spaniel, I suppose."

"Well, that is most odd. Lions are generally larger than that. Are you quite sure . . ."

"Oh! What does it matter what size the horrible creatures had grown to?" cried Lucy impatiently. "They had teeth enough and snarls enough for animals thrice the size! And so, Lord forgive me! I was frightened and I ran away! And supposing my poor mistress should come out of the house and the lions jump up at her! Supposing she does not see them in the dark until it is too late!" She began to cry.

"Hush, child," said David. "Do not fret. I will go and find your mistress."

"But it was not just the lions," said Lucy. "The whole town is peculiar. There are flowers everywhere and all the birds are singing."

David went out of the inn by the front door and immediately struck his head against something. It was a branch. There was a tree which stood next to The Wheel of Fortune. In the morning it had been of a reasonable size, but it had suddenly grown so large that most of the inn was hidden from sight.

"That's odd!" thought David.

The tree was heavy with apples.

"Apples in June," thought David. "That's odder still!"

He looked again.

"Apples on a horse-chestnut tree! That's oddest of all!"

In the moonlight David saw that Thoresby had become very peculiar indeed. Figs nestled among the leaves of beech-trees. Elder-trees were bowed down with pomegranates. Ivy was almost torn from walls by the weight of ripe blackberries growing upon it. Any thing which had ever possessed any sort of life had sprung into fruitfulness. Ancient, dried-up window frames had become swollen with sap and were putting out twigs, leaves, blossoms and fruit. Door-frames and doors were so distorted that bricks had been pushed out of place and some houses were in danger of collapsing altogether. The cart in the middle of the high street was a grove of silver birches. Its broken wheels put forth briar roses and nightingales sang on it.

"What in the world is Tom doing?" wondered David.

He reached Mickelgrave House and two very small lions trotted out of the gate. In the moonlight they looked more stony than ever.

"I assume," thought David, "that, as these lions are of Tom's creating, they will not harm me."

The lions opened their mouths and a rather horrible sound issued forth – not unlike blocks of marble being rent in pieces. David took a step or two towards the house. Both lions leapt at him, snarling and snapping and snatching at the air with their stone claws.

David turned and ran. As he reached The Wheel of Fortune he heard the clock strike midnight.

Eighty miles away in Cambridge an undergraduate awoke

from a dream. The undergraduate (whose name was Henry Cornelius) tried to go back to sleep again, but discovered that the dream (which was of a bridge) had somehow got lodged in his head. He got out of bed, lit his candle, and sat down at a table. He tried to draw the bridge, but he could not get it exactly (though he knew he had seen it somewhere quite recently).

So he put on his breeches, boots and coat and went out into the night to think. He had not gone far when he saw a very odd sight. Edward Jackson, the bookseller, was standing in the doorway of his shop in his nightgown. There was no respectable grey wig on his head, but only a greasy old nightcap. He held a quarto volume in one hand and a brass candlestick in the other.

"Here!" he said the moment he clapped eyes upon Henry Cornelius. "This is what you are looking for!" And he pushed the book into Cornelius's hands. Cornelius was surprized because he owed Jackson money and Jackson had sworn never to let him have another book.

The moon was so bright that Cornelius was able very easily to begin examining his book. After a while he glanced up and found he was looking into the stable-yard of an inn. There, in a shaft of moonlight, was Jupiter, the handsomest and fastest horse in Cambridge. Jupiter was saddled and ready, and seemed to wait patiently for someone. So, without giving any further consideration to the matter, Cornelius got upon his back. Jupiter galloped away.

Cornelius sat calmly turning the pages of his book. Indeed so absorbed was he in what he found there, that he did not pay a great deal of attention to the journey. Once he looked down and saw complicated patterns of silver and blue etched on the dark ground. At first he supposed them to be made by the frost, but then it occurred to him that the month was June and the air was warm. Besides the patterns more resembled moonlit fields and farms and woods and lanes seen from very high up and very far away. But, whatever the truth of it, it did not seem to be of any great importance and so he continued to examine his book. Jupiter sped on beneath the moon and the stars and his hooves made no sound whatsoever.

"Oh! Here it is," said Cornelius once.

And then, "I see."

And a little later, "But it will take a great deal of stone!"

A few minutes later Cornelius and Jupiter stood upon the riverbank opposite Thoresby.

"So!" said Cornelius softly. "Just as I supposed! It is not built yet."

The scene before Cornelius was one of the most frantic industry imaginable. Massive timbers and blocks of stones lay strewn about on the bank and teams of horses were bringing more every minute. There were workmen everywhere one looked. Some drove or pulled the horses. Others shouted orders. Yet more brought lights and stuck them in the trees. What was very extraordinary about these men was that they were dressed in the oddest assortment of nightgowns, coats, breeches, nightcaps and hats. One fellow had been in such a hurry to get to Thoresby that he had put his wife's gown and bonnet on, but he hitched up his skirts and carried on regardless.

Amidst all this activity two men were standing still, deep in conversation. "Are you the architect?" cried one of them, striding up to Cornelius. "My name is John Alfreton, master mason of Nottingham. This is Mr Wakeley, a very famous engineer. We have been waiting for you to come and tell us what we are to build."

"I have it here," said Cornelius, shewing them the book (which was Giambattista Piranesi's *Carceri d'Invenzione*).

"Oh! It's a prison, is it?"

"No, it is only the bridge that is needed," said Cornelius, pointing to a massive bridge lodged within a dreary prison. He looked up and suddenly caught sight of an eerie, silent crowd on the opposite bank. "Who are all those people?" he asked.

Mr Alfreton shrugged. "Whenever industrious folk have work to do, idle folk are sure to gather round to watch them. You will find it best, sir, to pay them no attention."

By one o'clock a huge mass of wooden scaffolding filled the river. The scaffolding was stuffed full of torches, lanterns and candles and cast a strange, flickering light over the houses of Thoresby and the watching crowd. It was as if a firefly the size of St Paul's cathedral had sat down next to the town.

By two o'clock Henry Cornelius was in despair. The river was not deep enough to accommodate Piranesi's bridge. He could not build as high as he wished. But Mr Alfreton, the master mason, was unconcerned. "Do not vex yourself, sir," he said. "Mr Wakeley is going to make some adjustments."

Mr Wakeley stood a few paces off. His wig was pushed over to one side so that he might more conveniently scratch his head and he scribbled frantically in a little pocket book.

"Mr Wakeley has a great many ideas as to how we shall accomplish it," continued Alfreton. "Mr Wakeley has built famous navigations and viaducts in the north. He has a most extraordinary talent. He is not a very talkative gentleman but he admits that he is pleased with our progress. Oh! It shall soon be done!"

By four o'clock the bridge was built. Two massive semi-circular arches spanned the river. Each arch was edged with great rough-hewn blocks of stone. The effect was classical, Italianate, monumental. It would have been striking in London; in Thoresby it dominated everything. It seemed unlikely that any one would ever look at the town again; henceforth all that people would see was the bridge. Between the arches was a stone tablet with the following inscription in very large letters:

THOMAS BRIGHTWIND ME FECIT
ANNO DOMINI MDCCLXXX[8]

David had spent the night inquiring of the townspeople if any of them knew where Tom had got to. As soon as the bridge was built he crossed over and put the same question to the workmen. But an odd change had come over them. They were more than half asleep and David could get no sense out of any of them. One man sighed and murmured sleepily, "Mary, the baby is crying." Another, a fashionably dressed young man, lifted his drooping head and said, "Pass the port, Davenfield. There's a good fellow." And a third in a battered grey wig would only mutter mathematical equations and recite the lengths and heights of various bridges and viaducts in the neighbourhood of Manchester.

As the first strong golden rays of the new day struck the river and turned the water all to silver, David looked up and saw Tom striding across the bridge. His hands were stuffed into his breeches pockets and he was looking about him with a self-satisfied air. "She is very fine, my bridge, is she not?" he said. "Though I was thinking that perhaps I ought to add a sort of sculpture in *alto rilievo* shewing God sending zephyrs and cherubim and manticores and unicorns and lions and hypogriffs to destroy my enemies. What is your opinion?"

"No," said David, "the bridge is perfect. It wants no further embellishment. You have done a good thing for these people."

"Have I?" asked Tom, not much interested. "To own the truth, I have been thinking about what you said yesterday. My children are certainly all very foolish and most of them are good-for-nothing, but perhaps in future it would be gracious of me to

---

8 Thomas Brightwind made me, the year of our Lord 1780.

provide them with responsibilities, useful occupation, etc., etc. Who knows? Perhaps they will derive some advantage from it."[9]

"It would be very gracious," said David, taking Tom's hand and kissing it. "And entirely like you. When you are ready to begin educating your sons and daughters upon this new model, let you and I sit down together and discuss what might be done."

"Oh!" said Tom. "But I have begun already!"

On returning to Thoresby to fetch their horses, they learnt that Mr Winstanley's servant had returned from Lincoln with the news that Mr Monkton had died in the night. ("There, you see," said Tom airily, "I told you he was ill.") The servant also reported that the English apothecary, the Scottish physician and the Irish wizard had not permitted Mr Monkton's dying to interfere with a very pleasant day spent chatting, playing cards and drinking sherry-wine together in a corner of the parlour.

"Anyway," said Tom, regarding David's disappointed countenance, "what do you say to some breakfast?"

The fairy and the Jew got on their horses and rode across the bridge. Rather to David's surprize they immediately found

---

9 Despite Tom's low opinion of his offspring, some of his sons and daughters contrived to have quite successful careers without any help from him. A few years after the period of this tale, at more or less the same time, several scholarly gentlemen made a number of important discoveries about electricity. Among them was a shy, retiring sort of person who lived in the town of Dresden in Saxony. The name of this person was Prince Valentine Brightwind. Tom was most interested to learn that this person was his own son, born in 1511. Tom told Miriam Montefiore (David's wife), "This is the first instance that I recall of any of my children doing any thing in the least remarkable. Several of them have spent remarkably large amounts of money and some of them have waged wars against me for remarkably long periods of time, but that is all. I could not be more delighted or surprized. Several people have tried to persuade me that I remember him – but I do not."

themselves in a long, sunlit *piazza* full of fashionably dressed people taking the morning air and greeting each other in Italian. Houses and churches with elegant façades surrounded them. Fountains with statues representing Neptune and other allegorical persons cast bright plumes of water into marble basins. Roses tumbled delightfully out of stone urns and there was a delicious smell of coffee and freshly baked bread. But what was truly remarkable was the light, as bright as crystal and as warm as honey.

"Rome! The Piazza Navona!" cried David, delighted to find himself in his native Italy. He looked back across the bridge to Thoresby and England. It was as if a very dirty piece of glass had been interposed between one place and the other. "But will that happen to everyone who crosses the bridge?" he asked.

Tom said something in Sidhe,[10] a language David did not know. However the extravagant shrug which accompanied the remark suggested that it might be roughly translated as "Who cares?"

After several years of pleading and arguing on David's part Tom agreed to forgive Igraine for getting married and her three sisters for concealing the fact. Igraine and Mr Cartwright were given a house in Camden Place in Bath and a pension to live on. Two of Igraine's sisters, the Princesses Nimue and Elaine, returned to the *Castel des Tours saunz Nowmbre*. Unfortunately something had happened to Princess Morgana in the nasty house in the dark, damp wood and she was never seen again. Try as he might David was entirely unable to interest any one in her fate. Tom could not have been more bored by the subject and Nimue and Elaine, who were anxious not to offend their grandfather again, thought it wisest to forget that they had ever had a sister of that name.

---

10 The language of the fairies of the *brugh*.

The fairy bridge at Thoresby did not, in and of itself, bring prosperity to the town, for Mr Winstanley still neglected to do any thing that might have made money for himself or the townspeople. However two years after Tom and David's visit, Mr Winstanley was shewing the bridge to some visitors when, very mysteriously, part of the parapet was seen to move and Mr Winstanley fell into the river and drowned. His lands, clay and coal all became the possessions of his baby son, Lucius. Under the energetic direction first of Mrs Winstanley and later of Lucius himself the lands were improved, the clay was dug up, and the coal was mined. Pewley Witts had the handling of a great deal of the business which went forward and grew very rich. Unfortunately this did not suit him. The dull satisfaction of being rich himself was nothing to the vivid pleasure he had drawn from contemplating the misery and degradation of his friends and neighbours.

And so nothing remains but to make a few observations upon the character of Lucius Winstanley. I dare say the reader will not be particularly surprized to learn that he was a most unusual person, quite extraordinarily handsome and possessed of a highly peculiar temper. He behaved more like Thoresby's king than its chief landowner and ruled over the townspeople with a mixture of unreliable charm, exhausting capriciousness and absolute tyranny which would have been entirely familiar to any one at all acquainted with Tom Brightwind.

He had besides some quite remarkable talents. In the journal of a clergyman we find an entry for the summer of 1806. It describes how he and his companion arrived at Thoresby Bridge (as the town was now called) on horseback and found the town so still, so eerily silent that they could only suppose that every creature in the place must be either dead or gone away. In the yard of The New Bridge Inn the clergyman found an ostler and asked him why the town was as quiet as any tomb.

"Oh!" said the ostler. "Speak more softly if you please sir. Lucius Winstanley, a very noble and learned gentleman – you may see his house just yonder – was drunk last night and has a head ach. On mornings after he has been drinking he forbids the birds to sing, the horses to bray and the dogs to bark. The pigs must eat quietly. The wind must take care not to rustle the leaves and the river must flow smoothly in its bed and not make a sound."

The English clergyman noted in his journal, ". . . the entire town seems possessed of the same strange mania. All the inhabitants go in awe of Mr Lucius Winstanley. They believe he can work wonders and does so almost every hour."[11]

But though the people of Thoresby Bridge were proud of Lucius, he made them uncomfortable. Around the middle of the nineteenth century they were forced to admit to themselves that there was something a little odd about him; although forty or so years had passed since his thirtieth birthday he did not appear to have aged a single day. As for Lucius himself it was inevitable that he should eventually get bored of Thoresby even if he did enliven it for himself by having great ladies fall in love with him, changing the weather to suit his moods and – as once he did – making all the cats and dogs talk perfect English while the townspeople could only mew and bark at each other.

On a spring morning in 1852 Lucius got on his horse, rode on to his father's bridge and was never seen again.

---

11 Journals of the Reverend James Havers-Galsworthy, 1804–23.

I N T H E S P R I N G of 1568 Mary, Queen of Scots, fearing the wrath of her subjects, crossed the border into England. Once arrived, she wrote a letter to her cousin, Queen Elizabeth, explaining her predicament and begging for her protection. Elizabeth wrote back, expressing her shock that subjects should behave so wickedly towards their lawful and divinely appointed Prince. But privately she considered how Mary had often laid claim to the English throne. She also thought how Mary had had a most baleful influence upon her Scottish subjects, how she had been an instigator of civil wars and the cause of several murders.

With many regrets, Elizabeth cast the Queen of Scots into prison for the rest of her life.

The Queen of Scots was given into the care of the Earl of Shrewsbury, a quiet gentleman of moderate abilities who was remarkable for two things – his vast wealth and his wife, a lady who was greatly esteemed by Queen Elizabeth. The Earl brought the Queen of Scots to Tutbury Castle, an ancient grey tower on the borders of Derbyshire and Staffordshire.

From the roof of this castle she looked down. Once she had laid claim to three thrones; now her world was shrunk to this view of a muddy ditch and a dark hillside.

How had this happened? In the royal courts of Europe her fall had been a matter of common prediction for many years. Her decisions had been catastrophic, her love affairs scandalous. She had been a comet; and her blazing descent through dark skies had been plain for all to see. But the Queen herself was amazed at this sudden change in her fortunes – amazed and very much inclined to blame someone.

Elizabeth, she thought, had done this to her. Elizabeth and England. The Queen gazed about her at the gloomy winter landscape. The pallor of the sky seemed to her to be Elizabeth's white complexion. The chill wind on her cheek was Elizabeth's breath. The glint of a river seen through winter trees was the bright spark of malice in Elizabeth's eye.

The Queen of Scots felt she had dwindled, until she was nothing more than a flea upon Elizabeth's body or, at best, a mouse in the hem of her gown. With a wail the Queen cast herself down and began to weep and to beat her hands on the stones. The soldiers who guarded her were amazed to witness such behaviour, but her French and Scottish attendants were not much disturbed. They had seen it all before.

They carried her to her chamber and laid her upon the bed. Her lady-in-waiting, Mrs Seton, sat down beside her and tried to distract her with gossip.

Mrs Seton told her how the Earl and Countess of Shrewsbury, though both middle-aged, had not been married long. She said that the Countess had not been born into any great family, indeed that she was scarcely more than a farmer's daughter, but had achieved her present rank by marrying four husbands, each richer and greater than the one before.

"*Quatre maris!*" exclaimed the Queen of Scots, whose first language was French. "*Mais elle a des yeux de pourceau!*" (Four husbands! But she has piggy-eyes!)

Mrs Seton laughed in agreement.

Four husbands! thought the Queen of Scots. And the first three dying in so convenient a manner! – just when the farmer's daughter had grown into her new rank and might be wishing for a greater. The Queen of Scots's husbands had never consulted her convenience in their dying. Her first, the King of France, had died at the age of sixteen and so she had lost the French throne – a circumstance that had caused her great pain. Her second husband (whom she had hated and wished dead) had fallen ill in the most tantalising way, but had utterly failed to die – until some kind person had first blown him up and then strangled him.

This suggested an idea to the Queen of Scots. "Did the Countess's husbands all die naturally?" she asked.

Mrs Seton snorted in ridicule and leant closer. "Her first husband was no more than a boy! The Countess – who was only plain Bess Hardwick then – embroidered him a coat all chequered over with black and white squares. And, after he had worn it a few times, he began to complain that the whole world had become to him nothing but black and white squares. Every dark tabletop seemed to him a gaping black hole that meant to swallow him up and every window filled with white winter light was ghostly to him and full of malicious intent. And so he died, raving about it."

The Queen of Scots was impressed. She had heard of a poisonous dart sewn into a bodice to pierce the flesh, but she had never heard of anyone being killed by embroidery before. She herself was very fond of embroidery.

She remembered how she had fancied herself a mouse in Elizabeth's skirts. A needle, she thought, was a most suitable weapon for a mouse – mouse-sized, in fact. And if Elizabeth were to die of that needle (or indeed of anything else) then the Queen of Scots would surely be Queen of the English too.

Tutbury Castle was cold and evil-smelling. It was also rather small and so they did not have to walk far before they found the Countess, seated at her needlework.

The Queen asked the Countess what she was embroidering.

"A picture of a beautiful palace in a sweet country," said the Countess and showed the Queen. "As I sew I like to fancy that my children and grandchildren will one day live in houses such as this. It is a foolish idea, no doubt, but it passes the time pleasantly."

The Queen of Scots rolled her eyes at Mrs Seton to express her astonishment at the presumption of the farmer's daughter.

The Countess saw what the Queen did but she was not in the least abashed.

Then the Queen of Scots began to talk of embroidery, and of husbands, and of the death of husbands; and just for good measure she threw in a few references to black and white chequering.

The Countess replied blandly that embroidery was a very charming way to pass the time, and husbands were generally a good thing, and their death much to be regretted.

The Queen frowned. She had heard that the Countess was a very clever woman. Surely she must understand what was meant?

The Queen said, "I should like to send a present to my dear sister, the Queen of England. A piece of embroidery that I intend to work with my own hands. The work will be nothing but a pleasure to me for I declare that I love the Queen of England better than anyone else in the world."

"As everyone must who sees her," agreed the Countess piously.

"Quite," said the Queen of Scots and then she began to speak of how great Princes rewarded those who helped them.

The Countess looked neither excited nor fearful at these hints and insinuations of future greatness. She gazed calmly back at the Queen.

The Queen brought out a book filled with quaint pictures which might be adapted for needlework. There were cockatrices and lions and manticores – all sorts of beasts which (the Queen hoped) might be made to tear Elizabeth to pieces through the means of magic and embroidery.

The Countess dutifully admired the pictures, but offered no opinion as to which the Queen should choose.

Henceforth every morning the Queen, the Countess and Mrs Seton sat down to embroider together. Gathered in the light of the window with their heads bent over their work, they grew very friendly. The Queen embroidered a pair of gloves for Elizabeth, which she decorated with pictures of sea monsters amid blue and silver waves. But though she filled the monsters' mouths with sharp-looking teeth, Elizabeth was not bitten by anything; nor did she drown.

The Earl of Shrewsbury sent a letter to Queen Elizabeth saying that the Scottish Queen passed her time very innocently. This was not in the least true: when she was not at her needlework, she was secretly intriguing with English malcontents who wanted to assassinate Elizabeth and she also wrote letters to the Kings of Spain and France cordially inviting them to invade England. But she did not forget to admire the Countess's needlework and to talk, every now and then, of black and white chequering.

But the years went by; Elizabeth was as healthy as ever, no one invaded and the Queen grew tired of paying the Countess compliments. She said to Mrs Seton, "She is obstinate, but I have magic of my own. And if she will not help me then I will use it against her. After all I know what it is that she loves the best."

Then the Queen combed and dressed her red-brown hair. She put on a gown of violet-brown velvet embroidered with silver and pearls. She called the Earl to her chamber and made him sit at her side and smiled at him and told him that of all the gentlemen who attended her, it was he whom she trusted the most. Day after day she made him many sweet speeches, until the poor old gentleman did not know whether he was on his head or his heels and was very near falling in love with her.

Mrs Seton watched all this with a puzzled air. "But I do not think it is the Earl that the Countess loves the best," she said to the Queen.

"The Earl!" The Queen burst out laughing. "No, indeed! Whoever said it was? But she loves his money and his lands. She desires that they shall be given to her children and grand-children. It is all she ever thinks of."

Word reached the Countess of what was happening, as the Queen knew it must, but no sign of anger appeared on her broad Derbyshire face. The next time that the three ladies were seated at their embroidery, the Queen revived the old question of what present would please the Queen of England best.

"A skirt," said the Countess of Shrewsbury in the most decisive manner. "A skirt of white satin. Her Majesty loves new clothes."

The Queen of Scots smiled. "As do we all. And what shall the devices be?"

"Let it be powdered with little pink carnations," said the Countess.

"Little pink carnations?" said the Queen of Scots.

"Yes," said the Countess.

So somewhat doubtfully (for she would have much preferred poisonous snakes and spiders) the Queen of Scots embroidered a skirt of white satin with little pink carnations; and sent it to the Queen of England. Not many weeks later she heard that Elizabeth had got the pox. Her white skin was all over pink pustules!

The Queen of Scots clapped her hands together in delight.

Over the next week or so she drew up a list of the great lords and bishops of England. She cast her mind back over the years of her imprisonment, recalling past slights and kindnesses, considering who should live and be rewarded, and who should be sent to the Tower and die.

Then a day came when the wind blew and the rain lashed the glass, and the Countess entered the Queen's room unannounced. Her eyes were bright with excitement. She brought news, she said. Queen Elizabeth's advisers and councilmen had been put into a great fright by Her Majesty's illness and what had terrified them most of all was the thought that the Queen of Scots might become Queen of England. "For," said the Countess heartlessly, "they hate you very much and dread the havoc you would certainly bring upon this realm. And so they have passed a law saying you shall never be Queen of England! They have dismissed you from the line of succession!"

The Queen of Scots was silent. She stood like a stone. "But the Queen of England is dead?" she asked at last.

"Oh, no. Her Majesty is much, much better – for which we all give grateful thanks."

The Queen of Scots murmured a prayer – she scarcely knew what. "But the pink carnations?" she said.

"Her Majesty was most disappointed in your present," said the Countess. "The embroidery came all unravelled." She cast a contemptuous look at the Queen of Scots' lady-in-waiting. "It is my belief that Mrs Seton did not knot and tie the threads properly."

Henceforth the Queen of Scots and the Countess of Shrewsbury were no longer friends.

That night in her chamber when the Queen lay in bed, it seemed to her that the curtains of her bed were parted by a breath of wind. In the light of the moon the bare winter branches appeared to her now like great, black stitches sewn across the window – like stitches sewn across the castle, across the Queen herself. In her terror she thought her eyes were stitched up, her throat was closed with black stitches; her fingers were sewn together so that her hands were become useless, ugly flaps.

She screamed and all her attendants came running. "*Elle m'a cousue à mon lit! Elle m'a cousue à mon lit!*" cried the Queen. (She has sewn me to the bed! She has sewn me to the bed!) They calmed her and showed her that the Countess had done no such thing.

But the Queen never again tried to steal the Earl's affections away from the Countess.

A year or so later the Earl moved the Queen from one of his own castles to the Countess's new house of Chatsworth. When they arrived the Earl smilingly showed her a new floor which his wife had caused to have laid in the hallway – a chequerboard of black and white marble.

The Queen shivered, remembering the boy who had died wailing that the black squares and the white were killing him.

"I will not walk across it," said the Queen.

The Earl looked as if he did not understand. When it was revealed that all the entrances to the house had black and white squares to their floors, the Queen said she would not go in. The poor Earl tore out his hair and beard (which was by this time completely white and rather wispy), and begged, but the Queen declined absolutely to walk across the chequering. They brought a chair for her in the porch and she went and sat upon it. The Derbyshire rain came down and the Queen waited until the Earl brought workmen to dig up the squares of black and white marble.

"But why?" the Earl asked the Queen's servants. They shrugged their French and Scottish shoulders and made him no answer.

The Queen had not known a life could be so blank. She passed the years in devising plans to gain this European throne or that, intriguing to marry this great nobleman or that, but nothing ever came of any of it; and all the while she thought she could hear the snip, snip, snip of Elizabeth and her advisers cutting the threads of all her actions and the stitch, stitch, stitch of the Countess sewing her into the fabric of England, her prison.

One evening she was staring vacantly at an embroidered hanging. It showed some catastrophe befalling a classical lady. Her eye was caught by one of the classical lady's attendants who was depicted running away from the dreadful scene in alarm. A breath of wind within the chamber kept bringing the hanging dangerously close to a candle that stood upon a coffer. It was almost as if the little embroidered figure desired to rush into the flames. "She is tired," thought the Queen. "Tired of being sewn into this picture of powerlessness and despair."

The Queen rose from her chair and, unseen by any of her attendants, moved the candlestick a fraction closer to the hanging. The next time the wind blew, the hanging caught the flame.

The moment they observed the fire the Queen's women all cried out in alarm and the gentlemen began to issue instructions to one another. They pleaded with the Queen to leave the apartment, to hurry from the danger. But the Queen stood like a statue of alabaster. She kept her eyes upon the embroidered figure and saw it consumed by the fire. "See!" she murmured to her women. "Now she is free."

The next day she said to her maid, "I have it now. Get me crimson velvet. Make it the reddest that ever there was. Get me silks as bloody as the dawn." In the weeks that followed, the Queen sat hour after hour at the window. In her lap was the crimson velvet and she sewed it in silks as bloody as the dawn.

And when her ladies asked her what she was doing, she replied with a smile that she was embroidering beautiful flames. "Beautiful flames," she said, "can destroy so many things – prison walls that hold you, stitches that bind you fast."

Two months later the Queen of Scots was arrested on a charge of treason. Some of her letters had been discovered in a keg of ale belonging to a brewer who had delivered beer to the house. She was tried and condemned to be beheaded. On the morning of her execution, she approached the scaffold where lay the axe and the block. She was dressed in a black gown with a floor-length veil of white linen. When her outer garments were removed there was the petticoat of crimson velvet with the bright embroidered flames dancing upon it. The Queen smiled.

The Countess of Shrewbury lived on for twenty years more. She built many beautiful houses and embroidered hangings for them with pictures of Penelope and Lucretia. She herself was as discreet as Penelope and as respected as Lucretia. In the centuries that followed, her children and her children's children became Earls and Dukes. They governed England and lived in the fairest houses in the most beautiful landscapes. Many of them are there still.

Antickes are grotesque figures. Frets are formal Renaissance devices. Both are used in sixteenth-century embroidery.

JOHN USKGLASS

and
the
CUMBRIAN
CHARCOAL
BURNER

THIS RETELLING OF a popular Northern English folk-tale is taken from *A Child's History of the Raven King* by John Waterbury, Lord Portishead. It bears similarities to other old stories in which a great ruler is outwitted by one of his humblest subjects and, because of this, many scholars have argued that it has no historical basis.

Many summers ago in a clearing in a wood in Cumbria there lived a Charcoal Burner. He was a very poor man. His clothes were ragged and he was generally sooty and dirty. He had no wife or children, and his only companion was a small pig called Blakeman. Most of the time he stayed in the clearing which contained just two things: an earth-covered stack of smouldering charcoal and a hut built of sticks and pieces of turf. But in spite of all this he was a cheerful soul – unless crossed in any way.

One bright summer's morning a stag ran into the clearing. After the stag came a large pack of hunting dogs, and after the dogs came a crowd of horsemen with bows and arrows. For some moments nothing could be seen but a great confusion of baying dogs, sounding horns and thundering hooves. Then, as quickly as they had come, the huntsmen disappeared among the trees at the far end of the clearing – all but one man.

The Charcoal Burner looked around. His grass was churned to mud; not a stick of his hut remained standing; and his neat stack of charcoal was half-dismantled and fires were bursting forth from it. In a blaze of fury he turned upon the remaining huntsman and began to heap upon the man's head every insult he had ever heard.

But the huntsman had problems of his own. The reason that he had not ridden off with the others was that Blakeman was running, this way and that, beneath his horse's hooves, squealing all the while. Try as he might, the huntsman could not get free of him. The huntsman was very finely dressed in black, with boots of soft black leather and a jewelled harness. He was in fact John Uskglass (otherwise called the Raven King), King of Northern England and parts of Faerie, and the greatest magician that ever lived. But the Charcoal Burner (whose knowledge of events outside the woodland clearing was very imperfect) guessed nothing of this. He only knew that the man would not answer him and this infuriated him more than ever. "Say something!" he cried.

A stream ran through the clearing. John Uskglass glanced at it, then at Blakeman running about beneath his horse's hooves. He flung out a hand and Blakeman was transformed into a salmon. The salmon leapt through the air into the brook and swam away. Then John Uskglass rode off.

The Charcoal Burner stared after him. "Well, now what am I going to do?" he said.

He extinguished the fires in the clearing and he repaired the stack of charcoal as best he could. But a stack of charcoal that has been trampled over by hounds and horses cannot be made to look the same as one that has never received such injuries, and it hurt the Charcoal Burner's eyes to look at such a botched, broken thing.

He went down to Furness Abbey to ask the monks to give him some supper because his own supper had been trodden into the dirt. When he reached the Abbey he inquired for the Almoner whose task it is to give food and clothes to the poor. The Almoner greeted him in a kindly manner and gave him a beautiful round cheese and a warm blanket and asked what had happened to make his face so long and sad.

So the Charcoal Burner told him; but the Charcoal Burner was not much practised in the art of giving clear accounts of complicated events. For example he spoke at great length about the huntsman who had got left behind, but he made no mention of the man's fine clothes or the jewelled rings on his fingers, so the Almoner had no suspicion that it might be the King. In fact the Charcoal Burner called him "a black man" so that the Almoner imagined he meant a dirty man – just such another one as the Charcoal Burner himself.

The Almoner was all sympathy. "So poor Blakeman is a salmon now, is he?" he said. "If I were you, I would go and have a word with Saint Kentigern. I am sure he will help you. He knows all about salmon."

"Saint Kentigern, you say? And where will I find such a useful person?" asked the Charcoal Burner eagerly.

"He has a church in Grizedale. That is the road over there."

So the Charcoal Burner walked to Grizedale, and when he came to the church he went inside and banged on the walls and bawled out Saint Kentigern's name, until Saint Kentigern looked out of Heaven and asked what the matter was.

Immediately the Charcoal Burner began a long indignant speech describing the injuries that had been done to him, and in particular the part played by the solitary huntsman.

"Well," said Saint Kentigern, cheerfully. "Let me see what I can do. Saints, such as me, ought always to listen attentively to the prayers of poor, dirty, ragged men, such as you. No matter how offensively those prayers are phrased. You are our special care."

"I am though?" said the Charcoal Burner, who was rather flattered to hear this.

Then Saint Kentigern reached down from Heaven, put his hand into the church font and pulled out a salmon. He shook the salmon a little and the next moment there was Blakeman, as dirty and clever as ever.

The Charcoal Burner laughed and clapped his hands. He tried to embrace Blakeman but Blakeman just ran about, squealing, with his customary energy.

"There," said Saint Kentigern, looking down on this pleasant scene with some delight. "I am glad I was able to answer your prayer."

"Oh, but you have not!" declared the Charcoal Burner. "You must punish my wicked enemy!"

Then Saint Kentigern frowned a little and explained how one ought to forgive one's enemies. But the Charcoal Burner had never practised Christian forgiveness before and he was not in a mood to begin now. "Let Blencathra fall on his head!" he cried with his eyes ablaze and his fists held high. (Blencathra is a high hill some miles to the north of Grizedale.)

"Well, no," said Saint Kentigern diplomatically. "I really cannot do that. But I think you said this man was a hunter? Perhaps the loss of a day's sport will teach him to treat his neighbours with more respect."

The moment that Saint Kentigern said these words John Uskglass (who was still hunting), tumbled down from his horse and into a cleft in some rocks. He tried to climb out but found that he was held there by some mysterious power. He tried to do some magic to counter it, but the magic did not work. The rocks and earth of England loved John Uskglass well. They would always wish to help him if they could, but this power – whatever it was – was something they respected even more.

He remained in the cleft all day and all night, until he was thoroughly cold, wet and miserable. At dawn the unknown power suddenly released him – why, he could not tell. He climbed out, found his horse and rode back to his castle at Carlisle.

"Where have you been?" asked William of Lanchester. "We expected you yesterday."

Now John Uskglass did not want any one to know that there might be a magician in England more powerful than himself. So he thought for a moment. "France," he said.

"France!" William of Lanchester looked surprized. "And did you see the King? What did he say? Are they planning new wars?"

John Uskglass gave some vague, mystical and magician-like reply. Then he went up to his room and sat down upon the floor by his silver dish of water. Then he spoke to Persons of Great Importance (such as the West Wind or the Stars) and asked them to tell him who had caused him to be thrown into the cleft. Into his dish came a vision of the Charcoal Burner.

John Uskglass called for his horse and his dogs, and he rode to the clearing in the wood.

Meanwhile the Charcoal Burner was toasting some of the cheese the Almoner had given him. Then he went to look for Blakeman, because there were few things in the world that Blakeman liked as much as toasted cheese.

While he was gone John Uskglass arrived with his dogs. He looked around at the clearing for some clue as to what had happened. He wondered why a great and dangerous magician would chuse to live in a wood and earn his living as a charcoal burner. His eye fell upon the toasted cheese.

Now toasted cheese is a temptation few men can resist, be they charcoal burners or kings. John Uskglass reasoned thus: all of Cumbria belonged to him – therefore this wood belonged to him – therefore this toasted cheese belonged to him. So he sat down and ate it, allowing his dogs to lick his fingers when he was done.

At that moment the Charcoal Burner returned. He stared at John Uskglass and at the empty green leaves where his toasted cheese had been. "You!" he cried. "It is you! You ate my dinner!" He took hold of John Uskglass and shook him hard. "Why? Why do you these things?"

John Uskglass said not a word. (He felt himself to be at something of a disadvantage.) He shook himself free from the Charcoal Burner's grasp, mounted upon his horse and rode out of the clearing.

The Charcoal Burner went down to Furness Abbey again. "That wicked man came back and ate my toasted cheese!" he told the Almoner.

The Almoner shook his head sadly at the sinfulness of the world. "Have some more cheese," he offered. "And perhaps some bread to go with it?"

"Which saint is it that looks after cheeses?" demanded the Charcoal Burner.

The Almoner thought for a moment. "That would be Saint Bridget," he said.

"And where will I find her ladyship?" asked the Charcoal Burner, eagerly.

"She has a church at Beckermet," replied the Almoner, and he pointed the way the Charcoal Burner ought to take.

So the Charcoal Burner walked to Beckermet and when he got to the church he banged the altar plates together and roared and made a great deal of noise until Saint Bridget looked anxiously out of Heaven and asked if there was any thing she could do for him.

The Charcoal Burner gave a long description of the injuries his silent enemy had done him.

Saint Bridget said she was sorry to hear it. "But I do not think I am the proper person to help you. I look after milkmaids and dairymen. I encourage the butter to come and the cheeses to ripen. I have nothing to do with cheese that has been eaten by the wrong person. Saint Nicholas looks after thieves and stolen property. Or there is Saint Alexander of Comana who loves Charcoal Burners. Perhaps," she added hopefully, "you would like to pray to one of them?"

The Charcoal Burner declined to take an interest in the persons she mentioned. "Poor, ragged, dirty men like me are your special care!" he insisted. "Do a miracle!"

"But perhaps," said Saint Bridget, "this man does not mean to offend you by his silence. Have you considered that he may be mute?"

"Oh, no! I saw him speak to his dogs. They wagged their tails in delight to hear his voice. Saint, do your work! Let Blencathra fall on his head!"

Saint Bridget sighed. "No, no, we cannot do that; but certainly he is wrong to steal your dinner. Perhaps it might be as well to teach him a lesson. Just a small one."

At that moment John Uskglass and his court were preparing to go hunting. A cow wandered into the stable-yard. It ambled up to where John Uskglass stood by his horse and began to preach him a sermon in Latin on the wickedness of stealing. Then his horse turned its head and told him solemnly that it quite agreed with the cow and that he should pay good attention to what the cow said.

All the courtiers and the servants in the stable-yard fell silent and stared at the scene. Nothing like this had ever happened before.

"This is magic!" declared William of Lanchester. "But who would dare . . .?"

"I did it myself," said John Uskglass quickly.

"Really?" said William. "Why?"

There was a pause. "To help me contemplate my sins and errors," said John Uskglass at last, "as a Christian should from time to time."

"But stealing is not a sin of yours! So why . . .?"

"Good God, William!" cried John Uskglass. "Must you ask so many questions? I shall not hunt today!"

He hurried away to the rose garden to escape the horse and the cow. But the roses turned their red-and-white faces towards him and spoke at length about his duty to the poor; and some of the more ill-natured flowers hissed, "Thief! Thief!" He shut his eyes and put his fingers in his ears, but his dogs came and found him and pushed their noses in his face and told him how very, very disappointed they were in him. So he went and hid in a bare little room at the top of the castle. But all that day the stones of the walls loudly debated the various passages in the Bible that condemn stealing.

John Uskglass had no need to inquire who had done this (the cow, horse, dogs, stones and roses had all made particular mention of toasted cheese); and he was determined to discover who this strange magician was and what he wanted. He decided to employ that most magical of all creatures – the raven. An hour later a thousand or so ravens were despatched in a flock so dense that it was as if a black mountain were flying through the summer sky. When they arrived at the Charcoal Burner's clearing, they filled every part of it with a tumult of black wings. The leaves were swept from the trees, and the Charcoal Burner and Blakeman were knocked to the ground and battered about. The ravens searched the Charcoal Burner's memories and dreams for evidence of magic. Just to be on the safe side, they searched Blakeman's memories and dreams too. The ravens looked to see what man and pig had thought when they were still in their mothers' wombs; and they looked to see what both

would do when finally they came to Heaven. They found not a scrap of magic anywhere.

When they were gone John Uskglass walked into the clearing with his arms folded, frowning. He was deeply disappointed at the ravens' failure.

The Charcoal Burner got slowly up from the ground and looked around in amazement. If a fire had ravaged the wood, the destruction could scarcely have been more complete. The branches were torn from the trees and a thick, black layer of raven feathers lay over everything. In a sort of ecstasy of indignation, he cried, "Tell me why you persecute me!"

But John Uskglass said not a word.

"I will make Blencathra fall on your head! I will do it! You know I can!" He jabbed his dirty finger in John Uskglass's face. "You — know — I — can!"

The next day the Charcoal Burner appeared at Furness Abbey before the sun was up. He found the Almoner, who was on his way to Prime. "He came back and shattered my wood," he told him. "He made it black and ugly!"

"What a terrible man!" said the Almoner, sympathetically.

"What saint is in charge of ravens?" demanded the Charcoal Burner.

"Ravens?" said the Almoner. "None that I know of." He thought for a moment. "Saint Oswald had a pet raven of which he was extremely fond."

"And where would I find his saintliness?"

"He has a new church at Grasmere."

So the Charcoal Burner walked to Grasmere and when he got there he shouted and banged on the walls with a candlestick.

Saint Oswald put his head out of Heaven and cried, "Do you have to shout so loud? I am not deaf! What do you want? And put down that candlestick! It was expensive!" During their holy and blessed lives Saint Kentigern and Saint Bridget had been a monk and a nun respectively; they were full of mild, saintly patience. But Saint Oswald had been a king and a soldier, and he was a very different sort of person.

"The Almoner at Furness Abbey says you like ravens," explained the Charcoal Burner.

"'Like' is putting it a little strong," said Saint Oswald. "There was a bird in the seventh century that used to perch on my shoulder. It pecked my ears and made them bleed."

The Charcoal Burner described how he was persecuted by the silent man.

"Well, perhaps he has reason for behaving as he does?" said Saint Oswald, sarcastically. "Have you, for example, made great big dents in his expensive candlesticks?"

The Charcoal Burner indignantly denied ever having hurt the silent man.

"Hmm," said Saint Oswald, thoughtfully. "Only kings can hunt deer, you know."

The Charcoal Burner looked blank.

"Let us see," said Saint Oswald. "A man in black clothes, with powerful magic and ravens at his command, and the hunting rights of a king. This suggests nothing to you? No apparently it does not. Well, it so happens that I think I know the person you mean. He is indeed very arrogant and perhaps the time has come to humble him a little. If I understand you aright, you are angry because he does not speak to you?"

"Yes."

"Well then, I believe I shall loosen his tongue a little."

"What sort of punishment is that?" asked the Charcoal Burner. "I want you to make Blencathra fall on his head!"

Saint Oswald made a sound of irritation. "What do you know of it?" he said. "Believe me, I am a far better judge than you of how to hurt this man!"

As Saint Oswald spoke John Uskglass began to talk in a rapid and rather excited manner. This was unusual but did not at first seem sinister. All his courtiers and servants listened politely. But minutes went by – and then hours – and he did not stop talking. He talked through dinner; he talked through mass; he talked through the night. He made prophesies, recited Bible passages, told the histories of various fairy kingdoms, gave recipes for pies. He gave away political secrets, magical secrets, infernal secrets, Divine secrets and scandalous secrets – as a result of which the Kingdom of Northern England was thrown into various political and theological crises. Thomas of Dundale and William of Lanchester begged and threatened and pleaded, but nothing they said could make the King stop talking. Eventually they were obliged to lock him in the little room at the top of the castle so that no one else could hear him. Then, since it was inconceivable that a king should talk without someone listening, they were obliged to stay with him, day after day. After exactly three days he fell silent.

Two days later he rode into the Charcoal Burner's clearing. He looked so pale and worn that the Charcoal Burner was in high hopes that Saint Oswald might have relented and pushed Blencathra on his head.

"What is it that you want from me?" asked John Uskglass, warily.

"Ha!" said the Charcoal Burner with triumphant looks. "Ask my pardon for turning poor Blakeman into a fish!"

A long silence.

Then with gritted teeth, John Uskglass asked the Charcoal Burner's pardon. "Is there any thing else you want?" he asked.

"Repair all the hurts you did me!"

Immediately the Charcoal Burner's stack and hut reappeared just as they had always been; the trees were made whole again; fresh, green leaves covered their branches; and a sweet lawn of soft grass spread over the clearing.

"Any thing else?"

The Charcoal Burner closed his eyes and strained to summon up an image of unthinkable wealth. "Another pig!" he declared.

John Uskglass was beginning to suspect that he had made a miscalculation somewhere – though he could not for his life tell where it was. Nevertheless he felt confident enough to say, "I will grant you a pig – if you promise that you will tell no one who gave it to you or why."

"How can I?" said the Charcoal Burner. "I do not know who you are. Why?" he said, narrowing his eyes. "Who are you?"

"No one," said John Uskglass, quickly.

Another pig appeared, the very twin of Blakeman, and while the Charcoal Burner was exclaiming over his good fortune, John Uskglass got on his horse and rode away in a condition of the most complete mystification.

Shortly after that he returned to his capital city of Newcastle. In the next fifty or sixty years his lords and servants often reminded him of the excellent hunting to be had in Cumbria, but he was careful never to go there again until he was sure the Charcoal Burner was dead.

A NOTE ON THE ILLUSTRATOR

Charles Vess's graphic narrative work has appeared in, among other publications, *Spider-man*, *The Sandman*, *The Books of Magic* and his own self-published *The Book of Ballads and Sagas* and has earned him two Will Eisner Comic Industry awards. In 1999 he received the World Fantasy Award for Best Artist for his illustrations for *Stardust* (a collaboration with Neil Gaiman). He lives in the Appalachian Mountains of Virginia. For more information about the art of Charles Vess please visit his website at **www.greenmanpress.com**.

A NOTE ON THE TYPE

The text of this book is set in Adobe Caslon, named after the English punch-cutter and type founder William Caslon I (1692–1766). Caslon's rather old-fashioned types were modelled on seventeenth-century Dutch designs, but found wide acceptance throughout the English-speaking world for much of the eighteenth century until being replaced by newer types toward the end of the century. Used in 1776 to print the Declaration of Independence, they were revived in the nineteenth century, and have been popular ever since, particularly among fine printers. There are several digital versions, of which Carol Twombly's Adobe Caslon is one.

ALSO AVAILABLE BY SUSANNA CLARKE

JONATHAN STRANGE AND MR NORRELL

'I was swept away. Absolutely the most magical thing, extraordinary on every level'
DONNA TARTT

The year is 1806. England is beleaguered by the long war with Napoleon, and centuries have passed since practical magicians faded into the nation's past. But scholars of this glorious history discover that one remains: the reclusive Mr Norrell, whose displays of magic send a thrill through the country. Proceeding to London, he raises a beautiful woman from the dead and summons an army of ghostly ships to terrify the French. Yet the cautious, fussy Norrell is challenged by the emergence of another magician: the brilliant novice Jonathan Strange. Young, handsome and daring, Strange is the very antithesis of Norrell. So begins a dangerous battle between these two great men which overwhelms that between England and France. And their own obsessions and secret dabblings with the dark arts are going to cause more trouble than they can imagine.

'Unquestionably the finest English novel of the fantastic written in the last seventy years'
NEIL GAIMAN

'A stunning achievement'
INDEPENDENT ON SUNDAY

'Ravishing lyricism and tart satire'
SUNDAY TIMES

ORDER BY PHONE: +44 (0)1256 302 699; BY EMAIL: DIRECT@MACMILLAN.CO.UK
DELIVERY IS USUALLY 3–5 WORKING DAYS. FREE POSTAGE AND PACKAGING FOR ORDERS OVER £20.
ONLINE: WWW.BLOOMSBURY.COM/BOOKSHOP
PRICES AND AVAILABILITY SUBJECT TO CHANGE WITHOUT NOTICE.

WWW.BLOOMSBURY.COM/SUSANNACLARKE

BLOOMSBURY